THE SCHUBERT CONNECTION

THE SCHUBERT CONNECTION

MARY LOCKE

authorHOUSE®

AuthorHouse™
1663 Liberty Drive
Bloomington, IN 47403
www.authorhouse.com
Phone: 1-800-839-8640

Published by AuthorHouse   10/26/2012

ISBN: 978-1-4772-7753-9 (sc)
ISBN: 978-1-4772-7752-2 (hc)
ISBN: 978-1-4772-7751-5 (e)

Library of Congress Control Number: 2012918568

Dedicated with thanks to all the Viennese who have welcomed and befriended me.

ACKNOWLEDGMENTS

The Schubert Connection is a work of fiction, and all of its present day characters are figments of my imagination. The historical figures, Schubert and others, were, of course, real people, but the missing song mentioned in this book does not exist, as far as I know. The streets and buildings of Vienna are genuine. Any mistakes in their description are mine alone.

I consulted many books and articles in my research. Foremost among them were Schubert: A Critical Biography, by Maurice Brown, Viennawalks, by J. Sydney Jones, Schubert's Vienna, edited by Raymond Erickson, and Music in the Romantic Era, by Alfred Einstein.

This book would not have been possible without the support and guidance of my dear friend, Dr. Anneliese Rohrer, who provided constant advice and thorough fact checking. We explored the streets and sidewalks of Vienna together. I cannot thank her enough.

Ständchen

Leise flehen meine Lieder
Durch die Nacht zu dir;
In den stillen Hain hernieder,
Liebchen, komm zu mir!

Serenade

My songs beckon softly
Through the night to you;
In the peaceful glade below,
Beloved, come to me!

Music by Franz Schubert
Text by Ludwig Rellstab

CHAPTER ONE

Vienna in winter is an enchanting city, veiled in shades of grey and white, as lovely and seductive as the melodies emerging from its concert halls. Stately buildings line the streets, stand solid as they've stood for centuries, elegant behind a creamy curtain of snow, windows aglow. Lights flicker along Kärtnerstrasse; streetcars hum around the Ring; students line up outside the Opera for standing room tickets. Dusk drops its pale blanket over the city; the evening begins; the Viennese make their way home.

It was because of Franz Schubert that I was walking through Vienna that January evening, walking the streets he had walked, humming one of his songs. The snow fell gently, stuck to my eyelashes and dampened my coat. It didn't crunch under my feet the way it did back home in Minnesota, but dissolved into wet footprints on the cobblestones.

It was one of my favorite songs, the one I was humming, the famous "Serenade." I'd studied the manuscript that afternoon, that one and several others, copies of manuscripts hand-written by Schubert himself. My shoulder bag was full of notes and observations, stuffed with ideas and hopes for another article. I needed to write something new and get it published. That's the rule in academia.

I'm a music history professor, actually an assistant professor, at a small Lutheran college near Minneapolis. Schubert was not Lutheran; the Lutherans generally prefer to study Bach and Buxtehude. They do love a beautiful melody, though, even one written by a lapsed Catholic, by a composer famous for "Ave Maria," rather than for "A Mighty Fortress." It's not easy for them to find Ph.D. music history graduates who are native Minnesotans, Scandinavians born and bred to live through winters so brutal that most professors say, "No thanks. I think I'll take that offer down south."

That's why they encouraged my love for Schubert, why they gave me the sought after job of teaching in their Vienna program that winter. Working on my research is a side benefit. I have to admit that all of this wouldn't have happened without Arthur though. Arthur Larson is my boss, the head of the music department, and he likes me. Well, like may not be the most accurate word for his feelings, but I do not encourage his adoration in any way. Arthur has been buried in Minnesota winters and medieval music history for so long that when I joined the faculty he saw me as the answer to his prayers, his muse, his new lease on life. Those clichés are his, not mine. Believe me, I don't want to be any of those things, but I do appreciate his interest in my research. The music of Schubert is a leap of centuries for a man who spends his days lecturing about liturgical and non-liturgical songs of the Middle Ages, although Arthur does appreciate a gifted composer and a beautiful melody as well as I do.

He's older than I am by at least ten years, but I don't think he can be much over forty. He's just terribly out of shape. He has the wan, washed-out look of someone who hasn't seen the sun for months. He doesn't enjoy the out-of-doors, not even during the short, sweet Minnesota summers. Until I joined the faculty, or so I'm told, he did nothing but read, write and lecture; he was rarely seen outside the music building. After I arrived, I became his new interest. Now he reads what I read, sits in on my lectures, follows me to the ice-skating rink, gives me tickets to concerts. Arthur would do almost anything for me. That's why he pulled the strings that allowed me to come here, why he sends numerous e-mails every day and calls at least once a week to check on me. I'm thankful for his interest, but I'm also glad to be living on another continent this winter, glad to be walking the streets of this beautiful old city without him trailing along behind me.

I'd been working all day, and it was already past four when I left the library of the *Gesellschaft der Musikfreunde*. That's the Society of the Friends of Music; it's on the second floor of the Musikverein, the building which houses the beautiful big concert hall glazed in gold and white, the one you see on the New Year's in Vienna Concerts, the one where the Vienna Philharmonic plays. They were just finishing their rehearsal, emerging from this very concert hall with their instruments tucked into sturdy canvas-covered cases, buttoning their dark overcoats, pulling on hats and gloves, when I reached the bottom of the steps from the library, and turned into the passage in the center of the building. Vienna is full of these covered walkways; once they were used for horses and carriages, but now they're filled with pedestrians. I followed a couple of violinists out onto Bösendorferstrasse, and stayed behind them to the corner of Dumbastrasse. They kept going straight, while I turned right to walk one block up to the Kärntnerring. The soft golden glow from the lamps in the restaurant of the great old Hotel Imperial filtered through delicate lace shades, made spidery shadows on the sidewalk.

The air had that smoky blue grey color Vienna takes on at twilight; the Viennese call these early evening hours *Die Blaue Stunden*,

"The Blue Hours." Lights flickered along the street; streetcars hummed on their tracks. The graceful buildings had little pillows of snow on their rooftops and window sills. I sniffed the damp air, smelled the sausages cooking in little stands on the street corners, hurried toward the escalator which would take me to the large underground passage full of shops and people and food.

I stepped on behind a stylish woman in a fur coat and leather boots. She had a bouquet of flowers in her gloved hand, roses and baby's breath wrapped in cellophane; the Viennese, gracious and well-mannered, take flowers to everyone. Music floated up from the underground, not Mozart or Schubert, but something more like a *Csárdás*, a Hungarian dance. I began to tap my foot to the beat; the woman turned slightly, but didn't look at me. I stopped tapping; she stepped off the escalator and headed for the stairs across the passageway, the ones that led up to the Opera. I spotted the source of the music, a thin, shabbily dressed violinist with his case open at his feet, dug into my bag and dropped a few coins into his case. The violinist nodded his thanks and launched into a polka; I tried not to hop along in rhythm as I moved toward the escalator which would take me up to the corner opposite the opera, to the Kärntnerring, where I'd catch my streetcar.

I dug out some more coins, exchanged them for a small paper sack of chestnuts. It was warm in my bare hand; I pulled out one roasted nut, peeled it, and then popped it into my mouth while I waited. There were others already waiting, Viennese bundled into dark wool coats and winter hats, clutching shopping bags and briefcases. The red and cream streetcar glided to a stop in front of us; the doors slid open; and we pressed toward them. A group of students rushed off, jostling each other, bumping backpacks, laughing and talking all at once. We had to wait for them to clear the doors before we could climb on.

The car was crowded; I stood in the aisle and held on to an overhead ring. I stuffed the chestnuts into my bag and braced myself as the streetcar closed its doors and moved on across the intersection. It was snowing harder now, and the lights of the cars on the Ring flashed golden beams through the swirling flakes. We passed the Opera, the Burggarten, the Heldenplatz, stopped to let people on and off. Each time they passed I had to press closer to the men sitting in the seats beside me. I sniffed the close air, tried to find something fresh to inhale, but what I smelled was a mixture of garlic and tobacco. It wasn't coming from me. I glanced down at the two of them; they were engrossed in their own conversation, but not in German. Was it Hungarian? It sounded like it. The one on the aisle, the one I leaned into each time the firm body behind me pushed closer to my back, had grey hair curling out of the unzipped top of his worn leather jacket. It matched the hair on his head. A gold chain nestled there at his throat, and it had a medallion dangling from it. I bent over a bit to get a closer look. Just as I did, though, the streetcar came to a halt in front of the Burgtheater, and I swayed backward into whoever was so warm and close behind me.

It was a man. He grabbed my elbow to steady me, and said, "*Vorsicht*" in a lovely deep voice. That means "Be careful." I tried to turn to look at him, but the tram started up again, and I had to simply hold on. I mumbled, "*Danke*" and got a better grip on the ring. Schottentor was the next stop, and I had to choose which door I could get to. The aisle was packed in front of me, so I decided to try for the rear exit. It wasn't going to be easy. I let go of the overhead ring as we stopped, pushed myself around to face the back, and grabbed the seatback. The man who had steadied me was in front of me now, pushing through to the rear exit. I followed his path, and stepped down onto the street beside him.

The pavement was slick with the new snow; my left foot slipped and I lurched into him. He grabbed my arm, held it, and said again in the voice I recognized from the tram, "*Vorsicht.*" This time I did look at him. He was taller than I, but I'm not very tall, only five feet five. He must have been close to six feet, so I found myself looking up at him. He looked good, I have to say. Dark hair dusted with snow, deep blue eyes, high cheekbones. I noticed all that in a few seconds. He was staring at me, but that was probably because I was staring at him and not moving. His hand was still on my arm, and he guided me to the sidewalk, out of the way of the people crowding on and off the streetcar.

"*Danke schön.*" I, who was fairly fluent in German, suddenly seemed to have very few words at my disposal. That was okay. He didn't have much to say either.

"*Bitte,*" was all he said as he removed his hand from my arm and stepped away. "*Auf Wiedersehen.*"

I took a deep breath and turned toward the steps to the underground. I had to go down again, this time to catch another streetcar out to the ninth district, where I live. The dark-haired man was a few steps in front of me. I watched him, watched his smooth, sure walk, the way his wool coat hugged his shoulders. Was he an Austrian? His German had been flawless, but then there had been very little of it. Somehow, he looked American. No matter how we dress or speak, we are recognizable. Is it our straight teeth, our healthy appearance? Could I get another peek at him if I caught up? His stride was so long and even, I didn't think I could do that, but maybe I wouldn't have to. All I had to do was work my way over to him, get within a few feet, check him out unobtrusively.

It was not to be. The number thirty-seven streetcar pulled in before I could get to him; the best I could do was climb on behind him, with a few people in between us. Most of the seats were taken; I spotted him halfway up the aisle, sitting behind the same two Hungarians who'd been beside me on the number one. Before I could get to the seat beside him, it was taken by a rather large woman in a fur hat. I was left standing again. I inched forward as far as I could before the streetcar started off, made it to the space behind his seat, and grabbed for the ring.

He had a good profile, straight nose, strong chin. I tipped my head to the side for a better view, then caught myself. Why did I need to keep looking at him? I don't usually do this, follow men and stare at them. I must have been spending too much time alone in the library. The woman beside him squeezed into him, took up more than her share of the seat. Her shopping bags were overloaded; bread and a bag of noodles stuck out of the top of one, bottles of beer from another. He didn't seem to notice though; he leaned slightly forward, intent on the garlic infused men in front of him, who were talking more intensely now, their hands gesticulating in front of them.

We were up on Währingerstrasse, and the streetcar came to its first stop, Berggasse, Freud's street. The passenger sitting across from the grey-haired Hungarian, the one with the curling chest hair and the gold chain, got off, as did a few others. I slid into the vacant seat, settled my shoulder bag on my lap, and reached into it for the chestnuts. I was hungry as only a woman who hadn't eaten since breakfast can be; I'd skipped lunch, too engrossed in my manuscripts to take time for it. I peeled one of the nuts as I watched the two of them. The man next to the window was shorter than the grey haired one, and younger and darker. He wore a wool jacket and a scarf around his neck. His hands were smaller than his companion's, and moved faster as he talked. He was very excited, and his voice grew gradually louder. I ate three more chestnuts before he stopped for breath.

I shouldn't have eaten so fast; my mouth was stuffed full and my bag was still open from reaching into it for the nuts when I noticed that we had already stopped at Strudlhofgasse and made the turn onto Nussdorferstrasse. I leaned forward, braced myself to stand and make my way to the door as soon as I saw the market on the corner of Alserbachstrasse, where I'd planned to pick up a few groceries

It may have been that I was thinking about what to buy for dinner, or it may have been that I found myself looking once more at the dark haired man who'd grabbed my arm and kept me from falling not that long ago, the one with the blue eyes and the smooth walk; who knows what it was that distracted me at that moment. All I know is that when I stood up, I bumped smack into the large woman with the overflowing shopping bags, dropped my own not quite closed bag and found myself hugging her ample form as the street car came to a stop just past the market.

My few remaining chestnuts scattered on the floor along with her packet of noodles and other assorted wrapped delicacies. At least the beer hadn't fallen out of her other bag, or I would have had broken glass to deal with too. As it was I scrambled to help her pick up her food, left my chestnuts rolling around in the aisle, apologized repeatedly, and hurried to follow her off the streetcar. This has to explain why I didn't realize until later that a few of the stray pieces of paper I had taken notes on that day had escaped along with the chestnuts. Among those strays was a copy of my request for the Schubert manuscripts I'd studied that day, and of course it had my signature on it. I have very good penmanship, so anyone who picked it up could have read my name clearly: Lily Lindstrom, Ph.D.

CHAPTER TWO

The market on the corner of Alserbachstrasse and Nussdorferstrasse with its familiar red, white and green logo carries gourmet items along with its other groceries, but I wasn't buying anything fancy this time. I selected some fresh fruits and vegetables, picked up eggs, milk and butter at the dairy counter, and, of course, rounded out my shopping with a visit to the bakery section. It didn't take long, but my shopping bag was stuffed full as I made my way up Nussdorferstrasse, heading toward home.

This was Schubert's old neighborhood, and after I'd crossed the street and turned off onto Säulengasse, I walked right past Number Three, where he'd once lived. It's a sturdy building with an arch in the middle which says, "Schubert Garage" in large green letters above double green doors. Over the arch there's an old grey plaque, with faded gold letters in German telling when he lived there and what he did during those years.

It's on the upper wall, between windows trimmed in green. You need to stand across the street to read it, and when you do, you may find someone looking back at you from one of those windows, someone who lives where he used to live. It gives me the shivers whenever I feel those eyes upon me.

I was shivering for a different reason now though. It was snowing harder, and the streetlights were flickering on the edges of the little square I had to walk through to get to my street, Sobieskigasse. It was a charming area, with an old fountain in the middle and small shops lining it. I really did love the neighborhood, and I was lucky that the college had rented this apartment for me. There was only enough space in their Vienna house for the winter quarter students and their faculty advisors, but it was fine with me not to be the resident advisor to all those college kids. I liked living on my own.

The pavement was slick and I was watching my step as I approached the end of the block. The snow was blowing in my face and I could barely see the outline of my apartment house. I stopped in front of the *Tabak* shop on the ground floor and started digging in my bag for my keys. Lights glowed through the shop window; it stayed open until six and did a good business selling chocolates, cigarettes, newspapers, magazines, stamps and streetcar tickets, among other things. The proprietor, Frau Frassl, probably would have been standing in the doorway watching the neighborhood if the weather had been better. As it was, she was a blurry figure through the frosty window. I could just make out the outline of her bright red hair as she hovered behind the counter.

My fingers were stiff from the cold, and it was hard to get them around my keys, but I pulled them out of my bag at last and had just stepped toward the outer door to my building when it burst open and two familiar forms rushed out of it, straight into me. It was the Hungarians from the streetcar, and they knocked me to the ground before they disappeared into the snowy night.

Everything seemed to happen at once after that, though it may have only seemed so from where I lay sprawled on the sidewalk. Frau Frassl was the first to reach me; I recognized her favorite cowboy boots as she bent over me. That's all I could see from my position. She began to shout, and her language was even more colorful than usual.

"*Gnädiges Fraulein Doktor Lindstrom!*" That translates roughly as "Most Honorable Miss Doctor Lindstrom." The Viennese do love titles and use them constantly. If I hadn't had a Ph.D. they probably would have given me some other designation to decorate my name. I won't go on to translate the rest of what she said. You'll have to trust that it was what my old German professor would have called common slang with a strong regional accent. He was very precise about language, but I'm getting off the track here.

Frau Frassl wasn't the only person bending over me now. A very distinguished man had emerged from a Mercedes idling at the curb. I knew it was a Mercedes from the low smooth purr of its engine. There are a lot of these cars on the streets of Vienna. His leather gloved hand brushed my cheek, and I looked up at a strangely familiar face crowned by a head of thick silver hair as he asked me if I was in pain.

I was too cold and shocked to know whether I was in pain, but I managed to lift my head and say, "*Es geht mir ganz gut, danke.*" Now that was not exactly correct. It means, "It's going well for me," which obviously it was not, but he and Frau Frassl were reassured enough to offer me a hand up on each side, and I staggered to my feet in front of the now open apartment house door. The helpful gentleman held my arm while Frau Frassl handed me my bag, my keys and my groceries. I was right about the Mercedes; it was a black one, and it had a uniformed driver behind the wheel. He pulled away from the curb only when the man holding my arm nodded at him. Who could this be, important enough to have a Mercedes with a driver, and why did he look familiar to me? I'd have to think about that later. Right now, I needed to focus on getting into my building.

There was only one stone step leading into the building and the silver haired gentleman held my arm and the door as I moved gingerly into the entrance hall. The Hungarians had left the elevator door open in their haste, and we stepped into it together. He pulled the metal door shut and asked which floor.

"*Drei*," I answered. He pushed the button and then continued to stand close to me as the small metal cage gave a little shake and began its ascent. He shook his head and uttered a low voiced imprecation. It translated roughly as "annoying tramps," though his expression wasn't actually quite that polite. In fact, it was impolite enough to cause me to lift my gaze to his, and as I did so, through the metal grid of the elevator, I caught a glimpse of a man coming down the stairs which wound their way around the open elevator shaft. It couldn't be, could it?

I swallowed the gasp which rose to my throat as those startling blue eyes met mine. He held a finger to his lips and stood perfectly still as the elevator shuddered to a stop on the third floor. He was standing in the shadows behind us, and the silver haired gentleman didn't see him as he pulled back the metal door and helped me out. I assured him that I was fine and thanked him again.

"*Bitte*," he replied as he stepped back into the elevator, closed the door and pushed the button. He was going up one more floor. Now that was interesting, but I didn't have time to think about who he could be visiting. My mystery man was standing beside me now as I inserted my key into my lock.

The voices of my parents resounded inside my head, those voices which had always warned me to beware of strangers. My hand was shaking as I turned the bolt, but I whispered, "I trust him."

His hand covered mine and helped me unlock my own door. "Trust who? Helmut Vogl? What were you doing in the elevator with the Minister of the Interior of Austria anyway?"

We were speaking English now. He followed me into my apartment, took my bag and groceries from me, and helped me out of my coat. He had already closed the door. I had to hope that my instincts were right. He hung up his coat next to mine on the hooks in my small foyer, and then turned his full attention toward me. I took a deep breath, and then let it out in a small whoosh.

"No wonder he looked familiar. I must have seen his picture in the paper." I shook my head. "But how would you know him?" I stared at the man standing so close to me. "Who are you anyway?"

He slid his hand into his pocket, brought out a leather wallet, and from it pulled a business card which he held out to me. I took it from him and read aloud.

"Stephen Cameron, M.D., Ph.D." it said in the middle, and in smaller print down below, "Research Associate, CDC." The address for the CDC, of course, was in Atlanta, Georgia.

What could I say to all of those titles? "You're a long way from home, Dr. Cameron." Oh my, the Viennese would love him. Not one doctorate, but two, and they would use both of them. I could hear it now, "Good Evening, Most Honored Doctor Doctor Cameron." But this didn't explain what he was doing in my building, not to mention in my apartment. That part would be hard to explain, even to myself.

"Yes," he turned and reached into a pocket of the coat he had just hung up. "Yes, I am." He paused before saying my name, "Dr. Lindstrom." When he turned back to me, he held in his hand my library request form, and a few other scraps of paper I'd scribbled notes on that day. I grabbed them from him and stuffed them into my briefcase.

"I think I need a glass of wine." I picked up my grocery bag and headed for my kitchen. He followed me. "And while I'm pouring it," I continued, "you can tell me how you got those pieces of paper and exactly what you're doing here, in my apartment, in my building, in Vienna, instead of in a lab in Atlanta where you belong."

I was quivering now, whether it was from indignation, nervousness, exhaustion, or hunger. Who knows. I dropped the bag onto the counter next to the stove and began pulling food out of it, suddenly desperate for something to eat. I took a large bite of the chocolate croissant I'd planned to have for breakfast and then reached into the cupboard for a frying pan.

Double Doctor Cameron, if that's who he really was, stood still, watching me. His gaze, I have to say, was a bit unnerving. I continued to chew my croissant, waiting for the sugar and chocolate to do its work, while I rummaged in the bag for butter and eggs. My plan was to make an omelet, but first I'd wash down my croissant with a bit of wine. I was reaching for the bottle when I felt his hands on my shoulders.

"You're shaking. Why don't you sit down and I'll pour." He pushed me down into one of the small wooden chairs at my kitchen table. Gently, I have to admit, but firmly. Then he leaned closer and brushed his fingers along my forehead, right at the very top, where I have an old scar from falling off my bicycle years ago. But it wasn't the scar he was interested in. "And you're bleeding." He frowned as he pushed my hair off my forehead, and then lowered his voice, as if he were talking to himself. "What is going on around here tonight?"

"Good question." I reached for the glass of wine he held out to me. He watched me take a swallow and then turned and began washing his hands at my kitchen sink. "Do you have a first aid kit?"

I took a sip of wine, swallowed and then waved my arms toward my bathroom. "I have some band-aids and first aid cream. In there, in the medicine cabinet."

He disappeared for a minute and then returned, pulled the other chair up directly in front of me, and began to dab at my forehead with something which stung. He must have found the hydrogen peroxide in there too. I kept my medicine cabinet well stocked. He leaned in very close as he dabbed. I tried to breathe evenly, but it wasn't easy, and it wasn't just the pain taking my breath away.

"At least it doesn't look as if you'll need stitches." He looked quite pleased with himself as he coated my wound with first aid cream and applied a small bandage. "There you go." He stood up, tossed his trash into the can and then headed for the stove. "How do you like your eggs?"

I took another swallow of wine and held out my glass for more before I answered. "I was going to make an omelet."

He began cracking the eggs into a bowl he'd found in my cupboard. The butter sizzled in the pan, and the pungent smell of the onions he was chopping filled the air as I leaned my head back against the wall and closed my eyes. My head was beginning to throb, and I set my wineglass down on the table.

He glanced my way. "I don't know what I was thinking, pouring you more wine." He transferred one omelet onto a plate and set it in front of me before he added more of the egg mixture to the pan. "Do you know how you hurt your forehead?"

My mouth was full, so I just shook my head. He sat down across from me, reached for the salt and pepper, and brought a forkful to his mouth. He ate European style, fork in his left hand, knife in his right.

"It must have been when the Hungarians knocked me down. I think it was the medallion on the chain of the grey haired one that hit me." I rubbed at the back of my head. "I think I may have a lump back here too."

"Medallion on a chain?" He reached across the table and ran his fingers through my hair until he found the lump.

"Ouch!" I pushed his hand away. "Yes, he was wearing it around his neck. I didn't get a good look at it though. It all happened too fast. I just wonder what they were doing in my apartment building and why they were in such a hurry to leave."

He looked away quickly as he withdrew his hand from my head. I remembered how he'd been watching them so closely on the streetcar.

"You know, don't you?" I sat up straighter, then leaned across the table until my face was just inches from his. "You were following them. That's what you were doing on the stairway! Ha! CDC! That's a likely story. Who do you really work for?"

I felt positively brilliant after a glass and a half of wine. I sat back and folded my arms across my chest as I waited for his answer. I have a very nice chest actually, and that's where his eyes rested as he cleared his throat and pushed himself back from the table. He tilted his chair back so that he could see me better and finally raised his eyes to my face. He was smiling.

"I do work for the CDC and I do have an M.D. and, by the way, I picked up your scraps of paper from the floor of the streetcar." He started to laugh, but stopped when I frowned at him. "It's not as if you made a quiet and graceful exit, you know." He reached toward me. "And I am going to check out that lump on your head."

Smug male. "I don't think so," I said as I stood up, pushed my chair back and carried my plate to the sink. "Number one. Anyone over the age of three can apply a band-aid; that doesn't prove you're a doctor. Number two. The CDC does not send double doctors to follow shifty looking Hungarians around Vienna; their employees keep busy doing research on dangerous bacteria." I paused, because I really didn't know exactly what the CDC did. Who knows what anybody working for a U.S. government agency does anymore? However, I had a point to make, so I kept talking as I rinsed off my plate. "Number . . ." I had lost count.

"Three," he said helpfully from behind me as he handed me his plate.

"Of course," I continued. "Three." How could I be out of points already? I turned around. Big mistake. Those eyes. That lovely dark hair brushing his forehead. There's no telling what I might have done in my light headed, injured, overtired state if someone hadn't started banging on my door at that moment.

CHAPTER THREE

I pressed my eye to the peephole in my apartment door. The dark haired double doctor stood so close behind me that his breath stirred the hairs on top of my head. The face of my upstairs neighbor, Mitzi, appeared, magnified and curved outward in that peculiar way that faces look when viewed through peepholes. I reached forward to slide open the bolt on my door, but of course, the would be heroic male behind me had other ideas.

"Wait!" He hissed in my ear. "Do you know who it is?"

"Of course I do. Do you think I'm an idiot?" I didn't give him time to answer that. "It's my upstairs neighbor, Mitzi. Now move back."

Amazingly, he did what I asked, and I opened the door just as Mitzi was lifting her hand to pound again. I grabbed her arm and pulled her into the apartment. Her hair was in disarray and she wore only a silk robe. Her feet were bare. This was not the perfectly coiffed, stylishly dressed woman I was used to seeing on the stairway.

Her mouth was open and she was gasping for breath. *"Hilfe. Ich brauche hilfe!"* Translation: She needed help, but I could have figured that out even without her words. She continued. *"Bitte! Komm' mit mir!"* She turned and started up the stairs; we followed right behind her.

Her apartment is directly above mine, and she had left the door open. She dashed through the living room and into her bedroom. I would have been the first one into the room after her, if my new friend hadn't cut me off and stopped me with his outstretched arm.

"Wait." It was only one word, but it was a definite command. I might have argued with him, if I hadn't seen the naked man on Mitzi's bed, the very man who had helped me after I'd been knocked down in front of the building. So this is where he'd been heading. Suddenly I was very glad that the double doctor was present, and hoped that he was, in fact a medical doctor.

He looked like the real thing at that moment. He was leaning over the undressed man, hand to his pulse. Too bad he didn't have a stethoscope handy, but he seemed to be doing fine without it. He lifted his head and began to question Mitzi, again in that quite perfect German I'd heard earlier from him, even as he continued to examine the man I thought of as my white haired gentleman. He was calm; his voice was firm; he gave no sign at all of being as upset as Mitzi about the man's condition. In fact, he had turned away from his patient to examine a container she produced from her bedside table, so I was the first one to see the man's eyes flutter open. He looked straight at me and groaned.

I kept my eyes on his, and said, "It's okay. We're here to help." I said this in German of course.

Mitzi, alerted by his groan, sank down beside him and began to stroke his face. "Darling. *Schatz. Liebling*. Helmut." She kept stroking, kept whispering endearments. All the while, my helpful doctor sniffed and touched, but, I noticed, did not taste whatever was in the container. He put it in his pocket and interrupted Mitzi.

"We need to get him to the hospital," he said. "Where's your phone?"

It seemed like a reasonable request, but she leaped from the bed and cried, "No ambulance," just before the man on the bed began to speak in that gravelly voice I'd heard earlier. "Call my driver." He lifted his head. "Use my phone."

Mitzi searched through the clothing folded neatly on her bedroom chair and pulled out a phone. Things happened pretty fast after that. Mitzi placed the call; Stephen helped the gentleman sit up and began to ease him into his clothes.

"Go down and get my coat for me, will you?" He was talking to me now. "And then you'll have to let the driver in. I'll need his help getting Herr Vogl to the car."

Helmut Vogl. The Minister of the Interior of Austria. Incredible. At least he was dressed now. That made it easier to look him in the eye.

"What are you waiting for?"

Good question. I rushed out of Mitzi's apartment and down the steps to my own place. I was slightly winded by the time I made it to the top of the stairs again, just in time to hand the helpful doctor his coat before heading back down to open the outer door for the driver.

The black Mercedes stood at the curb, its engine purring. The driver had already opened its back door and was striding toward me when the elevator rattled to a stop in the entrance hall behind us. Helmut Vogl, leaning heavily on Stephen Cameron, M.D., Ph.D., shuffled slowly toward us. He was pale, but he was alive. Mitzi was nowhere in sight. I watched from the doorway as they maneuvered the M of I, as I now thought of him, into the backseat of the car. My dark haired doctor slid onto the leather seat next to him, pulled the door shut, and they were off. I watched the taillights until the car turned right at the corner and I could see them no more.

The elevator door had been left open again, and I have to say I was thankful. I stepped in, pulled the metal door shut and reached out to push number three, but decided instead to push number four. I thought it would be a good idea to check on Mitzi. The lift rattled as it rose through the shaft, and I was grateful, as always, when it shook to a stop.

Mitzi's door was shut now, so it was my turn to knock. I shifted from foot to foot as I waited for her to open the door. It was a long wait. I had begun to count backward from one hundred, in German of course, when I finally heard the bolt slide open. She opened the door, but only a crack.

"I'm fine now," she said and made to close the door, but I put my foot in it.

"Herr Vogl asked me to check on you." I lied, but I figured that this might be my only way in. I slipped through the opening before she could change her mind, and then closed the door behind me.

Mitzi looked terrible. Her face was tear streaked, and her hair looked even worse than it had earlier.

"Do you have something to drink?" I headed for her kitchen—her apartment was arranged exactly like mine—but she directed me to her living room instead and headed for a cabinet opposite the couch. She pulled out a bottle of slivovitz, a potent plum brandy from the Balkans, and placed it on the table in front of me along with a couple of glasses. Then she sank down on a chair opposite me and poured the clear liquid.

I held the glass to my nose and inhaled the heady scent of the liquor before I took a sip. It formed a path of liquid warmth all the way down my throat, a warmth which gradually spread throughout my aching body; my head wasn't the only body part feeling the effects of that fall on the pavement. A low groan escaped my lips.

Mitzi set her glass down and leaned forward, but didn't say anything. I cleared my throat, took a breath, and asked her the question which had brought me up here, at least one of the questions. "Why me?" It seemed like a simple, reasonable inquiry, but she didn't respond immediately. She crossed her legs, pulled her robe together more tightly, poured herself another glass of slivovitz. She was drinking faster than I was.

Her answer, when she finally gave it, was short and clear. "I trusted you. I thought you could help me."

I took another sip while I thought about that answer. Really, I barely knew the woman. I had met her on the stairs and by the mailboxes several times, and we had exchanged friendly greetings, but that was it. She trusted me? Was that really it? Did my healthy Minnesota appearance reassure her? Or was there more to it?

"Did you know that I had a doctor in my apartment with me?" Crazy question. Even I hadn't known for sure I'd had a doctor in there with me, and it's not as if he'd ever been in my apartment before.

She shook her head, pushed her unruly hair out of her eyes, and choked out her next words. "No! No! I had no idea! I just panicked when he lost consciousness and ran to you. I don't know what I was thinking."

"It's okay. It's okay." I hadn't meant to upset her all over again. "I'm glad we could help." Now for the question I really wanted to ask, but I had to search for the best words. It can be hard to ask a delicate question, especially in German. "Has Herr Vogl been your . . ." I paused, hoping I'd chosen correctly. "Very good friend for a long time?" You could call me cowardly, but I wasn't quite ready to use the word lover for the Minister of the Interior. Plus, I did emphasize the very good part of that description.

Mitzi stared at me as if I'd lost my mind. Maybe I had, but after all, I had seen him naked on her bed. My curiosity seemed reasonable. She closed her eyes and sighed before answering. I had to strain to hear her.

"Not long." She whispered. "Just a few months."

"Oh." Now what? What else could I say? "Well, I'm sure he'll be fine." Of course I wasn't sure of that, but giving voice to the alternative didn't seem wise.

What did seem wise was making my exit. The room appeared to tilt slightly when I rose from the couch, and I had to walk very slowly toward the door. Mitzi followed me and surprised me again when she reached out to hug me and gave me a kiss on each cheek, European style, before sending me back to my apartment.

"*Danke schön*," she murmured, and then closed her door.

I had to hold tightly to the handrail as I descended the steps one more time. That slivovitz was powerful stuff. My apartment door was closed, but not locked. I'd been in a hurry the last time I'd been in there. I was a bit nervous going in, and checked behind all the doors and curtains before I slid the bolt, closed myself in for the night, and headed for the piano. I needed a little Schubert to steady my nerves.

As soon as I sat down at the piano I felt that relief which comes to me when my fingers touch the keys and the melody begins. I'd been playing the piano since I was old enough to sit on my mother's lap and press Middle C with one chubby finger; playing came as naturally to me as breathing, and I couldn't think of getting through a day without music. My Swedish immigrant ancestors had considered it as essential to daily life as sleeping and eating. "A musician," my Grandpa Lindstrom had once said to me, "is useful." Most of my relatives played instruments, and, of course, every one of us had grown up singing in Lutheran church choirs.

The piece I began to play, the first of the Six *Moments Musicaux*, was one of my favorites. It was tender; it was lyrical; it had that sweet melancholy I so loved in Schubert. Whether he was writing for piano, orchestra, or voice, whatever he wrote turned into a song; mystery and enchantment poured from his soul into his music, and, whenever I heard it or played it, into mine. I could almost feel his heart beating in the deep bass notes of the piano. The music took me away, soothed me as nothing else ever did. I could play when I was tired, when I was sick, when my head was throbbing, as it was now. To live without music would be unthinkable for me.

I don't know how long my phone had been beeping before I noticed it. I finished the piece—I never stop in the middle of a piece unless there's blood or a life threatening emergency involved—and picked up the mobile, as the Viennese call their cell phones. It was a text message from Arthur Larson, my boss, back home in Minnesota. I sighed.

For someone who lived and breathed the history of the middle ages, Arthur was amazingly adept at the latest technology. He'd picked up the art of text messaging from his students; e-mail was second nature to him, and now he had added internet telephoning to his repertoire. All in all, it was an annoying skill for someone as determined as Arthur was to stay in touch with me. I didn't bother to answer his text message, which said only "Where are you?" Instead I went straight to my computer, opened my e-mail and sent off a message to him. I told him about my day of research at the Musikverein library, but left out everything after that. If Arthur picked up even a hint of what had happened to me since leaving the library, he'd be over here before I could say, "Richard the Lion Hearted." As it was, I fully expected him to appear as soon as the weather warmed up and the lilacs started blooming. He dreamed of a pilgrimage to Dürnstein, where legend has it that Richard was imprisoned and a famous troubadour, Blondel de Nesle, sang outside his window. Most serious musicologists called this story total fiction, but Arthur is a romantic, if ever there was one, and he wanted to believe it. Dürnstein is just outside Vienna, in the area known as the Wachau, and it really is a lovely place to visit, just not with Arthur.

I made sure that my internet telephone icon was set at "not available," so that if Arthur was at his computer, he wouldn't call me immediately. The problem with this technology he so loved was that he'd have a full view of me through the automatic camera on my computer; I didn't want him to see the bandage on my forehead, not to mention the dark circles under my eyes. Arthur had a strong tendency to worry and fuss over me.

He sent a message straight back to me: "Have you found any lost love songs yet?" It was Arthur who'd urged me to expand my Schubert research beyond the early keyboard sonatas I'd focused on for my dissertation. Actually he could be on the right track in his suggestion; an unpublished Schubert manuscript had been found not that long ago in the stacks of the Vienna City Library, the other place I liked to do research. The thing was, only the librarians were allowed back in the stacks, and the whole question of lost love songs was a bit dicey anyway, but I didn't want to get into that with Arthur right now. I just wanted to take some aspirin, soak in a bathtub full of hot scented water, and crawl into bed. I had to teach the next day and needed a good night's sleep. I sent him one more message, which said, "Not yet. I'll tell you more about my research tomorrow." Then I closed my laptop and turned off the lights.

CHAPTER FOUR

The face which appeared in my mirror the next morning didn't look as bad as I thought it would. Sleepy grey green eyes looked back at me, and my straight blonde hair covered the band-aid on my forehead. I'd slept through the night, though I still felt a bit groggy. It turns out that slivovitz is an excellent painkiller. My dreams, I have to admit, had been somewhat strange and filled with naked men. That's all I'm going to say about them.

I blinked at my reflection, pushed my hair back, and tugged gently at the band-aid. A purplish bruise was blossoming around the small cut; it was not a lovely sight, but what could I do? I washed it, applied more first-aid cream and a new band-aid, and then reached for a tube of make-up. I don't usually wear much make-up, but I did my best to cover the bruise, let my hair fall back over my forehead, and hoped that no one would look at me too closely today. How would I explain it? I'd have to think of a story, but meanwhile I drank another cup of coffee and finished getting dressed.

The lump on the back of my head was still tender, but at least it didn't show. By the time I had bundled myself into my coat and boots and pulled on my wool hat and gloves, I felt almost normal. I was the only one on the stairs this morning; the elevator stood empty on the ground floor. My own echoing footsteps were the only sounds to be heard, until I pulled open the outer door to my building.

It had stopped snowing, and the sun shone brightly. Frau Frassl stood on the sidewalk in front of her shop, broom in hand, sweeping the remains of the snow to the curb. She was wearing her cowboy boots again, along with a heavy sweater over her blue smock. The red of her hair seemed even brighter than usual, with the sunlight beaming down on it. She had left the door to the shop ajar, and Willie Nelson's voice drifted out to us. "The last thing I needed the first thing this morning was to have you walk out on me," he sang. Frau Frassl hummed along in her off key alto and swayed back and forth to the beat as she swept. I hated to interrupt, so I stood and watched for a moment, until the song came to an end, and then I cleared my throat.

"*Grüss Gott.*" I addressed her with the traditional Austrian greeting. She stopped her sweeping and turned to me.

"*Guten Morgen, Gnadiges Fräulein Doktor Lindstrom.*" She used the full title again. There was no stopping her. I turned and headed into her store, and she followed me, closing the door behind us. Willie was still singing. I asked for my morning papers; she handed me a copy of the *International Herald Tribune* along with a daily Vienna paper, and I dropped the correct change into her outstretched hand. She was wearing knit gloves with the fingertips cut off, the kind I used to wear to practice back in Minnesota to help keep my fingers warm. I tucked the newspapers into my shoulder bag and was reaching for the door just as it opened.

There was Mitzi, looking elegant and beautiful in a fur trimmed coat and tall leather boots. Her hair was as sleek as the mink on her collar, dark and glossy with just a hint of henna, and her eyes were as dark as her hair. She was clearly much more expert at applying make-up than I was, and she smelled like expensive perfume. I had to wonder where she could be going, looking so elegant, so early in the day. Even without the substantial heels on those boots, she would have been a couple of inches taller than I am, so I had to tip my head upwards when I greeted her. I smiled and said, "*Guten Morgen,*" and she smiled back. Frau Frassl seemed to know already what Mitzi would ask for, and had a fashion magazine and chocolate bar ready for her. She paid for them and then followed me out the door. I paused, not sure what, if anything, to say to her after our evening together, but she solved my problem when she waved and hurried into a waiting taxicab.

I watched it for a moment, and then turned and headed the other direction, toward Schubertgasse. I walked one block over to Nussdorferstrasse, crossed the street, then stood not far from Number Fifty-Four, the house where Schubert was born, to wait for the streetcar which would take me out to the nineteenth district, Döbling, where the college's Vienna house is located.

The streetcar was on time, as always; it was a relief to climb on and find it almost empty. There were no Hungarians and no double doctors, just a few other passengers, and lots of empty seats. I slid into one and looked out the window as we left the ninth district and headed away from the center of the city, watched as the tram glided past the shops and apartments lining Billrothstrasse on the route to Döbling.

Döbling is a beautiful area, once you get off the busy thoroughfares leading into it. Its streets are lined with large trees and old villas, and the wine gardens of Grinzing are just beyond it. Sometimes you can even see the hillsides of the Vienna Woods in the distance. I couldn't sit and enjoy the view right now, though, because the next stop was mine. I stood and headed for the door, pushed the button which would open it, and stepped down once the streetcar came to a stop.

I made a much more graceful exit than I had the day before, not that anyone was watching. I could have waited for a bus to take me to within a few blocks of my destination, but it was such a beautiful day that I decided to walk instead. It was almost a mile to the house, which the college had named "Villa Christina," for Christina Anderson, an alumna who had inherited a fortune and had used some of it to buy this place for the college. I enjoyed my walk though; it's a lovely neighborhood. The house itself is one of those yellow stucco ones common to the area; in fact, the color is such a favorite around here that it has its own name, *Schönbrunner Gelb,* the hue associated with Schönbrunn Palace, the former summer residence of the imperial family. The story is that people tried to elevate their social status by painting their houses that same shade of yellow.

Villa Christina, like many of the houses in the area, is surrounded by an ornate iron fence. Because it used to be a consulate, it has a state of the art security system. I pushed the button at the gate and the secretary buzzed me in. There was another buzzer for the front door, but I stopped on the front porch to scrape the slush from my boots before I pushed that heavy carved door open.

It was warm in the entrance hall, and the aroma of freshly brewed coffee wafted out from the kitchen. The secretary, a Viennese named Helga, nodded at me and continued working at her computer and talking on her phone at the same time; she had a terrific ability to multi-task, and her knowledge of the city and how to get things done here was invaluable. That would probably explain why the college put up with her habit of arriving late, taking a two hour lunch break and leaving early. These are not habits common to Minnesotans. I had just finished hanging up my coat when I heard my name.

"Good Morning, Lily!"

That deep voice belonged to the faculty director of the house, German professor Tom Thornquist, a tall and robust man a few years older than I am. He and his wife, Eva, lived in the house with the students and taught them German language and European history. Austrian professors taught courses in art history and current political events, and I supplied the music history component of the curriculum. I was teaching an overview of Viennese composers from 1750 to 1950, from the Classical Era through Expressionism, a fairly daunting course. Fortunately for me, the city itself helped me do my work, with all of its fabulous concerts, as well as its small museums devoted to composers, the ones found in the numerous apartments where they had lived, worked, or died.

"Come join us for some coffee." Tom called out from the dining room, and I followed his voice down the hall to a beautiful, light filled room. At one end of the long table sat Tom, between two women, one of them his wife Eva, the other an elegant woman who looked a bit like my mother. She was slim, petite, and had silvery blonde hair and clear blue eyes. People often said that I looked like a younger version of my mother, but believe me, no one would ever think that I was related to this stylish woman, who looked much richer than I would ever be.

"Pull up a chair, Lily." Tom gestured to the place next to the exquisitely dressed guest. "Have you met Christina?" I took in her perfectly tailored suit, flawlessly done hair, and sparkling diamond rings. A woman like that can make the rest of us feel positively shabby. I sat up a bit straighter, tugged at my sweater, tried to look dignified.

"Christina Anderson," Tom continued, oblivious to my effort to spruce myself up. "This is Lily Lindstrom."

"How do you do." She held out one of those diamond laden hands to me, and I shook it carefully before sinking into the chair next to hers. This was the very woman who had donated the house and started the program of study in Vienna. I had never met her, probably because she spent very little time in Minnesota, but Arthur absolutely adored her. It wasn't hard to guess why.

Shrewd eyes met mine and assessed me as I poured the cream into my coffee.

"We were just talking about you." Her gaze shifted to my coffee and I stopped pouring the cream an instant before my cup would have overflowed.

"Tom is very enthusiastic about all the outings you've planned with the students."

I cleared my throat. "Yes, well." I took a small sip of the strong Viennese coffee. "The city has so much to offer. What's hard is choosing the best concerts and places to take them."

To my own ears, it sounded like a pretty glib and self-evident statement, but it was the best I could do while she was staring at me so intently. Fortunately, she didn't seem to expect anything more profound at that moment. She merely nodded and kept her eyes on me.

"I'm sure it helps that you studied here yourself, and that you know the city so well." I wondered what else she knew about me, but decided that there were some things that no one else could possibly know, or so I hoped. Wisely, I said nothing and she continued.

"Arthur assured me that you were the very best person for this position." She turned toward Tom. "And Tom agrees."

I glanced at Tom, who grinned back at me.

"Yes, indeed. Our Lily knows what she's doing."

Our Lily? What could I say after that? "I do my best."

I shifted in my chair, struggled to shift the conversation from me to the students.

"We're all going to *The Magic Flute* tonight."

She smiled, showing teeth which gleamed almost as brightly as her diamonds. This woman took good care of herself.

"Wonderful!" She turned toward Tom again. "I'll be there myself. Let's meet during the intermission." She smiled again, and this time she positively glowed. "There is someone I'd like to introduce you to."

Then she stood up, smoothed out her fine wool suit, and said her farewells. I didn't move until I heard the front door close behind her, and then I let out my breath and slumped down in my chair. I reached for one of the Viennese confections I hadn't wanted to eat while our benefactress was sitting next to me, and let the sugar do its work while Tom talked. He answered the question I hadn't asked, since my mouth was full.

"Christina arrived yesterday. She keeps an apartment here, over in the third district, near the Belvedere. She likes to be here during *Fasching*."

That's the season between New Year's and the beginning of Lent when the Viennese have several balls to choose from every night, from large formal dances to small costume parties. Every organization, from electricians and plumbers to lawyers and doctors, throws a party. It's the Viennese version of "Carnival."

I poured myself some more coffee to wash down the delicious pastry. Tom just kept talking.

"This program is dear to her. Since her husband died and left her all that money, it seems to help fill her time." He lifted his eyebrows when I took another pastry, but he didn't say a word about my eating habits. Instead, he continued to talk about Christina.

"She'll probably be around here a lot this winter. Eva thinks she's lonely." His gaze left me and went to the doorway to the kitchen. A second later, his two year old son, Jack, came toddling into the room, followed by one of the students. They adored him, and I liked him too, but not so much when his fingers were as sticky as they looked right now. Of course he came straight to me. Children and dogs gravitate toward me for some reason. My dad says it's the hope for crumbs from whatever I'm eating.

He scrambled into my lap and patted my face with those sticky fingers. I can't imagine that he would have done this to Christina Anderson, but then she probably never dropped a morsel of anything. Eva dipped her napkin in water and held it out to me. I grabbed one of Jack's little hands, but the other one had moved to my forehead. I winced when he rubbed the bruise around my band-aid.

"Ouch!"

Eva got up from her chair and plucked her son from my lap while I dabbed at my now sticky cheek with the damp napkin.

Tom leaned in to get a better look at my forehead.

"What happened to you, Lily?"

"Oh." I had forgotten to come up with a good story, so I had to improvise. "Nothing really. I just bumped my head, that's all." Fortunately, Tom seemed satisfied with that explanation, and I decided to escape while I could, before Eva got interested.

"I'd better go over my notes." I pushed my chair back, stood up, brushed the remains of the pastries from my lap, and headed for the door. "See you later."

I crossed the hall to the classroom I used, closed the door behind me, and pulled today's lecture from my bag. By the time my students had joined me, I was prepared to continue their education in the composers of Vienna. I was almost finished with Mozart, if you overlooked the fact that it was impossible to ever finish with Mozart, and looking forward to getting started with Schubert. The timing was perfect; his birthday was coming up.

There were ten students this winter, all living in this large house, all experiencing Vienna for the first time. Young, fresh faced, earnest, steeped in the Protestant work ethic; they were as diligent and quiet as we expect Minnesota Lutherans to be. I figured that they'd be able to relate well to Schubert's sweet melancholy, accustomed as they were to endless grey winters. What I wondered was how they would deal with the underlying romanticism, his and Vienna's, how they would react to the abundance of feelings fully expressed, rather than concealed beneath a stoic Scandinavian surface.

I'd already taken them to several concerts, but tonight would be our first visit to the opera. They had good questions, and by the time I'd answered them, I was ready for a few minutes to myself. As soon as the door closed behind them, I pulled the newspapers I'd bought that morning out of my bag. Frau Frassl handed me a different Vienna paper every day, depending on her mood and what Willie was singing when I came in. Today it was *Die Presse*; I scanned the lead articles a bit anxiously, I have to admit. I hadn't seen any photographers lurking in the street the night before, but then I had been pretty distracted. Could anyone possibly know about the Minister of the Interior's visit to Mitzi or his trip to the hospital? Did the Viennese even care about such things? I hoped not, but I kept turning pages, kept looking.

I really didn't expect what I saw though. There toward the back of the paper on the society page was a picture of Helmut Vogl with a lovely woman at his side. It wasn't Mitzi. I looked closely at the fine print beneath the photo. It was his wife. Did Mitzi know he had a wife? More importantly, did his wife know about Mitzi?

I thought about this all the way back to my apartment, on the streetcar, as I walked the couple of blocks back to Sobieskigasse. I thought about the tears in Mitzi's eyes, the way she'd called him

"*Liebling.*" That would be "darling" in English. Her feelings for him had seemed to be quite genuine, but then maybe she was just very good at expressing emotion. I thought about his wife, who had looked quite lovely in a long evening gown in the picture, next to her tuxedo clad husband. The photo had been taken at one of the many Viennese balls being held this winter. And, of course, I thought about how he'd looked when I'd last seen him, and I even thought about who had been helping him into his car.

I didn't expect to see that helper when I reached my apartment house though, not really, and I especially didn't expect to see him coming down the stairs with Mitzi, or standing so close to her with his hands on her shoulders, or receiving what looked to me like an overly affectionate Viennese kiss on each cheek from Mitzi. They didn't notice me for a moment, and that was a good thing, because it took me that long to get my own emotions under control. I had an overwhelming urge to swing my heavy shoulder bag at them, but instead I cleared my throat and stomped my feet harder than I needed to on the stone floor.

Double Doctor Cameron turned away from Mitzi and met my gaze without blinking.

"Well, Dr. Lindstrom," he said. "It's good to see you again."

CHAPTER FIVE

I like to think of myself as an even tempered and logical person, someone who thinks before she acts, someone who is unfailingly polite, someone who, with typical midwestern courtesy, says, "after you," rather than pushing to be the first in line. That's why it's hard to explain why I felt the way I did at that moment, why my fingers itched to pull Mitzi's beautifully arranged hair, why my arms tensed with the urge to push her out the door. I don't even want to mention what I felt like doing with the maddeningly calm man in front of me.

Of course, all I did was stand there while Mitzi finished kissing his cheeks, pivoted gracefully on her high heels, and said, "*Auf Wiedersehen*," in her husky voice. I watched her make her exit and then turned my attention back to the double doctor. He looked even better than I had remembered. A dark blue sweater matched his eyes, which were now focused unnervingly on me. I cleared my throat again.

"It's good to see you too, Dr. Cameron."

He flashed a smile which I felt all the way to my toes. "We need to talk," he said, and he stepped to my side, placed his hand at the small of my back, and guided me into the elevator. He really must be from Atlanta. Minnesota men didn't move like this, at least not the ones I knew.

The elevator vibrated its way to the third floor; we stepped out together, and I pulled out my key. It felt like déjà vu all over again, as my Viennese friend Sophie liked to say. She would certainly have plenty to say if she knew what had happened to me during the past twenty-four hours. Sophie would have to wait, though, for once more Dr. Cameron and I were in my small foyer, hanging up our coats. Once more we headed for the kitchen, but this time I pulled a tall bottle of my favorite Austrian beer from the refrigerator and rummaged in the cupboard for some pretzels to go with it. He already had the glasses out and took the bottle from me. The man certainly knew his way around my kitchen already.

"Can we sit someplace more comfortable?"

I nodded and led the way to my living room. I sat on my favorite chair close to the piano and left the couch for him.

He raised his glass to me, "*Prost.*"

I returned the toast and took a sip. Ah. Exactly what I needed. I glanced at my watch and then at him. "You wanted to talk?"

"I thought you might like to know the rest of what happened last night." He leaned toward me across the small coffee table. I tried not to do the same, though it was difficult to sit still, so close to him. I watched his hands as he reached for the pretzels. They were good hands, I have to say, long fingered and graceful. When I lifted my eyes to his face again, he was looking at me intently and this time I did meet his gaze. Wham.

What can I say about that feeling, that squeezing of the heart, that breathless sense of familiarity and anticipation mixed with longing? Some would call it infatuation; others would call it simple attraction or desire. Sophie would snort with laughter and call it lust. I couldn't have reached my age without having experienced this before, and I had the bruises on my heart and the bittersweet memories to prove it. My brain was shouting "Caution!" while my body was saying something else all together.

Dr. Cameron, meanwhile, was talking about Herr Vogl, or so I gathered. I hadn't been listening, but I began to pay attention. Perhaps my brain was winning the battle after all.

"Have you heard a word I've said?" He leaned back against the couch cushions and took another sip of beer. I watched him lick his lips. Good grief.

"Oh. I'm so sorry. I was thinking about my students and the opera tonight." I took a sip of my own beer and forced myself to concentrate on the matter at hand. "Can you explain it one more time?" At least I didn't bat my eyes at him, but I did my best to sound innocent and contrite.

He sighed. "As I was saying." He stopped and looked at me, to make sure that I was paying attention this time. "Herr Vogl had coronary angioplasty this morning at the Rudolfinerhaus; that's a private hospital up in the nineteenth district."

I nodded. I knew about the Rudolfinerhaus; it's a few stops beyond where I got off the streetcar today. It's a favorite of the rich, the famous, the politicians, those who can afford state of the art treatment, discreet staff, and elegant surroundings.

Stephen kept talking. "It turns out that his loss of consciousness while he was . . ." He paused here as if searching for precisely the right words. " . . . with Miss Tauber last night was fortunate. It served as a warning that his heart needed attention."

"I'll say his heart needs attention!" I set my beer glass down on the table with a quick staccato motion. If I'd been at the piano, it would have produced a fine forte ending. As it was, it elicited just a wince from the man on my couch. I dashed to my foyer, pulled this morning's paper out of my bag and came back into the room, waving it in his face.

"Look at this. Just look at this!" I opened it to the picture of Herr Vogl with his wife. "He has a wife!" I paused for breath; I was all but gasping with indignation. "Do you think Mitzi knows he's married?"

He didn't seem to have anything to say, so I kept going. He just sat there sipping his beer and watching me.

"Is that what you were telling her? Is that why you were with Mitzi?" At least I stopped before I added, "And is that why you had your hands on her shoulders and and looked so pleased to have her kiss your cheek?" I did have some self control.

He set his beer down much more carefully than I had and tipped his head back so that he could look me right in the eye as he finally began to speak. "Back when you were thinking about tonight's opera, or whatever it is you were thinking about . . ." He stopped to smile, and I was distracted but didn't move. "I was about to tell you that I had come to see Miss Tauber to tell her about Herr Vogl's surgery." He stopped. Maybe he expected me to say something, but I didn't, so he continued. "His marital status was not discussed."

"Oh." I thought about this for a moment. "Well, I may have to tell Mitzi myself. I'm sure she'd want to know. I mean, I'd want to know if someone I had a relationship with was married, wouldn't you?"

His smile was starting to twitch. He began to speak, hesitated, then tried again. "Relationship? What kind of relationship exactly do you think Miss Tauber has with Herr Vogl?"

I was pleased that he kept calling her Miss Tauber and not Mitzi, but I wasn't sure where he was headed with this conversation. "They have," I paused, replaying the picture of Helmut Vogl naked on Mitzi's bed last night. "a rather intimate relationship." I decided to elaborate. "It looked like love to me."

His smile twitched again, and then his shoulders started to quiver; if I didn't know better, I'd think he was laughing. I couldn't tell, because he had lowered his head into his hands. Wait. I strained my ears. I could hear him now, hear the soft chuckle. He was definitely laughing. So much for infatuation. I wasn't even sure that I liked the man right now.

"What in the world is so funny about that?"

He looked up at me, but it took him a minute to get himself under control. "You are priceless, a true romantic." There it was again, that deep rumbling laugh. "No wonder she came to you for help!"

"Well, she did call him *'Schatz'* and *'Liebling.'* You were there. You must have heard her." My explanation didn't seem to satisfy him, so I tried again. "And you didn't see how he looked at her." I sat back down and reached for my beer while I waited for him to respond.

"I can just imagine how he looked at her." He grinned.

I frowned at him, and he quit grinning.

"Lily," he said, and his tone had become more serious. This was the first time he'd called me by my first name, rather than "Dr. Lindstrom." I tried not to be thrilled. I was beginning to be concerned by the absence of my usual good sense and balance when he was around. He'd called me a romantic. Was I really? I didn't usually think of myself that way. He kept talking.

"Listen carefully." He leaned toward me again, and this time I did let myself lean toward him too. "Mitzi Tauber has many," he paused, apparently considering his words, "relationships. Helmut Vogl is not the only man she sees. Furthermore, she's receiving deliveries of questionable substances from those Hungarians who knocked you down."

I sat perfectly still now, and struggled to make sense of what he was saying.

"Questionable substances?"

"Yes." He ran his fingers through that thick dark hair. "That's all I can tell you, except that you need to be careful, not quite so trusting."

Was he talking about my dealings with Mitzi, or himself now? I didn't know, but said, "Okay. I was just trying to be a good neighbor."

He sighed. "I know, and it's very admirable of you, but . . ."

"But?"

Those deep blue eyes, only inches from mine now, didn't waver. "But I don't want you to get in the middle of this and get hurt."

Just when I thought he might lean in even closer, he sat back, reached into his pocket, and pulled out a pen and small notepad. He scribbled something on a page, then ripped it off and handed it to me. "That's my phone number in Vienna. I want you to call me if you see or hear anything unusual. Or if you're frightened, or . . ."

Now it was my turn to smile. "Or?"

"Lily, just be careful."

He stood then, picked up his beer glass, and headed toward the kitchen. Here was a man who cleaned up after himself; that was something in his favor. I followed him and his example, but by the time I reached the front hall, he was already shrugging into his coat. I watched him, watched the strength and grace of his hands as he buttoned the last button and pulled his scarf into place.

"No hat?"

He paused as he reached into his pockets for his gloves. "I guess I'm used to Atlanta." He shrugged. "At least it's stopped snowing."

He reached out then, lifted my hair from my forehead, and ran his fingers gently around the band-aid. His eyes narrowed when he saw me wince, and he dropped his hand to my shoulder. I held my breath as he closed the space between us, but I kept my eyes wide open. I wanted to watch whatever he did next. What he did next was brush first one cheek, then the other, with those lips I had imagined might be heading toward mine.

"You can breathe now, Lily."

His nose was about an inch from mine, and his eyes were so close that I could almost feel him blink. I could see the fine ends of those thick dark lashes curve upward as he opened his eyes wider.

I tried to take a deep breath, I really did, but my lungs weren't cooperating. In fact, my entire body felt as if it belonged to someone else, as if it could no longer follow my instructions. Only when he finally stepped back, dropped his hands from my shoulders and began to pull on his gloves did I manage to suck in some air. It didn't help that what I inhaled contained his scent, a mixture of fresh soap and woodsy aftershave.

I sniffed the air again. I liked that smell. I didn't realize that I'd closed my eyes until I felt his gloved hand lift my chin. When I opened them he was leaning in again, and this time those lips did brush mine, but very gently and only for a second. Had I imagined it?

He had his hand on the doorknob already, and I struggled to find the right words to say. All I came up with was, "*Wiederschauen,* Dr. Cameron," and that came out in a husky whisper. You would think that someone with a Ph.D. could manage something slightly more eloquent, but I did at least elicit a smile and a flash of deep blue from those eyes.

"I think you can call me Stephen now," he said as he opened the door. And then he added as he started down the stairs, "Enjoy the opera."

CHAPTER SIX

The Vienna State Opera House is an impressive building, its stone façade a strong and graceful presence on the corner of the Ring and Kärtnerstrasse. Lights glittered behind its windows, shone through the glass in the entrance doors, cast a welcoming glow toward all of us hurrying toward those doors.

I'd bolted down a quick dinner and dressed in record time: black dress, black boots, black coat. It was much easier when everything matched. Even so, when I joined the crowd in the gorgeous cream and gold foyer, I was out of breath and had to push my way to the end of the line at the coat check counter. I rubbed shoulders with elegant Viennese, squeezed past groups of casually dressed students, stepped around and between conversations about the newest singing sensation and tonight's conductor.

By the time I'd checked my coat and started up the main stairway, only minutes remained before the overture would begin. I moved as fast as I could up that green carpeted walkway, turned right when I reached the balcony level, and found my seat just as the chimes sounded to let us know that the opera was about to start. Thank goodness I was at the end of the row. I nodded to Tom and Eva at the other end, whispered "Hello" to the student next to me and sat down as the lights dimmed and the conductor made his way to the podium.

I love this moment, the moment when the conductor lifts his baton, the musicians sit poised and ready to play, their eyes on the baton, the lights on their music stands casting a glow on their instruments. I held my breath, watched those arms, sat on the edge of my seat waiting for the first chord, and there it came, that powerful resonant sonority, and then again, those rich full tones repeated like someone knocking on a huge door. Finally the strings moved into their smooth opening melody, and I could exhale. When I began to breathe again, I was in rhythm with the orchestra, my eyes on the conductor's arms, my excitement building with the increasing tempo. Then the strings took off, bows flying through the opening allegro section, joined by the winds as the fugue built until the anticipation was almost unbearable. My fingers drummed along on the arm rests; my feet tapped the beat. It was all I could do to stay in my seat. The curtain hadn't even opened yet, and I had already been swept away. By the time the final chords of the overture sounded, I was ready to stand and cheer.

I didn't though. I watched mesmerized as the curtain opened and Tamino appeared, running to escape a huge snake, singing, *"Zu hilfe, zu hilfe!"* I knew this opera; I knew that Tamino would survive. Nevertheless I was completely caught up as soon as he appeared. I rummaged in my handbag for my opera glasses, managed to get them out and focused on the stage in time for the ladies who had rescued him to sing their song of triumph. Ah. I exhaled, sank back into my seat and awaited the arrival onstage of my favorite baritone, Vienna's beloved Fritz Gerling. I didn't have to wait long; the ladies finished their song, exited stage right as Fritz, playing Papageno, the Queen's bird-catcher entered stage left, singing, *"Der Vogelfänger bin ich ja."* "I am the bird catcher." Covered all in feathers and playing his pan pipe, he may not be everyone's idea of a leading man, but his full, robust voice and cheerful presence captivated me as easily as if I were one of his birds. I must have been humming along, because the student next to me prodded me gently.

"Professor Lindstrom," came the whisper. "You're singing."

I nodded.

"You'd better stop."

"Oh."

I managed to rein myself in during the rest of the first act, or at least I did my best. By the time the curtain came down at the end of Act One, I was ready for something to drink.

The lights came up; I stuffed my opera glasses back into my handbag, then stood and stretched. The student next to me was looking at me as if he had never seen me before. Odd. Hadn't he been in my class just this afternoon? I followed his gaze to where it rested on the neckline of my dress, realized what it was he didn't recognize, and cleared my throat.

His eyes jumped back to meet mine; he coughed and said, "Glad you made it, Dr. Lindstrom." He paused, and then gestured toward the aisle. "Are you going out for some refreshments?"

"Yes, right. Of course." The whole row seemed to be waiting for me to move, so I started up the aisle, pressed through the packed hallway, and headed toward the main stairway. Tom and Eva were there ahead of me; they'd had the aisle seats at the other end of the row.

"Good. There you are. We're supposed to meet Christina in the Schwindfoyer."

"Of course." How could I have forgotten that? We moved shoulder to shoulder down the magnificent staircase, advanced with the crowd flowing toward the sumptuous reception rooms. There, under the painting of *Fidelio,* near the bust of Beethoven, stood Christina

Anderson, dazzling in a silver dress, her diamonds glittering under the light of the crystal chandeliers. She lifted one hand toward us in an elegant summons. We threaded our way through the crowd to join her.

"There you are." Her voice sounded like a low purr tonight. She had one of her diamond laden hands on the arm of a handsome, well dressed man, a man who looked as if he were used to having those hands on him.

"Michael, I'd like you to meet two of our faculty members, Dr. Lily Lindstrom." She nodded in my direction. "And Dr. Thomas Thornquist, and his wife, Eva." Her smile was positively radiant. "This is my friend and neighbor, Michael Fodor." She turned back to him. "We like to call him, *"Der Graf,"* though of course they don't allow that anymore."

In English, that title would translate to "The Count," and as Christina had said when she introduced him, those titles aren't used officially anymore in Austria. Nevertheless, you do still hear them occasionally. There will always be people who are fascinated by those things, I guess. I was a bit surprised by Christina though. Minnesotans generally aren't impressed by titles, unless one of the Scandinavian monarchs comes to visit.

Michael Fodor looked nothing like the King of Sweden, but that didn't seem to matter to Christina. I would never say that she actually giggled, though the sound coming from her well made up lips was rather bubbly. Maybe it was caused by what she was drinking. I looked longingly at the flute she held in her hands. She caught my gaze.

"Graf, mein Schatz." She angled her head closer to his. "We need *Sekt* all around." *Sekt* is the Austrian version of champagne. Wonderful stuff.

He turned away for a moment, said something to a short, dark haired man behind him, and in moments, the man reappeared with a tray full of flutes filled with the bubbly beverage. Very impressive. That man, who looked strangely familiar to me, must have stood in line earlier and had the loaded tray ready for Christina's Graf and his retinue.

The Count, as I'd begun to think of him, lifted his glass. We all joined the toast and then sipped the sparkling liquid. Ah. This was exactly what I had needed ever since that moment at my door, that moment with Stephen.

Christina's voice pulled me back from that moment to this. "As I was telling Michael," she was saying, "You're quite an expert on Schubert, aren't you, Lily?"

I choked on a bubble, caught my breath, and tried not to sputter as I focused on the man standing opposite me. He was taller than Christina, but not by much; his shoulders were broad under his beautifully tailored jacket; his head was topped by expertly trimmed dark hair threaded with silver. Altogether an attractive package, if you like the wealthy, domineering type, the kind who can make you nervous with just one glance from eyes which are no doubt accustomed to quick calculations and shrewd decisions. Those eyes were traveling up and down my black clad body, and met mine only when I spoke.

"Schubert. Franz. Yes." I paused and took a deep breath, willed myself to concentrate. "I did my dissertation on his early keyboard sonatas, but right now I'm studying some of his songs." I certainly wouldn't mention my Arthur inspired search for those lost love songs.

He smiled then. "Ah. Good. Do you like *Die Winterreise?*"

There was only one correct answer to that question about Schubert's song cycle, "The Winter Journey," asked in that tone of voice, by a man staring at me the way he was. "Well, of course."

"Wonderful!" He lifted his glass, took a sip, then continued. "You must come to my *Schubertiade* tomorrow night then, don't you think so Christina?"

I don't know how she managed to squeeze even closer to him, but somehow she did, and her answer, when it emerged from those well-glossed lips, was somewhere between a breathy sigh and an intimate whisper.

"Of course, Michael."

"Very good then." He turned toward the hallway, just as the bell signaling the end of the intermission sounded. Over his shoulder he said, "Christina will give you the details." Then they were gone, and I was left to gulp the rest of my champagne and hurry back to my seat.

The second act of *The Magic Flute* begins in a grove of palms outside a large temple. It's all very dark and mysterious. The plot revolves around freemasonry; in fact, the main characters have been identified with some of the most powerful people of Mozart's time, including Empress Maria Theresa. I won't go into the details now, except to say that the story is fascinating, and the music is among the finest ever written. So when the lights dimmed and the singing began, I should have been totally mesmerized by what was happening onstage. Instead, I was pulling my opera glasses from my purse and aiming them toward the box seats to my left and below me, searching for the flash of diamonds and silver which would identify Christina Anderson and her Count.

My opera glasses are quite powerful; my dad gave them to me years ago and they were the best he could afford. Right now, they framed a view of Christina and Michael Fodor in a pose which could certainly be called operatic, if it was the part where the hero and heroine finally got to embrace each other. She was leaning toward him, and his hands were, well, I won't go into any more detail about where his hands were, except to say that he was skirting the outer edges of Viennese propriety.

I must have gasped, because the student next to me squeezed my arm and whispered, "Are you all right, Dr. Lindstrom?" Fortunately, the priests were blowing their trumpets at that moment, and the full volume of the music covered both my gasp and his whisper. The Viennese do not tolerate any noise or distractions during performances; I'm pretty sure that what Christina and the Count were doing would not be condoned either.

I whispered "Yes, I'm fine," and then refocused my opera glasses. I couldn't resist just one quick check of Christina's box before I returned to the action on the stage. They were still there, sitting very close to one another, but now they were watching the opera, hands in their own laps. Had I dreamed what I'd observed a few moments earlier? I didn't think so, though I remembered the lump on my head and had to wonder whether my brain had been affected by my encounter with the running Hungarians, not to mention my moments with Stephen Cameron.

Fortunately, Mozart's music has a way of carrying me off to another plane of existence; some people talk about entering the zone or experiencing a runner's high. All I have to do is listen to those heavenly notes and I'm transported. Once I refocused on the opera, I was pulled back to that musical sphere and away from my questions about Christina and her companion.

I shed a few tears during Pamina's exquisite aria, *"Ach, ich fühl's, es ist verschwunden."* "Ah, I feel it, it's gone forever," she sings, when she thinks that her true love has abandoned her. I do that every time I hear it. It may be just a more elegant version of "Breaking up is hard to do," but it gets to me every time, and I feel the pain right along with her. At least for Pamina, the suffering came to an end, and she was finally united with her beloved, Tamino. Papageno and Papagena ended up together too. I love a happy ending. Beautiful music, incredible voices—it doesn't get much better than this. I love this city!

"Well, I do too, Dr. Lindstrom. What's not to love?"

Good grief. How much had I said aloud? Sometimes I worry that everything I think comes straight out of my mouth. It's a danger we musicians face, trained as we are to express emotions directly through our bodies. Never mind that I am a pianist, not a singer. Fortunately my student didn't seem to think it was odd for me to say this while everyone else was cheering and applauding. He was smiling at me and nodding.

I took that as a cue to keep talking. "Yes, it doesn't get any better than this, does it?"

We continued this conversation about the incredibly high quality of Vienna's music all the way down to the coat check counter, where he helped me into my black wool coat. I do appreciate a polite young man. He stuck with me as I pushed open the doors, stepped out into the cold starry night and made my way toward the street car stop. I didn't expect him to stay with me all the way to my apartment house, but he did, and he was still standing there as I inserted my key in the outer door and pushed it open.

I turned to thank him. To say that I didn't like the adoring look in his eyes is an understatement. I hate it when this happens to young, impressionable male students. I held out my hand, grasped his and shook it energetically before he could do anything else with it.

"Thank-you so much! See you in class!" With these words I slipped inside and closed the door in his face.

CHAPTER SEVEN

I had delightful dreams filled with luscious melodies, magic flutes and dark haired heroes. I woke up slowly, reluctantly, snug under my down comforter, still hearing Fritz Gerling's mellow baritone floating through my head.

"Ein Mädchen oder Weibchen wünscht Papageno sich," he sang. Like many others, he's wishing he had a sweetheart. I hummed along, opened my eyes slowly, wondered why my memory wasn't filling in the glockenspiel part, then shot out of bed when I realized that the voice I was hearing wasn't emerging from my memory, but from somewhere in my building. It sounded as if my favorite baritone was singing in the stairwell.

"It can't be." I threw on my robe, raced through the living room to my front hall, pressed my eye to the peephole in my front door and saw nothing but the opposite wall.

The voice was stronger now, resonating within the stone enclosure. *". . . so ein sanftes Täubchen wär' Seligkeit für mich,"* he continued. "Such a gentle little dove would be bliss for me." Those are not my words; they are the words of the librettist, a friend of Mozart named Emanuel Shikaneder. I do like them though.

I couldn't help myself; I pulled the door open and stuck my head out. There he was, not ten feet from me, coming down the stairway.

It was Fritz Gerling, no doubt about it. He was well into his aria and didn't see me, not yet. I drew back, left my door open just a crack, and watched him descend. His step was light; he looked as cheerful as the song he sang. He could have been onstage, so perfect was his diction, but he was wearing a wool suit instead of Papageno's feathered outfit.

He was close to my door now, and close to the end of the aria too, when another voice floated down from above us. It belonged to Mitzi.

"Wiedersehen, mein Schatz."

He stopped, turned, gave a sweeping bow in her direction, and, hand to his heart, as if receiving applause from an audience, called out, *"Bis später, meine Liebe."* Then he blew a kiss up the stairwell and continued right past my door without stopping. His eyes were still looking upward. I hoped he wouldn't miss the next steps. He didn't.

I eased my door shut and leaned against it. "Good-bye my treasure? Until later my love?" What did this mean? What about Helmut Vogl? How many sweethearts did this woman have? Stephen had been trying to tell me about her, but I'd been distracted. That's putting it mildly. I'd have to pay closer attention next time, if there was a next time. Meanwhile, my phone was ringing.

I ran back through my apartment, picked it up, and managed a breathless "Hello."

"Dr. Lindstrom?"

I recognized that voice, though the last time I'd heard it, it had sounded softer and more seductive. Of course, Christina Anderson hadn't been talking to me the last time I'd heard her voice.

"Yes. Good Morning."

"I hope you enjoyed the opera last night."

Not half as much as you did, I thought, but what I said was, "It was wonderful. I loved every moment." That was true.

"Oh, so did I, but that's not the reason for my call." She cleared her throat and I waited. "Michael asked me to give you directions to his apartment."

I searched for a pen and paper and she continued.

"He lives on Metternichgasse, off Rennweg. You know, opposite the lower Belvedere."

I did know, and I jotted down the address, as I listened to the rest of the details about tonight's gathering. Michael Fodor, Christina's Count, was planning a *Schubertiade*, an evening of Schubert's music, in celebration of his coming birthday. Franz was born on January 31st, 1797. Today was the 29th.

"Yes. Right. I've got it. Eight o'clock. I'll be there."

We said good-bye; I slipped the phone into the pocket of my robe and headed for the kitchen. I was on my second cup of coffee when it rang again. At least this time I didn't have to run across the apartment to answer it.

"Hi friend." I loved hearing those words. It was Sophie. I'd met her during my Fulbright year here, and we'd stayed in touch ever since. She taught in a private school in Vienna.

"I have a half day off. Let's have lunch." Before I could reply, she continued, "I know you skip meals unless someone feeds you, so I won't let you say no."

You have to love a friend like that. "Sure Sophie. I'm planning to do some research at the Vienna City Library today, you know, the one on Bartensteingasse with the Schubert Collection." While I'd immersed myself in Schubert, Sophie had chosen to major in Mahler. "How can you go wrong with *Das Lied von der Erde?*" she had asked. Well, I never did answer that, especially since I knew that Sophie's real interest was in Alma, Mahler's wife. Now there was a woman with a story, one we loved to talk about over glasses of wine. Today though, we planned to meet for something more nourishing, and once we'd set the time and place, I finished my coffee and headed for the shower.

I was fresh and clean and clothed in wool from head to toe. I pulled on my boots, grabbed my bag and keys and headed down the same steps Fritz Gerling had used barely an hour before. I looked carefully, but he hadn't dropped anything. The only evidence that he'd been there was stored in my memory. Would anyone believe it? I hoped so, because I was dying to tell someone.

I pulled open the outer door and stepped into the pearly gray dampness of winter in Vienna. The lights were on in Frau Frassl's shop, and Willie Nelson's voice greeted me as soon as I walked inside. "You were always on my mind," he sang. I liked that one. Frau Frassl was swaying along to the melody, eyes closed, head nodding to the beat. I hated to interrupt, but Mitzi, who was standing in front of the counter, clad in fur and leather, had no such reluctance. She leaned so close to Frau Frassl that their noses were almost touching and shouted, *"Schocolade, bitte! Sofort!"*

Frau Frassl's eyes flew open and she jerked as if she'd been slapped, but she handed Mitzi a chocolate bar and a magazine, took her money, and watched her hurry out the door to the waiting taxi.

"Business is good for that one," she muttered, in German of course. The rest of it I won't translate except to say that it wasn't very complimentary. I figured that could have been because of the lack of respect Mitzi had shown for Willie, but I was curious enough to ask just what business Mitzi was in.

"You'll have to ask her," was the only reply I got, as Frau Frassl handed me my newspapers. She was moving to the music again, so I turned toward the door and stuffed them into my bag. It was pointless to try to converse with her when she was thinking only of her favorite cowboy. I walked the few blocks to Nussdorferstrasse and waited for the number thirty-eight streetcar. I was headed for the library.

I admit that I was looking for a blue eyed, dark haired Georgian as I scanned the passengers on the streetcar, but I was probably as likely to see him today as Frau Frassl was to meet Willie Nelson. He wasn't on the number thirty-eight. I didn't see him when I changed to the number two at the Schottentor. I kept watching for him when I got off at the Rathausplatz across from the Burgtheater and strolled past the skaters on the rink in front of the gothic Rathaus. Nevertheless I jumped when I heard his voice in my ear and felt his hand on my arm.

"How was the opera?"

I turned and gazed directly into those eyes. Big mistake. I couldn't think straight, let alone talk. I blinked, looked away, took a deep breath.

"Good. It was good. I mean fabulous, of course. Superb." I looked at him again. I could breathe now, a good sign.

He was smiling.

"And Fritz Gerling? Was he in fine form?"

Why would he ask particularly about Fritz, but not about the gorgeous soprano or any of the other singers? Why was I so suspicious? Did I really think that he lurked outside my building waiting for Hungarians making deliveries to Mitzi or watching the men who came and went up and down my stairway. Okay, I admit it. I did think that, but all I said was, "Yes, of course."

The cobblestones were still slick from yesterday's snow; he held me steady as we walked one block up Stadiongasse and then turned left onto Bartensteingasse. We stopped at number nine, the entrance to this section of the Vienna City Library. I didn't pull away from his supporting arm. Leaning on him felt good, I have to say.

"Lily." His smooth deep voice vibrated in my ear. I took a step toward the door, then turned to face him.

He was reaching toward me, but he didn't seem to have the same thought in mind that I did.

"May I borrow your newspapers while you're doing your research?"

"You want my newspapers?"

"Did you think I wanted something else?"

I shook my head, "What else could you possibly want from me?" I pulled the papers out of my bag and held them out to him.

He held my gaze as he took them from me. I wasn't sure what I saw in those eyes.

"I can't answer that right now." He paused, looked at his watch, then continued. "Can you meet me for lunch?"

I couldn't believe it. I hadn't had lunch with anyone in days, and today Sophie was expecting me and now Stephen was asking too.

"I'm awfully sorry, but I already have lunch plans."

He didn't say anything but he didn't go anywhere either. There was really only one polite thing for me to do, and I did it.

"I'm meeting an old friend. I guess there's no reason you couldn't join us."

He smiled. "Are you sure?"

"Of course." Sophie would love this. "Meet me here at noon and we can walk together." I turned toward the entrance. "And don't lose my newspapers."

I watched him walk away, watched until he turned the corner and moved out of sight. Then I entered the building, climbed the steps to the first floor, pressed the button next to the library, and pushed the door open when the librarian buzzed me in.

We were old friends, this librarian and I. His name was Kurt Baumgartner and he'd worked here for years. He was a typical Viennese in appearance, with his wire rimmed glasses and neat brown hair. He wasn't as tall as Stephen, but he wasn't short either. Kurt was a very nice guy, a scholar with a good heart. He was waiting when I got to the top of the steps, and I was glad to see him.

"*Gröss Gott.*" That's a colloquial Austrian expression, which translates literally as "Greet God." Don't ask me where it came from; that would be the subject of another research paper. Just believe me that it's the customary greeting in Vienna. I said the same thing in reply and followed him into the catalogue room. He was whistling, as usual. It sounded like a Schubert melody.

"Which song is it?"

"Now that is a good question, Lily, one you should try to answer."

Franz Schubert had composed more than six hundred songs, and I was working my way through them one at a time, starting with the most famous. Kurt had helped me back when I was doing my research on the piano sonatas and loved it that I was finally doing what he thought I should have done long ago. "How can you study Schubert," he had asked, "without investigating his songs?'

It was a reasonable question, and all I could say was that we music majors have to choose our areas of concentration, and it was only natural that I should gravitate toward compositions written for my own instrument. I can sing, but no one would pay me to do so. The great thing was that Schubert, with his incredible gift for melody, had not only written beautiful songs, but also extraordinary piano parts to accompany them. In fact for Schubert, the piano accompaniment was integral to the song; it set the mood and created a framework for the words.

"Well?" He was waiting for me to identify his tune. He kept whistling. I kept listening.

"*Lachen und Weinen*." In English, "Laughing and Crying," a lovely song.

"Yes! You're improving!"

He waited for me for me to finish filling out my request forms, and then disappeared into the stacks while I found a seat in the reading room. I couldn't possibly examine the manuscripts of every single song Schubert had ever written, even if they were all in Vienna, which they were not. Many of them were here, though, either in this library or in that of the *Gesellschaft der Musikfreunde*, where I'd been working the day I'd met Stephen. What I had to do was go through the Thematic Catalogue put together by Otto Deutsch, choose the manuscripts I wanted to study that day, fill out the request form with the name of the composer, the title of the work, and the catalogue number. Then I had to sign it, print my name under my signature, and hand this request with its two copies to the librarian.

This reading room was a bright room; it had pale yellow walls and windows with views to the street corner. Except for the hum of traffic outside, the only sounds to be heard were those common to every research library I'd ever worked in: the rustling of papers, the clearing of throats, the scraping of chairs as they were pulled out from the small desks, and, now, the footsteps of Kurt as he approached with the copies of the Schubert manuscripts I'd requested.

"Here you are, Lily." He placed them on the desk in front of me. "The first two songs of *Die Winterreise*." I would like to say that it was coincidental that I was about to study the very songs I would be hearing tonight at the Count's evening of Schubert, but of course, it wasn't. I like being prepared.

I don't know if I am ever truly prepared to see Schubert's handwriting, though, to look at the notes he'd written and then scratched out almost two hundred years before, to observe the date he'd inscribed at the top of the first page, as was his habit, to gaze at his signature. I had to take a deep breath and close my eyes for a moment before I could continue.

"It's magical, isn't it?" Kurt whispered over my shoulder. "Just to look at it and to imagining him writing it."

Kurt and I were kindred spirits when it came to Schubert. All I could say was, "Yes," but that was enough. He gave my shoulder a squeeze and left me to my work.

I scrutinized every note, every mark, every word of both songs. I jotted down what I observed, hummed the tunes, heard the words inside my head. I could have worked all day, and usually did, but today I remembered to check the time, and to gather my research together shortly before noon.

"Did you find whatever it is you're looking for?" Kurt took the manuscripts from me and watched as I pulled on my coat. I hadn't told him yet about Arthur's idea to look for lost love songs. I don't know why, because if anyone would be interested in finding more Schubert songs, Kurt would be. I decided to confide in him.

"Well, you know, I've spent these first few weeks familiarizing myself with his song writing style, just the way he put the music together, the way the pages look." I had his full attention, and I chose my next words carefully. "I think I may be ready to move on to the next phase of my research soon though."

His gaze didn't waver. "And that is?"

"I think that there may be some love songs which have never been published. I suspect that they may be in a private collection

somewhere in Vienna. I'm just not sure how or where to begin looking."
He still said nothing, so I continued. "I was hoping to find some hint
in his manuscripts, some idea in the chronology or themes of his songs,
but he wrote so many that I could spend my entire life looking for
hints. And, yes, I've read every book and article I could get my hands
on. You know that about me. You know that I do my research."

Kurt was smiling now, and nodding his head. "Wait here a
minute." He turned and headed into the stacks with the manuscripts
I'd been studying and I filled the time buttoning my coat and pulling
my gloves out of my bag. It was only a few moments, though, until
I heard his returning footsteps. I thought that he was empty handed
until he reached out to me and pressed a card into my hand.

"Look at it later," he whispered, and then out loud he said,
"*Wiedersehen*, Dr. Lindstrom."

I slipped the card into my pocket and opened the door.

CHAPTER EIGHT

Stephen was waiting for me outside. He leaned in and brushed a kiss on each cheek. Then he handed me my newspapers and I stuffed them into my bag.

"Where are we headed?"

"The Café Eilis, on the corner of Josefstädterstrasse and Lenaugasse. It's not far."

He took my arm and linked it with his. We walked to the corner, turned left, and headed up Stadiongasse. Our steps were in synchrony, as, apparently, were our thoughts.

"Did you find what you were looking for?"

"You knew that I was looking for something?"

"Lily. You're doing research. Of course you're looking for something."

"Oh. Of course." We had stopped at the end of the block and were waiting to cross Landesgerichtstrasse. The street was slushy from yesterday's snow and the passing cars sent up sprays of the wet dirty stuff. It was not a beautiful day in Vienna. The sky was the same sooty gray color as the street and there was a darkening mist hanging between the buildings.

We hurried across the street toward the solid old building housing the Café Eiles. It was one of those venerable Viennese coffee houses which had been in business back before Freud walked the streets. The Turks were responsible for bringing coffee to Vienna way back in 1683 when they laid siege to the city. When the siege ended, they left sacks of coffee beans behind, and the story goes that a Polish courier between the Viennese and the Turks asked for the sacks as payment. So a Pole, Franz Kolschitszky, started the first coffeehouse in Vienna, and the coffee house tradition is centuries old here.

The Eiles is not one of the most famous coffee houses in Vienna, not like the Café Central, or the Griensteidl, or the Hawelka, or a dozen more you could name. Schubert didn't come here; he died before it was built in 1839, but there had been a coffeehouse on this site since 1821, six years before he took his last breath. I came here so often mostly because it was convenient to the library. At lunchtime it was often full of politicians, since it's also close to the City Hall and the Parliament. The mood and atmosphere of a coffeehouse is determined to a great extent by its clientele, and this one was usually bustling with customers engaged in spirited debates.

Today its big windows glowed through the gloom, drawing us toward the warmth inside. We stomped the slush off our boots and pushed the door open. I paused inside the entrance, scanning the room for Sophie. My eyes traveled over the pale yellow walls, the gleaming wood, the black bentwood chairs and round tables. There was carpet underfoot and soft cushions on the benches lining the walls. The aroma of fresh coffee filled the space and the air hummed with conversation. I was very aware of the warm male body right behind me, but I didn't see Sophie until Stephen said, "Do you know that woman across the room who's waving and calling your name?"

There were a lot of people in there, and there are two sections, one for smokers and the other for non-smokers, but it was still embarrassing not to have noticed her. My excuse is that my vision was quite blurry from having slept in my contact lenses. That plus straining my eyes all morning while squinting at notes written over two hundred years ago could account for my lapse. It could. Or it could be that Sophie is not a tall person, so that even while waving her arms, she could be tough to spot, at least from my vantage point. Stephen, after all, is taller than I am. I didn't even want to contemplate the notion that my focus could have been diverted by his close proximity to me. Surely not.

We skirted the racks of newspapers, made our way through the non-smoking section, down the middle of the room lined on both sides with booths full of patrons sitting alone reading, around groups discussing philosophy and politics as they do all day in Viennese coffee houses, between waiters carrying small silver trays holding coffee cups and water glasses. Sophie stood to greet us, her brown hair curling wildly around her head. She hugged me, kissed me on both cheeks, and then stood back and looked over my shoulder at Stephen.

"Have you brought a friend, Lily, or is this man following you without your knowledge or permission?"

I took a step to the side, so that Sophie wouldn't have to strain her neck trying to see around me, and then performed the introductions.

"Sophie, I'd like you to meet Dr. Stephen Cameron. Stephen, this is my dear friend, Dr. Sophie Mayer."

While they shook hands and exchanged polite greetings, I removed my gloves and unbuttoned my coat. I was pulling it off my shoulders when I felt Stephen's hands helping me at my task. I admit that I loved the feel of those hands on my shoulders. He hung our coats on the bentwood rack closest to our table and then held my chair for me. Sophie was lifting one eyebrow and giving me that intense look which said, "You'll tell me all about this later."

When Stephen sat down though, all she said was, "So, Dr. Cameron, how did you meet Lily?"

"We bumped into each other on the streetcar a couple of days ago." He paused at this point and smiled at me. "We discovered that we had common interests." That was all he said, and Sophie surely would have asked for more details, if our waiter hadn't appeared at that moment.

Vienna coffee house waiters are nothing like their American counterparts. This was no eager, eternally smiling college student, introducing himself and saying he'd take care of us. Indeed not. Our waiter was a middle aged male, dressed in an impeccable suit, standing over us with practiced authority. In Vienna, it is the job of the customers to charm the waiter and convince him that they deserve to be served. Until you've proven yourself worthy of their time and effort, they can be grumpy and even sarcastic. It's part of the coffee house tradition here, probably caused at least in part by the fact that they stay in their jobs for a lifetime; they don't lose their positions for being rude. Fortunately for us, we were regulars here and had already proven ourselves. This waiter seemed almost to like us on his better days. This appeared to be one of them.

"*Guten Tag,*" He didn't actually smile when he greeted us, but he didn't frown either. That was a good sign. "*Was wollen Sie heute?*"

The Eiles served lunch, along with a full array of coffees and pastries. We ordered and then continued our conversation while we waited for our food. I was right about Sophie wanting details.

"Common interests?" she asked, as if there had been no interruption. "Does that mean that you're as crazy about Schubert as Lily is?"

Stephen didn't so much as blink at the mention of Franz, didn't reveal in any way that we had never spoken of him. On the contrary, he acted as if he knew all about my devotion to this Viennese composer.

"I'm not sure that anyone can be as passionate about Schubert as Lily is." Here he paused, for dramatic effect I guess, and aimed his devastating smile straight at Sophie. It didn't seem to have the same effect on her that it had on me, but then Sophie has always been incredibly level headed, except for her intense devotion to Gustav Mahler. He kept talking as if her reaction, or lack thereof, didn't matter to him.

"It makes perfect sense, though, when you think of the kind of woman Lily is, that she would love Schubert, the beauty of his melodies, his tenderness, the way he can express any emotion, and especially." He paused here before he finished. "Especially, his romanticism."

My mouth must have dropped open, and even Sophie looked a bit stunned. Where had he come up with this speech? Fortunately, our waiter, with flawless timing, chose that moment to place our orders in front of us. I reached for my spoon and dipped it into my soup, thankful to have a moment to collect my wits. Sophie was ahead of me though.

"You found out all of this about Lily on a streetcar?" She started to snort, something she does when really amused, but caught herself. "That must have been some ride."

"It was actually." That was my voice, though I was surprised to find myself talking. "I was on my way home from the Musikverein; I'd been poring over manuscripts all day, and Stephen apparently couldn't help picking up on my fervor for Franz."

Whatever game he was playing, I could play it too. However, as soon as I said the words "picking up," I remembered that he had, in fact, picked up some of my dropped notes from the floor of the streetcar. That must have been how he'd come up with all of that stuff. It's not as if he were a music professor, though he'd just given a pretty good imitation of one.

Sophie must have thought so too, because the next thing she asked was, "And what was your area of study, Dr. Cameron? Did you specialize in Schubert too?"

He swallowed, cleared his throat, and glanced sideways at me. What was that look in his eyes supposed to mean? Was he going to keep pretending that he was an expert in my field?

"Ah, no, actually." He lowered his coffee cup as he spoke. "My degrees are in medicine and chemistry."

Sophie's eyes widened at that information and she opened her mouth, ready with another question, but Stephen hadn't finished yet.

"My mother is a piano teacher, though, and so I grew up hearing her play his pieces, and talk about them too."

He turned toward me finally, and I tried to read the message in his eyes. I wouldn't call his expression sheepish exactly, but those eyes seemed to be pleading for something. Could it be mercy he was after? Maybe it was the phrase "the kind of woman Lily is" which swayed me, but I decided to help him out.

"That explains a lot, doesn't it? My mom is especially fond of Bach; she talks about him all the time. She's a very logical and orderly person, isn't she Sophie?"

Sophie nodded. She'd met my parents when they'd visited during my Fulbright year. She looked as if she'd like to jump into the conversation, but I kept going, not ready to let her talk yet.

"Mom always says that Bach's slow movements are among the most tender pieces ever written though."

"Ah," said Stephen, and then stopped. What did that mean?

I had time to think about that word, not to mention all the others he'd uttered, while the waiter cleared our dishes and asked if we'd like more coffee. Sophie and I both said yes to that, but Stephen shook his head.

"I have to go," he said. "An appointment."

"Ah." If he could use that word, so could I.

He called for the check and shrugged into his coat while he watched for the waiter who could take his cash, since not all of them can. It took awhile for the head waiter, *Herr Ober*, as he's called, to appear, so Stephen filled the time saying his good-byes.

"It was very nice to meet you," he said politely to a skeptical looking Sophie. To me, he said, "I'll talk to you later." He gave my shoulder a gentle squeeze, paid *Herr Ober*, who had finally shown up, and then he was gone.

Sophie waited until he'd left before she started her interrogation.

"You met him on a streetcar? Two days ago? And he's already talking about the kind of woman you are?" Sophie's voice was rising with each word. Thank goodness the coffee house was humming with other conversations, but I still worried about being overheard. I stirred another cube of sugar into my coffee and thought hard about how much to tell her.

"Keep your voice down, Sophie," I whispered. "I'll tell you everything, but you have to promise not to shriek.

"I never shriek."

That was not true, but I decided not to argue with her. Instead, I launched into the full story of the Hungarians on the streetcar, Helmut Vogl naked in Mitzi's apartment, Christina Anderson clinging to her count, and, oh yes, Fritz Gerling on my stairway. By the time I was finished, she was looking slightly dazed, and it takes quite a bit to surprise Sophie.

"Lily, if it were anyone but you telling me this, I'd think you were making it all up."

"You saw Stephen. I didn't make him up."

"I have a feeling that you may just have left something out of the story when it comes to him though."

I felt the blush rising up my neck. Sometimes I hate being a fair skinned Scandinavian.

"What could I possibly have left out? I've barely met the man."

This time she did snort. "A lot can happen between a man and a woman in two days." She leaned over the table and murmured the next part. "It looked like lust to me."

I choked on my coffee, sputtered, lowered my cup to the saucer carefully, and looked her right in the eye as I replied.

"I knew you would say that." My teeth were clenched together so hard that it was difficult to talk. "You're so fascinated by the life of Alma Mahler Gropius Werfel, that you've lost your perspective." I was glad to have remembered all of Alma's husbands. Listing her lovers would have been too much for me. She had cut a wide swath through Vienna's artistic community. Sophie was not to be sidetracked though.

"And? I'm right, aren't I?"

I didn't answer. She didn't blink.

"Oh no. It's even worse, isn't it? You think you're falling in love again, don't you?" All I could do was nod. She groaned. "Lily. Have you forgotten what happened with Fritz already? And Günther?"

I shook my head. "Of course I haven't forgotten, Sophie. I remember them very well." And a few more she didn't know about back in Minnesota, but I decided not to mention them.

"Well? Haven't you learned anything?"

I pondered that question for a moment. "Of course I have." I took another sip of coffee. "In fact, I've learned many things, some of them quite painful, I admit." I paused to consider my next words. "But Sophie, I can't lock up my heart just because it's been bruised a few times." Had I just said that? Willie Nelson must be getting to me. Maybe I should give Frau Frassl some new CD's.

"A few times?" Sophie had an excellent memory.

At moments like this, I had to remind myself that she was one of my dearest friends. I chose my words carefully. "You know how serious I am about my work. I've never thrown myself at any man. They just seem to find me. I can't help it if a couple of them have touched my heart."

"Touched it and broken it."

I finished my coffee. There was nothing more to say.

Sophie signaled the waiter; we paid for our lunch and coffee, pulled on our coats, and made our way through the crowded cafe.

CHAPTER NINE

The weather was even gloomier than it had been earlier. A cold sleet falling from the heavy clouds overhead pelted us as soon as we stepped outside. I pulled on my hat and gloves, then blinked to try to clear my vision. Everything looked blurry; Sophie grabbed me before I bumped into a man hurrying toward the corner.

"You slept in your contacts again, didn't you?" I nodded and she grumbled. "*Bist du nicht recht gescheit?*"

Sophie is Viennese, after all, so we often speak in a mixture of German and English. What she had said this time was, "Are you half-witted?" It was a reasonable question, even if it wasn't terribly polite. She's right. It's a stupid thing for me to do, though in my own defense, I don't do it very often. What can I say? It's one tiny bit of laziness in an otherwise well disciplined life. We all have our flaws. I gave her my excuse for this time. "It was a late night at the opera. I'll try not to do it again." I meant it too.

"Right. If you say so." I did pick up on her sarcasm, but I ignored it. The light changed; we hurried across the street, and she changed the subject, thank goodness. "Are you going back to the library?"

I shook my head. "No, I think I'll head home. I need to practice and plan next week's lectures." I stifled a yawn. I was thinking of taking a nap too.

"I'll walk a few blocks with you." Sophie loves to walk in all kinds of weather. We were in front of the Rathaus now. No one was skating. That should tell Sophie something, but no, she kept marching along. She was humming the part of Mahler's First Symphony that sounds like a minor version of "Frère Jacques" and looking perfectly content. "We've come this far. We might as well keep going to the Schottentor." That's where I could get the number thirty-eight back out to my neighborhood. Sophie lived in the other direction, so I hugged her and left her on the Ring in front of the University waiting for a number two.

I was so thankful for the warmth of the streetcar that I didn't even care that there were no seats left. I found a spot in the aisle and braced myself between two students with backpacks. They smelled of onion and one of them had drops of mustard on his jacket, a sure sign that they'd stopped at a *Würstelstand* before they got on the streetcar.

These little stands selling different kinds of hot sausages can be found all over the city, and Viennese have their favorites, just as they prefer certain coffee houses or wine gardens. The one I like best is behind the Opera.

I tried not to lean on the mustard stained teen-ager as the streetcar glided up my regular route. I could have called out all of the stops myself, from Berggasse to my stop on Nussdorferstrasse, but I didn't. I spent the time gazing out the window at the outlines of buildings obscured by the falling sleet and wondering what Stephen was up to. When we stopped near Schubert's house, I maneuvered around the boys to the exit, pushed the button to open the door, and stepped off not far from Number Fifty-Four.

The house where Franz Schubert was born is a museum now, and I'd been there many times. The building is typical of Vienna, pale yellow stucco, with a big arched entrance. Like all museums and historical sites in Vienna, it's marked by a plaque and red and white flags. I planned to take my students to see it, once we got into our overview of his life and work, but today I hurried past it, crossed the street and moved as fast as I could through the neighborhood toward my apartment house.

By the time I reached my doorstep, my face was stinging from the icy crystals lashing it, and I was breathless from the cold. All I wanted was to get in out of this weather, so I groaned when Frau Frassl called out to me.

"Dr. Lindstrom! *Bitte! Warte!*"

I obeyed her command to wait, paused with my key in the door, and turned to see her holding a large bouquet of roses out to me.

"A handsome young man left these for you a little while ago." She said this in German, of course, and smiled as she handed them to me, showing the gap between her front teeth. "There's a note."

And I bet she'd read it already, if it was in German. I wasn't sure about her command of English, but I suspected that she knew more than she let on. You couldn't listen to Willie Nelson day and night without picking up a few words.

I took the roses, thanked her, and let myself into my apartment building. Whoever had bought these for me had spent a bundle. They were gorgeous long stemmed red ones. My mind went directly to Stephen, but I couldn't figure out when he would have done this, not to mention why. I held them to my nose and inhaled the sweet scent as the lift shuddered its way up to my floor. I loved roses. Had I told him that? Or did he think that of course a woman like me, one who loved Schubert, would have to love roses too? I was all but breathless with anticipation by the time I pulled the card out.

"Last night was wonderful," it said. "I can't wait to see you again." I couldn't quite make out the signature, but it really didn't look as if it said Stephen. Maybe it was my vision, rather than bad penmanship. I had to get these contacts out of my eyes and clean them. I left the roses and the card on my kitchen counter, pulled my coat off and dropped it on a chair. I'd hang it up later.

I hurried into my bathroom, removed my contacts, found my glasses and returned to the kitchen minutes later. The card was waiting for me where I'd left it, but this time when I picked it up I could read the signature. "Kevin." Who in the world was Kevin? Had Frau Frassl made a mistake? I looked at the envelope to check the name. It said, "Dr. Lily Lindstrom." No mistake. That was me. I thought back to last night, to everything that had happened starting with Stephen's visit, going on to the opera and then home again. Uh-oh. Kevin must be the student who'd sat next to me at the opera, and who'd walked me all the way back to my apartment. I pulled my student list out of my bag and sure enough, there he was, close to the top, Kevin Carlson, a junior from Minnetonka. This was not good, not good at all. I'd have to call Eva, but first, I put the roses in a vase. No sense in letting them wilt just because the wrong person had given them to me.

It was when I was hanging up my coat that one of my gloves fell out of the pocket where I'd stuffed it, and with it came the card Kurt Baumgartner, the librarian, had pressed into my hand. I'd forgotten all about it. I held it up to the light. It looked like the kind of business card everyone in Vienna seemed to carry. It had his name, his title, his phone number. I turned it over and found the short message he'd written: "Call me. I can help you"

Kurt and I had gone out a few times back during my Fulbright year, but we were just friends and, in fact, he was married now. I didn't think this was about me. It must be about Schubert. I have to admit that a shiver of excitement pulsed through me. At least I hoped it was the excitement and not the freezing walk which caused it. I put his card on the small table in my foyer next to the roses and the card from Kevin. I couldn't call him while he was at work, and in the meantime, I planned to swaddle myself in sweaters, drink a cup of hot chocolate and read my newspapers.

I settled myself on the couch in my living room and started with *Der Kurier*, the Vienna paper Frau Frassl had chosen for me today. The sweaters and hot chocolate were doing their work, and I was feeling warm and content, even a bit drowsy. I scanned the paper, skimming the articles about politics in Europe, skipping the editorials about corruption in Vienna, flipping the pages until I came to an article which caught my attention. It would have been hard to have missed it, considering that it was circled in red ink. The headline said, "Minister of Interior Helmut Vogl is reported to be recovering from coronary angioplasty in a private Vienna hospital. His condition is said to be stable. According to reliable sources, he was stricken while in a closed meeting with top officials. He is not expected to return to work for at least ten days."

I guess you could call it a closed meeting, but Mitzi did not look like a top official to me. Then again, who was I to argue with a "reliable source?" I have to admit that I was relieved that my part in the events leading up to his surgery was omitted. I was curious, though, about what else Stephen might have circled, and I turned to the next page. Aha. There was more red ink, this time around a picture of a balding man of indeterminate age, standing stiffly behind a podium. The caption read, "Otto Heimberger, Chief of Staff, speaks at a gathering honoring top officials of the Ministry of Interior." He did not look happy to be there, but the photographer could have caught him at a bad moment.

There was no more red ink to be found in the Vienna paper, so I stopped for a sip of hot chocolate and then turned to the *International Herald Tribune*. I really didn't expect to see anything circled in this paper, so I was surprised to see more red ink. It was around one of those very small articles on an inside page. The first sentence said, "The CDC is reported to be investigating mysterious deaths in Chicago traced to an imported aphrodisiac. Those seeking enhanced lovemaking experiences are cautioned to avoid products sold under the names 'Love Stone' and 'Rock Hard' and to call the CDC for assistance if they have already purchased this product." I'm not kidding. I couldn't make this up. Apparently Stephen had told me the truth about his work. Had he known the article would be in today's paper? Was that why he'd borrowed it? I had wondered, since newspapers are readily available at Viennese coffee houses.

I scanned the rest of the paper, but there were no more circles, not that I had expected any more. I had hoped for a more private message though, something along the lines of "I can't wait to see you again." Sophie was right about me, and I resolved to take her advice. I would be very careful. I fell asleep on the couch while thinking that thought, and woke up to an insistent beeping sound. It was my cell phone, signaling another text message from Arthur. I sent a message back and then headed for my computer. I'd better bring him up to date.

While I was composing a very careful e-mail message to him, Arthur called me on the internet phone connection he'd set up. I pulled off my extra sweaters, smoothed the hair over my forehead, though the bruise was fading, and leaned in toward the built in camera on my laptop. When I clicked on the little green telephone icon, he'd be able to see me and I'd be able to see him. Yes, there he was, looking as pale as ever. Arthur wouldn't be a bad looking guy if he'd take better care of himself. Of course, I couldn't tell him that. It would only encourage him.

"Hello, Lily! *Wie geht's?*" Arthur prided himself on his linguistic ability, so I humored him by conversing in German for a while. In response to his question, I assured him that I was fine, and then I told him about the miserable weather, and about my continued Schubert research.

"Any new love songs, Lily?"

"Not yet, Arthur. You'll be the first to know if I find something."

That was true too. It was the least I could do for him. That plus talk to him when he called like this. The trouble with these internet phone calls is that they're free, so Arthur tends to go on forever, and he did, telling me everything about life there on the campus in Minnesota, facts I didn't need to know. I struggled to stay alert, and just to change the subject, I told him about meeting Christina. I left out the details about the count and the *Schubertiade.* I figured I could save that for another day, especially the part about the count, which I would have to edit. By the time I clicked the little red icon and signed off, I was ready for another nap, but I made myself go to the piano.

I started with some scales to warm up and then played a Bach Invention before I launched into a Schubert Impromptu. If Sophie could be inspired by miserable weather to think of Mahler, then I could be equally inspired by warmth and coziness to take pleasure in my favorite composer. I enjoyed myself for more than an hour, before I moved back to my computer to work on my lecture notes for the coming week.

That's what I was doing when I heard the knocking on my door. Strange. Ordinarily people have to buzz me from down below first. It had to be someone who lived in the building. I put my eye to the peephole, difficult to do with my glasses on, but I could still make out Mitzi's face, slightly magnified and distorted. I turned the bolt and unlocked the door. When I opened it she smiled brightly and handed me a bottle of slivovitz.

"I wanted to thank you for your help," she explained. "If it hadn't been for you and your friend . . ." Her voice quivered at this point, and I would swear there were tears in her eyes. I pulled her into the apartment and shut the door.

"Come in and sit down. Let's have some of this."

She took off her coat and hat, hung all that expensive looking leather and fur on a hook in my foyer, and followed me. I had already pulled two small cognac snifters from the cabinet, plus some cashews I'd been saving for a special occasion. This seemed to be it. I poured. She lifted the small glass and took a sip. I did the same, and it was a moment before either of us said a word. Finally I broke the silence.

"It sounds as if he's going to recover." She nodded, but didn't say anything, so I kept talking. "There was an article about his surgery in today's *Kurier.*" She took another sip of the slivovitz, but still didn't say anything. I plunged ahead.

"Did you know that he had a wife?" There, I'd said it out loud.

Finally, she responded, but not until she'd poured herself some more of the potent liquor. "Yes, I did know that."

Somehow, I'd thought that she might have more to say, but she lapsed back into silence, sipping her slivovitz.

"Does that bother you?"

She looked directly into my eyes as she answered, "Do you think it should bother me?"

Mitzi seemed genuinely puzzled by my question, and I wasn't sure what to say next, until I remembered her quivering voice and her tears. "Well, you seemed to care about him." Would she laugh if I said what I'd said to Stephen? I didn't know, but I decided to take a chance. "I thought you might be in love with him."

Mitzi didn't laugh, but she did set her glass down rather abruptly. This time she stared at a spot over my shoulder as she answered. "No, I wouldn't say that I'm in love with Helmut." She paused and pulled at her sweater. "I am very fond of him though."

"Oh." I let my breath out slowly. "Well then." How could I ask my next question? "Maybe I was hearing things, but I could have sworn that Fritz Gerling was singing in the hallway this morning." I decided not to mention seeing him, or hearing her call out to him.

Now she did look surprised. "Oh yes, he was here. He comes every Thursday."

"Every Thursday? And he stays all night with you?" I didn't want to believe what she seemed to be telling me, but even a naïve Lutheran from Minnesota has to believe the evidence eventually. It was hard for me though, so I decided to ask just one more question. First I fortified myself with another sip of slivovitz.

"What is it that you do for a living, Mitzi?"

"You don't know?" She looked truly surprised, but then she dug into her handbag and pulled out a business card. Did everyone carry these except me? I made a mental note to get some printed for myself. What would they say, "Lily Lindstrom, Schubert Scholar Extraordinaire?" Meanwhile, Mitzi pressed hers into my hand and I focused my attention on it. It said, "Mitzi Tauber, Human Relations Specialist," in German and English. It had her address and phone number on it too, and it was printed on an especially elegant ivory background.

"Well, of course." I placed it carefully on the table, next to the bottle of slivovitz, and then picked up my glass and raised it to her. "Here's to successful relationships!"

She tilted her head back, emptied her glass, and then erupted in peals of laughter. When she was finally able to speak, she said, "I do like you, Lily Lindstrom!"

I surprised myself by reaching over to squeeze her hand. "I like you too, Mitzi." It was true. Amazing. I'd never known anyone in this profession. She squeezed back, and then she stood, smoothed out her skirt and turned toward the foyer.

"I have to get ready for my next appointment." She paused, seeming to consider her words carefully. She smiled at me. "Business is very good these days."

What could I say? I wondered who was on her schedule tonight. Who could compete with the Minister of Interior and Vienna's favorite baritone? She must have seen the question in my eyes, because she said, "It's better if you don't know."

"Oh. Yes. Of course."

She picked up her coat and hat, opened the door and stepped out into the hallway.

"See you later, Lily."

I watched her start up the stairway to her apartment, and then I closed the door and leaned against it. Incredible. My mother wouldn't believe it. In fact, my mother would never know about it, if I could help it. I started to laugh at the very thought of my family and friends back in Minnesota dealing with the idea of Mitzi's work. I could have leaned on that door even longer if my stomach hadn't growled and reminded me that I needed to eat something and change my clothes. I stood up straight and headed for the kitchen. I had a long evening ahead of me.

CHAPTER TEN

I'm a frugal person and I'm used to riding public transportation everywhere I go in Vienna, but it was dark and cold and the sleet had turned to snow so I called a taxi to take me to the count's place on Metternichgasse. I waited in the front entrance hall of my building, just inside the door. It wasn't heated in there, but at least it was dry. When I saw the taxi pull up, I let myself out and stepped carefully to the curb. Even though the walk had been scraped earlier, the new snow was sticking to the remains of the sleet, and I didn't want to fall and add to my bruises.

The taxi was a silver Mercedes, not uncommon in Vienna, but a luxury for me. I sank into the cushioned warmth of its back seat, gave the driver the address, and then leaned back and looked at my neighborhood through windows glazed with ice. From inside the car, the streetlights shone like beacons, each one surrounded by a nimbus of swirling snowflakes. The streetcars gliding down the middle of Währingerstrasse sent out flashes of light as they rolled by.

We turned right onto Swarzspanierstrasse to take a route parallel to the Ring, since that thoroughfare is one way from the Opera to the Danube Canal. Too bad, since I love seeing it at night, and it would have been especially lovely from the back seat of a taxi, rather than from the aisle of a streetcar, where I usually ride. It's Vienna's grandest boulevard, Franz Joseph's monumental urban renewal project. The Viennese have plenty to say, much of it laced with irony and humor, about all of those lavish buildings built during the last half of the nineteenth century where the old town walls used to stand. From the neo-Gothic Rathaus to the neo-Renaissance Burgtheater to the neo-Classical Parliament building, they form a fabulous spectacle, especially when it's snowing. All lit up, glowing against the backdrop of tonight's deep purple sky, they would be magnificent. Unfortunately, I'd have to wait to see all of that until my taxi ride back home.

I couldn't complain of my view, though, as I watched the shadowy silhouettes of the museums appear behind the curtain of snow. The traffic was heavy and moving slowly, so it took several minutes to reach Karlsplatz and the brightly lighted dome and spires of the Karlskirche on our right. Then as we inched forward to Lothringerstrasse, I could see the rose and cream façade of the Musikverein on the left, illuminated from within and without. There must be a concert tonight.

"Don't you just love driving through this incredible city all night long!" Even though my German was correct and my enthusiasm was genuine, the driver didn't seem to be impressed. In fact, he grunted his reply.

"I'd rather be watching the hockey game." His accent was so strong that he was difficult to understand, but I picked up his meaning, and kept quiet for the rest of the drive. We proceeded through the brightly lighted Schwarzenbergplatz, turned right on Rennweg, and passed the Lower Belvedere. I was still feeling fairly dreamy from the comfortable ride and the radiant spectacle of Vienna at night, when the driver turned left onto Metternichgasse, the street where Michael Fodor, Christina's count, lived.

The area is full of beautiful old apartment houses, and the driver stopped in front of one of them. He had to double park, since there's rarely a space to be found on Vienna's crowded streets. I handed him the correct amount and stepped out onto the snowy pavement. He didn't even acknowledge my thanks or my farewell; he had the radio tuned to his game. I'm just glad that I made it to the curb before he pulled away in a spray of cinder laced snow.

The door to the count's house was one of those huge old wooden ones common in Vienna. I was not the only person heading for it; there was a small group gathered in front of it waiting to be buzzed in. We stepped through into an arched stone passageway. Beyond it was a courtyard where a few expensive cars were parked: a Porsche, a BMW and an Audi. I could imagine Michael Fodor behind the wheel of the Porsche. I must have stopped to stare at it, because one of the group called out to me, "Do you want to get into the lift with us?" I glanced at the antique elevator inside the stairwell, and decided to walk. Even though the contraption looked quite elegant, I wasn't convinced that it could carry one more passenger.

It began its ascent with a squeak and a shake, while I stomped the snow from my leather boots and started up the stairway curving around it. The design was the same as in my apartment building, but ever so much more tasteful. The stairs were considerably wider and there were ornate lanterns on each landing, casting a soft glow over the stucco walls. Voices floated down from next floor, and in the background I could hear a piano. The group in the elevator had already entered the apartment, so when I reached the door I had the undivided attention of the uniformed attendant.

"*Guten Abend,*" he said, and then pointed to his right as he told me where I could leave my coat. I tried not to gawk at the splendor of the apartment, tried to act as if I were used to being invited to homes like this, tried to walk down the gleaming parquet floor of the hallway without gasping at the expensive antiques lining the walls. I thought I was doing well until I came face to face with Christina Anderson, who guided me gently through a doorway to our right.

"It is breathtaking, isn't it?" All I could do was nod in agreement as she continued. "He is descended from royalty, you know." Then she proceeded to outline his family tree while I added my coat to the collection in the exquisite parlor. "There's no one like him in Minnesota," she finished. Then she pointed to a doorway toward the back of the room. "You can freshen up in there, my dear." I must not look as good as I thought I'd looked when I left home. Of course, I would probably never look as perfectly put together as Christina. For one thing, I suffered from a serious deficit in the diamond department. Nevertheless, I mustered all my grace as I walked away from her, through the door she'd pointed out, and into the adjacent powder room.

I don't know what I was expecting to see in there, but it wasn't multiple reflections of myself bouncing back from the mirror lined walls. I was thankful that I was fully dressed, or I might have taken cover under the gilt encrusted dressing table. As it was, I simply took a deep breath, placed my evening bag on the gleaming surface in front of me, dug into it for my comb and lipstick and went to work. Really, I didn't look too bad, even in comparison to Christina. I was wearing a cashmere sweater dress which matched my eyes, a Christmas present from my parents; it was quite lovely. My hair was neat and shiny; my make-up was understated and tasteful, the only way I knew how to apply it, and my lipstick was a subtle neutral shade. It was true that I had no diamonds, but the silver hoops in my ears were genuine sterling, as was the necklace which matched them. All in all, quite respectable, as my dad would say. I gave myself a nod of approval, opened the door, and stepped back into the parlor, now quite empty. I'd have to find my own way to the party.

It wasn't hard. I followed the hum of conversation and the melody of a Schubert waltz to a grand salon opening off the same hallway I'd walked down earlier. The tall doors to the room stood open, and I stopped in the entrance to examine the exquisite space. It had incredibly high ceilings, plastered in elaborate swirling patterns and painted in shades of cream and gold. Chubby little angels looked down at me, each one playing a different instrument, each one glowing in the reflected light from the crystal chandeliers.

Opposite the doorway stood a wall of glittering windows with a view of the snowflakes swirling outside. On each side of the room there were more tall doors opening to adjacent chambers. It definitely had the feel of a small palace, at least of the few I had toured. I must have stood there a few minutes longer than most guests, because the same attendant who'd greeted me at the main entrance earlier approached me now.

"Would Madam care to partake of the buffet?" the man asked as he pointed toward a long table loaded with platters. He said this in German of course, and my translation is just as stiff as his delivery. He spoke as if he were concentrating on getting each word absolutely right, as if he might not be a native speaker. "Or perhaps Madam would prefer something to drink first?" He waved one hand in the air, and, as if by magic, a uniformed waiter appeared in front of me holding a tray loaded with tall crystal glasses, each one filled to the brim with champagne. I reached toward the tray, and as I did so met the eyes of the waiter. They were dark, and keen, and not at all what I would call professional; in fact, his gaze went far beyond being impolite to what I'd call rude bordering on insolent. He was examining me from my head to my toes as if he were memorizing every detail, with a definite smirk on his face.

It was the sort of scrutiny which made me want to turn and leave the room, but instead of doing so, I stared back. One of my older brothers had taught me this technique. The point, he had said, was to prove that I wasn't intimidated, so with that fraternal voice in my head urging me on, I looked right back at the ill-mannered server, took in the details of his appearance, from his greasy dark hair to the scar on his cheek to the gold ring in his left ear. He was about my height, but then, inspired by Mitzi, I was wearing boots with high chunky heels, so he might actually be a tiny bit taller. He was not a large man, though. In fact, he was so small and lean that his uniform hung rather loosely on his body; the sleeves of his jacket fell to the middle of his hands and his trousers were almost dragging on the floor. Where in the world had the Graf found him? He was certainly out of place in such an elegant setting.

Christina's voice broke the spell connecting me with him. "There you are. I wondered what had become of you." She frowned at the gaping server; he turned away; and I watched him as he offered beverages to a well-dressed couple standing nearby. Why did he look so familiar to me?

"I don't know where Michael found his servers tonight. They're totally untrained and unprofessional. I'll have to talk to him later." Christina linked her arm through mine and steered me toward the other side of the room. "Right now though, I need to introduce you to my friend Trudi." That's how I met Helmut Vogl's wife.

She looked as lovely in person as she had in the photo I'd seen in the newspaper earlier that week, the one where she'd been standing next to her husband at a Fasching Ball. Tonight she was wearing a beautifully tailored velvet skirt and matching jacket, with an elegant lace blouse underneath. It was a very attractive, very Austrian outfit. Her hair was a rich auburn color, and it was held away from her face by diamond clips. In fact, in the quality and quantity of her diamonds, she could compete with Christina, who was busy introducing us.

Trudi Vogl held out a slender hand for me to shake as she said, *"Sehr angenehm, Sie kennen zu lernen."* In English that would be, "Very pleased to make your acquaintance." I murmured the polite response and then listened as Christina gave a summary not only of my reason for being in Vienna, but especially for being here tonight. She made me sound like the ultimate Schubert expert, and, believe me, I would have clarified my qualifications if Trudi Vogl hadn't jumped into the conversation at that point.

"Oh, my husband would love to meet you. He is passionate about Schubert!"

I had in mind what else her husband was passionate about, as well as the memory of him as I'd seen him in Mitzi's apartment. Of course, I didn't mention this. What I said was, "I would be honored to meet him."

"Unfortunately, Trudi's husband is recovering from surgery and couldn't join us tonight." That was Christina speaking. I acted as if I knew nothing about his recent angioplasty, and, in fact, listened attentively to Trudi Vogl's explanation. It followed the same story line I'd read in the article Stephen had circled for me, and I was certainly not going to share the actual scenario with his wife.

"He's a descendent of the famous Michael Vogl, you know."

"Michael Vogl, the famous singer, the one who sang Schubert's songs?"

Trudi Vogl nodded politely. "The very one."

I was tingling with excitement. In fact my toes were twitching inside my boots, and I had to take a quick sip of champagne to calm myself. That turned out to be a poor idea. I inhaled a few bubbles, began to choke and found myself being patted on the back by the wife of the Minister of Interior. She was totally cordial about it, though, and said only, "You should be careful, my dear."

"You're right. I'm so sorry." I would have gone on, because Lutherans love to apologize, but at that moment we heard a resounding chord from the piano, followed by the voice of Michael Fodor, our host. We turned toward the front of the room, where he stood next to the piano. He looked even more distinguished than I had remembered, but perhaps it was where he was standing, with those huge sparkling windows in the background, and Fritz Gerling next to him. Good grief. Fritz Gerling. I tried not to choke again.

"And as you know," the Count continued. "Our own dear Helmut Vogl, who unfortunately couldn't be with us tonight, is descended from the very singer who helped make Franz Schubert's songs famous." Here he stopped and gestured toward Trudi, who smiled briefly in acknowledgement. I was thinking that it went both ways, that it was Vogl who was remembered these days primarily because he'd sung Schubert's songs. How many other court opera singers of the early nineteenth century can you name?

The Count was still talking while I was thinking about Michael Vogl.

"However," he continued, "We are fortunate to have with us tonight Vienna's favorite baritone, Fritz Gerling." The audience erupted in applause. Fritz Gerling bowed in response. Michael Fodor continued his speech, introducing the pianist, and finishing by asking us to please seat ourselves in the chairs arranged in the front of the room.

I sat between Christina and Trudi, who acted as though they were my favorite aunts, with only a few rows of Viennese aristocrats between me and the musicians. I'd already placed my glass on the tray of a passing server, thankfully not the one who'd ogled me earlier. The pianist played the rather mournful introduction to *"Gute Nacht,"* the first song of *Die Winterreise* song cycle, based on poems written by Wilhelm Müller. It's not one of Schubert's more cheerful collection of Lieder; in fact, I'm sure there are many who would say that Schubert has no truly cheerful songs in his vast collection. I'd have to agree with that assessment. Schubert's songs can be tender, sensual, and intensely emotional; his melodies are so enchanting that it's easy to get lost in them, at least for me. The man revealed his heart in his music. It's why people still loved him, two centuries after he'd walked the streets of Vienna.

Fritz caressed the last words of the first song. "I have been thinking of you," he sang, and I must have sighed out loud, because the dowager in front of me turned and aimed a reproving glance at me. I was saved from having to apologize by the wave of applause rippling through the audience, followed by the arpeggiated introduction to the next song. What can I say? It was captivating for me, being so close to the performers that I could see the beads of sweat forming on Fritz Gerling's forehead and feel his round tones vibrating through my body. I did try very hard not to sigh again, even when he sang my favorite, *"Der Lindenbaum."* After that one, which was clearly loved by the rest of the listeners too, Fritz Gerling and his accompanist bowed to the audience and made their way out of the room. Michael Fodor announced an intermission and urged us to enjoy the buffet while the performers rested and refreshed themselves.

The woman in front of me, the one who'd disapproved of my sigh, stood and whispered something to her companion, who added an unfriendly glance to the one I'd already received. "Don't worry about them." It was Trudi Vogl speaking. "They are old Viennese society matrons, trying to enforce their idea of correct manners wherever they go." Once more, I would have apologized, but she continued. "It's good to see someone who is truly touched by Schubert's music." She guided me away from the chairs and toward the food as she talked. "We must have you over once Helmut is feeling better."

It was a good thing that I didn't have anything to choke on at that moment. As it was, all I could do was breathe deeply and smile my thanks to her. Later on, I'd have plenty of time to reflect on the irony of meeting and liking both Helmut Vogl's wife and his paramour. At the moment, though, my attention was focused on the vast array of food in front of me. It was a typical Austrian buffet, from the platters of chicken and schnitzel to the bowls of potatoes and kraut, the cucumber salads, and, of course, the obligatory goulash, this time served thick like a stew with spaeztle to accompany it. In addition to all of this, there were tureens of steaming soup and baskets of bread.

I had eaten a snack before leaving home, but I was hungry again, so I loaded my plate and balanced it in one hand while I carried a bowl of soup in the other and followed Christina and Trudi to one of the adjoining rooms, where tables and chairs were set up. They gestured to a vacant place, and I seated myself next to a balding, bespectacled man in a grey tweed jacket, a man who looked vaguely familiar to me. He rose to help me with my chair, and as I spread my napkin on my lap, he introduced himself.

"Otto Heimberger," he said, and waited for my name, while I struggled to deal with the peculiar reality of another newspaper photo coming to life. Fortunately, Trudi Vogl, with her innate courtesy and charm, helped me, and after telling Otto who I was, she continued. "Otto works with my husband," she explained, and I pretended that this was something I didn't know. I must have succeeded, because she was still talking, this time about tonight's *Schubertiade*. "Dr. Lindstrom," she said, "is a true lover of Schubert. She is probably one of those, like my dear Helmut, who would have attended these gatherings during Franz' lifetime."

She saved me, I have to admit. I was able to concentrate on what I knew quite a bit about, and talk about the history of these friendly gatherings of Schubert's friends and acquaintances, where he'd had the chance to share his compositions. They were supposed to have been comfortable evenings of poetry and music, of eating, dancing, playing and talking attended by the artists and writers closest to Schubert. I'd never read anything about any aristocrats or politicians being in attendance, but of course, I didn't mention this fact.

Otto looked much more at ease than he had in the picture I'd studied earlier that day, but he was readily identifiable as a bureaucrat, rather than an aristocrat. When I'd asked which was his favorite song, he'd said, "Well, *"Der Lindenbaum,"* of course, and that had been the end of it. If it hadn't been for the others at the table, I would have had trouble conversing with Otto. The rest of them, however, were talking about everyday Viennese concerns, rather than about two hundred year old musical gatherings, and he seemed very comfortable with their topic. That was fine with me, because it gave me a chance to eat. I had just finished my last bite, and placed my napkin on the table next to my plate, when I became aware of the itching. I rubbed at my throat, ran my finger around the neckline of my new cashmere dress, and reached for the glass of mineral water in front of me.

"Lily, dear, are you all right?" That was Christina's voice and it sounded as if it were coming from far away, though she was right next to me. "Your face is looking red and splotchy."

By then, I was feeling other symptoms, the itchy eyes and the dizziness that let me know when I'm in trouble. I wheezed out my next words as I opened my evening bag. "No. I may need help." I managed to pull out the small case containing the EpiPen I always carry, some Benadryl tablets, and a printed synopsis of my allergic reactions and treatment protocol. I yanked the activation cap from the EpiPen, jabbed the black tip of the device into my outer thigh right through my knit dress, and held it there for several seconds. When I pulled it out, Christina took it from me, looked to see if the needle was showing, and then stowed it back in its carrying tube, just as if she'd done this before.

I was rubbing my thigh around the spot where I'd stabbed the needle in, and I was about to ask about her unusual expertise, when I felt that faintness which often follows these episodes. I did manage to whisper, "Thanks," just before I slid from my chair.

When I opened my eyes, I saw faces hovering over me, distorted and wavy as if I were viewing them through the peephole in my front door, and I heard a commanding voice say, "Sandor, Andreas, carry her to the front parlor." If I could have protested, I would have, believe me. Whoever Sandor and Andreas were, they were not gentle. I wondered if they'd ever carried a living, breathing person before. By the time they had deposited me on a cushioned chaise in the parlor where I'd left my coat earlier, I was wishing I could slip into unconsciousness again. Instead, I opened my eyes, looked up at the men who'd just dropped me and gasped. It was the insolent dark haired waiter I'd encountered earlier, and next to him, a burly grey haired man with a gold chain around his neck, a chain with a medallion dangling from it. There wasn't a saint on the medallion as I'd expected though, nothing as prosaic as that. Instead there was an intricate swirling pattern forming a background for the letter 'S.' This had to be Sandor, unless the 'S' stood for something else. The small dark one must be Andreas. I could identify them now. These were the two Stephen had been following, the ones who'd delivered something to Mitzi before they knocked me down in front of my apartment building.

Michael Fodor came into my line of vision while I was staring at them. "You can go now." They left without a word, apparently accustomed to obeying the Graf, who now directed his words to me. "Christina has called your doctor. He should be here momentarily."

My doctor? What doctor? Who could Christina have called? While I was trying to solve that mystery, the Count kept talking. "I'm sorry to leave you now, but I need to get back to my guests." He turned and left the room, and his place was taken by Christina, who knelt next to me.

"You're looking better already, Lily." She stroked my hand as she spoke. "Thank God you had that EpiPen with you." She adjusted a pillow under my head, and I murmured my thanks. "My late husband had to carry one too." She stopped stroking my hand and reached for something on the table beside the chaise. It was my evening bag. "How smart of you to carry your doctor's phone number. I called him as soon as you slipped off your chair and dropped your bag. He's on his way." She held up a familiar slip of paper and I knew now who was on his way. I'd jotted down Michael Fodor's address on the back of the piece of paper Stephen had handed me a couple of days ago; it contained his

Viennese mobile phone number, and it was imprinted with his name and degrees. What could I say, except, "Thank-you, Christina." Then I leaned back and closed my eyes again. I would have dropped off to sleep if Stephen's voice hadn't disturbed me.

"Lily. Look at me." It was a command, and I obeyed. This time when I opened my eyes, Stephen's deep blue ones were looking into them. He was placing a tablet on my tongue, helping me lift my head, holding a glass to my lips, and ordering me to swallow. The man could multi-task.

"It's a good thing you had the EpiPen and the Benadryl with you." Aha. That's what I had just swallowed. "What are you allergic to?"

"Shellfish." I was so tired I wanted to drop my head back again, but he wouldn't let me. "I didn't see it." I paused to take another sip of water. "Or taste it. It must have been in the soup. There was so much paprika it concealed the other flavors." I know the danger of eating shellfish, obviously, or I wouldn't have been as well prepared as I was. I had just never expected to encounter it at a Viennese party.

"Oh yes. It says so right here." He was scanning my treatment protocol sheet. "You're well prepared, Lily. I'm impressed."

Maybe I should have felt complimented. Instead, I felt irritated. "I do have a Ph.D." I snapped and then dropped my head back. "If you'll leave me alone now, I think I'll just rest a bit."

"Oh, no you don't. Not yet. We need to get you out of here first." He turned to Christina who was hovering over his shoulder. "Do you know which coat is hers?"

"It's black wool." I croaked. My voice wasn't quite right yet. Ordinarily this description wouldn't be helpful, but at this gathering, it could separate my humble wrap quickly from the stacks of fur and leather in the room. "And it has my name in it."

"Why am I not surprised?" That was Stephen.

"It's good to be organized," I mumbled.

"It certainly is." Christina agreed as she handed my coat to Stephen. I liked her better all the time. Underneath that glamorous, diamond laden exterior there was a sensible and pragmatic Minnesotan.

Stephen helped me to my feet and into my coat. He wrapped his arm around me and held me close as we made our way down the hallway. From the music room the haunting, mournful notes of *"Einsamkeit"* came floating out to us. In English that's "Loneliness," and it's Schubert at his most poignant and melancholy. I admit that it pulled at my heartstrings. I'd like to say that I leaned into Stephen just because I still felt a bit weak and dizzy, but the truth is, it felt good to be supported by his solid warmth. We were a few steps from the entrance to the apartment when Christina stopped us.

"Don't forget your evening bag, Lily." She handed it to me, and then she continued. "I'll check on you tomorrow. In the meantime, I'm going to talk to Michael's new chef and find out exactly what he put in that soup." Her last words were directed to Stephen. "Take care of her."

"That's what I intend to do."

I was enjoying the sound of those words when I looked up and saw who was standing between us and the doorway. Stephen must have felt the shiver which vibrated through me, because he whispered, "Hold on. We're walking right past them without a word."

And that's exactly what we did. Not until we were in the elevator and making our descent did I whisper back to him. "What was Otto Heimberger doing with Sandor and Andreas?"

CHAPTER ELEVEN

Several minutes passed before he answered my question and then it was with another question. "Sandor and Andreas? How did you find out their names?"

I settled myself in the back seat of the grey, slush spattered Skoda which had been idling in the street outside Michael Fodor's apartment house. The elevator had delivered us safely to the ground floor, and no one had stopped us or followed us outside, at least as far as I knew. Really, there was no reason for me to think anyone would do so, but I kept glancing over my shoulder as we drove down Metternichgasse and through the count's neighborhood, making our way to the Ring.

Stephen sat beside me in the back while the man who had been introduced to me as "my friend Janos" drove the small car. I couldn't see his face, just the back of his head, which was covered with a dark wool cap. He drove well, and he drove fast. The buildings of the Ring flew by in a blur of light. Ahead I could see the Opera, its arched façade gleaming through the darkness. As we crossed Kärntnerstrasse, I craned my neck to see around Stephen for a dazzling view of the patterned rooftop and steeple of St. Stephen's Cathedral. We cruised past the Hofburg on our right, the Parliament on our left, followed by the Rathaus, and then the Burgtheater on the right. They were all glistening through the snowfall, a truly lovely sight, but Stephen and Janos didn't seem to be as moved as I was by the beauty of Vienna at night.

"Your place or hers?" That was Janos speaking. His voice was a deep, smooth bass, but his question caused me to lift my head from Stephen's shoulder where it had been resting.

"Hers. She'll be more comfortable in her own bed." He gave him directions but then lapsed into silence. Neither of them said another word until Janos brought the car to a stop in front of my apartment house.

"Stay there. I'll come around." Stephen said that to me as he opened the car door on his side.

While he walked through the snow covered street to my side of the car, I thanked Janos, said I hoped we'd meet again when I felt better, and listened to his polite, but puzzling response. "That's up to Stephen," he said. That was one more thing he could explain later. I had a long list of questions now.

The entrance to my apartment house was hard to see with only the faint glow from the streetlight on the corner, but I managed to find the lock and fit the key into it. Stephen pushed the door open, and as he did so, Janos pulled away from the curb.

We didn't talk as the elevator rattled its way to the third floor; in fact, not a word was spoken until we'd entered my apartment and Stephen had hung up our coats. I don't know what I'd thought he would say, but it wasn't, "Roses? Someone sent you roses?"

There they were, all those long stemmed fragrant red roses, in a vase on the little table in my entry hall where I'd left them earlier, and the card from Kevin was right next to them. He picked it up, of course, and read it. "Last night was wonderful?" He turned to look at me. I hoped that I was looking so pale and weak that he'd put down the card and think only of taking care of me, as he'd promised Christina he would do, but no, he kept reading. "I can't wait to see you again?"

I decided to take matters into my own hands. "Do you think you can help me with my boots?" Unfortunately, my wish to be weak was being fulfilled. I was longing to sit down, but didn't want to track through my apartment in my slushy boots.

"Sure. In a minute." Now he was picking up the other card, the one from Kurt, which said, if I remembered correctly, "Call me." It said more than that though. I remembered the rest when Stephen read it aloud too, and got to the "I can help you" part.

"You've been busy." He said that right before I swayed toward him. I wasn't kidding about needing to sit down. He caught me and helped me to a chair in my kitchen.

"Put your head between your legs. I'll get you a glass of water."

Fine doctor he was. I could have figured all of that out by myself, but I did what he told me. While I had my head down so close to my boots, I tried to unzip them, but my fingers wouldn't obey my brain. His would though, and he pulled the snug leather boots from my feet very efficiently.

"I should have taken you to the hospital. What was I thinking?"

"You were following the instructions in my treatment protocol which say very clearly that as long as someone stays with me for twelve hours and makes sure that I take my Benadryl and rest, I don't need to be hospitalized."

"Right." He had his hand on the pulse at my wrist and his eyes on his watch. My eyes were on his face, on the strong line of his jaw, the dark shadows under his eyes. He looked up and our glances met and locked. "I'll stay with you tonight, Lily."

It was not exactly what I might have imagined for our first night together, if I had even allowed myself to imagine such a thing. He made me sit in the kitchen until I felt steady enough to walk to my bedroom and change into my pajamas. He offered to help me, but I said, "No thanks," and made him wait just outside the door, where he could hear if I called out. He hovered outside the bathroom too, while I washed my face and brushed my teeth. He made me take another Benadryl and drink some more water, and he watched as I sank into my bed and curled up under my down comforter. He stayed very close, I have to say.

It was lovely, it really was. The snow was falling outside my window; "Love Songs from Your Favorite Operas" was playing on my CD player. I like to listen to it at bedtime; I have found that listening solely to Schubert has a melancholy effect on me. He was, after all, not lucky in matters of the heart, at least as far as we know. Stephen was pacing back and forth in my living room, talking to someone on his phone, pausing to peek in at me every minute or two. I really had no excuse for feeling so grumpy, except that I wanted to talk to him before the Benadryl knocked me out. I had a lot of questions.

The next time he stuck his head in to look at me, I waved at him. He waved back and kept pacing and talking. Okay. I'd have to try something else to get his attention. I pushed back the comforter, sat up, and put my feet on the floor. It worked.

"What do you think you're doing?"

"Trying to get your attention."

He mumbled something into his phone, then shoved it into his pocket. "You've got it. You can get back under the covers now."

"Not unless you promise to stay in here with me until I fall asleep."

"I'm not sure that's a good idea."

I patted the bed next to me. "Sure it is. You sit here on top of the covers and I'll snuggle down under, and we can talk. It will be just fine."

He didn't look convinced, but he did it. He actually reclined next to me with his head against the pillows, folded his arms across his chest and said, "Here I am. You can go to sleep now."

I was awfully tired, I must admit. It had been a long day, and Benadryl makes me drowsy, but I wanted to know a few things. "Can you tell me what's going on before I go to sleep?"

He turned on his side facing me, propped his head on his hand, and spoke softly.

"Lily, it's a very long, complicated story. How about if I promise to fill you in over breakfast?" He smiled in response to my unvoiced question. "Yes, I'll still be here."

Then he did a very sweet thing. He reached out and stroked my hair. I closed my eyes, but not my ears. I heard him say, "And you can tell me about Kevin and Kurt and those flowers." Then I floated off to sleep, while Rodolfo and Mimi sang to me of their love. Ah Puccini. Ah love. Did I imagine that Stephen's arm came around my shoulders and that he murmured, "Sleep well, Lily" to me as I rested my head on his shoulder? I hope not.

I woke up to the smell of coffee and the sound of a piano. Was someone playing a Beethoven Bagatelle? I sat up, stretched, and rubbed my eyes. I did not feel wonderful. Benadryl leaves me feeling as groggy as if I had a hangover, and my body ached in odd places. I must not have slipped to the floor quite as gracefully as I'd thought the night before, or else it was the rough way Sandor and Andreas had picked me up which was causing this pain. Whatever it was, it made me pause before I tried to get out of bed. I leaned back against the pillows, turned my head to where I last remembered seeing Stephen, ran my hand over the empty pillow, and felt the indentation his head had left.

Then I pulled that pillow close to my face and inhaled the scent he'd left behind. I could have stayed there for quite a while, sniffing that pillow, if the Bagatelle hadn't come to an end. I waited a minute, listening for another one to begin, but instead I heard the sound of footsteps coming toward my room. I shoved the pillow back into place and closed my eyes. The footsteps stopped next to my bed, and I felt a hand on my forehead.

"Good morning." How did he know I wasn't asleep?

I mumbled a reply and opened my eyes. Oh my, he looked good. He must have taken a shower, because he smelled fresh too.

"Are you hungry?"

I had to think about that. "Maybe."

"I have chocolate croissants."

"Oh. Well then. I'm hungry." I sat up and pushed the comforter aside. He watched me.

"Are you in pain?"

How could he tell? "Just a bit."

"Do you feel up to taking a shower?"

Did I blush? I must have, because he was quick to say, "On your own, I mean."

"Of course. What else could you mean?" I stood up and headed for the large antique armoire which held my clothes. He didn't move until I said, "I'll be fine. You can leave the room now." He did.

I felt much better after a hot shower. Clean hair, clean body, clean clothes, plus the prospect of a chocolate croissant and a cup of coffee made me smile. It didn't hurt that the man who'd made the coffee was waiting for me in the kitchen. His eyes traveled from the top of my freshly washed head to the tips of my sock encased toes, and he smiled too.

"You look good, Lily."

Good? Was that a compliment? I met his eyes, and decided that it was, even though it seemed a bit understated to me. I was hoping for something more along the lines of "lovely" or "irresistible," adjectives which had been used often and enthusiastically by the men Sophie had mentioned. My older brothers would definitely approve of him though. Not only did he refrain from throwing overblown praise at me, but more importantly, he had rescued me when I needed help, and then had spent the night watching over me, without making any romantic overtures whatsoever, at least none that I could remember. Was something wrong with him? Or with me? I'd have to think about this. Meanwhile, I sat down across from him, poured a little cream into my coffee, and reached for a croissant.

"How did you get the croissants?" I was thinking of the walk to the market, and looked out the window to see whether it was still snowing. It was.

"Janos brought them when he came by with my clean clothes and other stuff."

"Ah, well then. That explains everything, except of course who Janos really is, how you two got to me so fast last night, what Sandor and Andreas are doing working for Michael Fodor, not to mention what Otto Heimberger could have been talking to them about." I paused to take a bite of the croissant. There was nothing like the combination of chocolate and sugar to improve my brain function. "And while you're explaining things, you can tell me about those articles you circled in red in my newspapers. Is this the latest government technique for sharing clues? It seems a bit rudimentary to me."

"Is that all you need to know?" He didn't look a bit bothered by my list of questions. In fact, he didn't look bothered about anything. He sat calmly across from me, peeling an orange. He placed a few segments on my plate. "A woman can't live on chocolate alone."

"Sure she can." I picked up a piece of the fruit and popped it into my mouth though. The juice dribbled down my chin and he reached over and wiped it with his napkin, as he talked.

"First, Janos and I were already in the car and close by. That was lucky. Second, as I told you last night, Janos is a friend. Third, I don't know yet what Sandor and Andreas were doing working at Michael Fodor's party, or why Otto Heimberger was talking to them, but I'll see what I can find out." He peeled another orange. I had finished the first one. It did go well with the croissant and coffee. "As for clues, I just thought you'd be interested in those articles, and the red pen seemed like the best way to bring them to your attention."

He seemed to be answering my questions, but really the man hadn't revealed much. "In the car and close by?" That could mean anything. Where specifically had they been and what had they been doing? I must have been thinking out loud again, because he answered me.

"You don't need to know exactly what we were doing, Lily. Isn't it enough that we got there quickly to help you?"

Now I was embarrassed. Had I ever thanked him? "Yes, of course it is, and I don't mean to sound thankless. Really. If you hadn't come, I don't know what I would have done. Believe me, I do thank you, Stephen."

"But?" He had finished the orange and sat across from me, totally focused on me. It was a bit unnerving, but I kept talking.

"There's more going on than you're telling me."

"Of course there is." He sipped his coffee. "If it will make you feel better, there's more going on than I know about yet." He stood and started to clear the table. "The thing is, Lily, I'm not free to share everything I know, and even if I were, I'm not sure that you should be informed of every single detail."

"Why not? It hardly seems as if knowing about aphrodisiac peddling Hungarians endangers national security." I started to laugh. I couldn't help myself. "Really. 'Rock Hard' and 'Love Stone.' Couldn't they think of something more subtle?"

"Do they look like subtle guys to you?"

I thought of the last time I'd seen Sandor and Andreas and I stopped laughing.

"They scare me, if you want to know the truth." I carried my plate to the sink, refilled my coffee cup, and headed for the living room. We settled ourselves on the couch this time, and I made a strong effort to keep a little distance between us. It wasn't easy. He put his arm on the back of the couch, just above my shoulders.

"You're right to be scared, Lily. The names of those aphrodisiacs may sound funny, but Sandor and Andreas and their employer are dealing in illegal drugs, and they're illegal for good reason. People have died from using that stuff. Helmut Vogl is lucky to have survived. The aphrodisiac wasn't the only drug he took that night. They're selling black market pharmaceuticals too. This is a big ring, Lily, with a network not only here, but reaching across Europe to the United States. Those deaths occurred in Chicago."

He paused to sip his coffee. "So you're right. National security is not an issue in this situation." His fingers caressed my neck, gently as he continued. "But your security is, Lily, and it's important to me. You need to fill me in now, beginning with how you know their names, and what you were doing at Michael Fodor's party." His fingers had moved on to my earlobe. "And then you can tell me about Kevin and Kurt, and those roses."

My breath caught in my throat, but I cleared it and tried to proceed as if I didn't notice those skillful fingers. Apparently the man did know how to make a romantic overture after all.

"It's a bit complicated actually."

"You're good at complications. You can explain it all to me."

And so I did, starting with Christina Anderson's connection to the college's Vienna program, her apparently amorous relationship with Michael Fodor, their invitation to the *Schubertiade*, and my encounter there with Sandor and Andreas. I finished with my description of the medallion which had struck my forehead the night we'd met. He didn't seem nearly as interested in Sandor's neckware as I was though. He had something else on his mind.

"And where do Kevin and Kurt and the roses fit into this story?"

Since he wasn't going to let that go, I told him about Kevin at the opera, insisted that I'd done nothing to warrant or even encourage the gift of the roses, and that, in fact, I was going to have to discourage his little crush on me. As for Kurt, that was easy to explain, and it did remind me that I needed to call him. I was feeling quite satisfied with my explanation, and he must have been too, because his lips had stopped asking questions and were now otherwise occupied.

The man had good technique, I have to say. Who knows how long we would have stayed there on my couch, enjoying the sweet sensations of our lips and hands on each other, if the insistent buzzing of my doorbell hadn't disturbed us.

"Ignore it. I'm not expecting anyone." I'm not sure how I managed to get those words out. It was hard to think, let alone talk, while those skilled hands were doing what they were doing. He lifted his head and dropped one more kiss on my pleasure softened mouth.

"I wish I could."

And then he moved away from me, stood, and turned toward my front hallway. I watched him, watched how those fine fingers ran through his rumpled hair and then pulled his sweater back into place. I wanted to do that for him. He must have seen the message on my face, because he grinned and said, "Next time."

CHAPTER TWELVE

While Stephen answered the buzzer, I pulled myself together as well as I could, and then hurried to the bathroom to brush my hair and reapply my lipstick. The woman who looked back at me from the mirror looked very pleased with herself, as well she should. Becomingly flushed cheeks and eyes with a contented gleam told their own story. I must have stood there communing with my own reflection longer than I thought, because Stephen's voice at the bathroom door startled me.

"What are you doing Lily? Hurry! Christina Anderson is in the elevator on her way up."

I opened the door, walked right into that solid male and indulged in one more kiss before I followed him to my front hallway. The elevator was quivering to a stop just as I arrived at my threshold. Christina Anderson pulled back the metal grille and stepped out onto the stone landing. She was swathed in fur from head to toe, and she carried a bulging shopping bag.

"Lily! You're looking much better this morning." She looked over my shoulder and smiled. "And Dr. Cameron. How nice to see you again." She didn't blink, or even pause when she saw him. "I've brought you some gifts from Michael. He's feeling just terrible about your allergic reaction."

She set the shopping bag on the floor, pulled off her snow covered hat, and ran her fingers through her hair, which fell perfectly into place. Stephen helped her out of her coat, and while she bent to pick up the shopping bag, I reached over to rub my fresh lipstick from his lips. Had she noticed it? Did it matter?

"Won't you come in and join us for a cup of coffee?"

"Thank-you. That would be delightful." Stephen led her into the living room, while I fetched the carafe and a fresh cup from the kitchen. I added a chocolate croissant to the tray, just in case she was hungry. They were already seated and conversing when I returned.

"I was just telling Dr. Cameron how relieved I was to see him here. "She aimed her charming smile at me. "I remember watching Lars all through the night after he had these episodes." She paused to stir cream into her coffee. "Lars was my husband," she explained. I knew that she was a widow, but Stephen didn't. Her suddenly moist eyes must have given him a clue, along with her next statement. "I still miss him."

"How long has it been?" Stephen leaned toward her, his voice low and soothing, his attention totally focused on her response.

She pulled a tissue from her purse and dabbed at her eyes.

"Not quite a year." She blew her nose. "I'm sorry. The grief still takes me by surprise."

It took me by surprise too. How did Michael Fodor fit into her sorrow? While I was contemplating that question, Stephen was talking. He was clearly more experienced at this topic than I was. "Grief takes all of us by surprise," he said gently, "And we never stop missing the ones we've lost."

That was almost as eloquent as a Schubert melody. Where had he learned to say things like that? Now my eyes felt moist too, and I sniffed. Christina reached across and squeezed my hand.

"You two are so precious. I'm not able to talk about this with very many people. I just try to keep living as bravely as I think Lars would have wanted me to."

Maybe that helped to explain her relationship with Michael. Maybe she was just doing what the Viennese called *fortwursteln*, muddling through what had to be a very tough year. If so, she was certainly doing it with great style.

"In the south we call that "keepin' on keepin' on," Stephen said, "And it's never easy." What did he just say? Believe me, this is not a phrase we use in Minnesota. I glanced over at him, but his eyes were still on Christina.

"Thank-you, both of you, for understanding." She pulled her hand back from mine and reached into her bag. From it she pulled a bottle of champagne, a box of chocolates, and an envelope with my name on it.

I examined the bottle of champagne first; it was, as I might have expected, one of the finest labels. The same was true of the chocolates, which were actually truffles. I thanked her profusely, of course, and she responded with, "You're welcome, but remember that these gifts are from Michael, not from me. Do open the envelope, though, Lily. It has the information you deserve."

I pulled two sheets of paper from the envelope, unfolded them, and began to read. It wasn't easy, because they were hand written in an almost undecipherable script. Christina must have noticed my difficulty, because she said, "It's the recipe for the soup, plus an apology from Michael's new chef. It turns out that he's another one of those cousins he rescued from the family estate in Hungary. In fact, the two men who carried you after you fainted last night are the chef's brothers."

If I'd thought that Stephen was attentive to Christina when she was talking about her late husband, Lars, it was nothing compared to the focus he aimed at her as she spoke about Michael Fodor and his Hungarian cousins. "He's given them all jobs?" Even though he put no special emphasis on his words and his tone of voice was perfectly neutral, I had a pretty good idea of one of the jobs he might be thinking of.

"Oh yes. He has such a generous heart." She waved toward my gifts as she spoke. "He's put them to work in the family business, in addition to paying them to help out in his home. I did speak to him about the need to train them better, and he promises that he'll work on it." I assumed that she was talking about their serving and cooking skills, but Stephen had latched onto the first part of her statement.

"Family business? I thought that he worked for the diplomatic corps." How had he known that? Maybe he was better at this undercover intelligence business than I'd given him credit for.

"Oh that. Yes, he's in their protocol department here in Vienna now, but that's not really a full time job, just a duty to fulfill. It comes with the family lineage, you know. His family business is where his heart is; he has such responsibilities. Nothing like my Lars and his company, of course, but still, it's quite impressive how he's been able to renovate the Hungarian estate, keep up the apartment in Vienna, and help his cousins, all with his import/export business."

"Impressive indeed," said Stephen quite calmly. He took the papers written by the Hungarian chef from me and studied them as if he could make sense of the badly scrawled words. Maybe he'd learned to do this in medical school. "Did he say anything specific to you about what he put in the soup?"

"Oh. Yes, he did. I asked, because I had trouble reading that too." She pointed at the recipe Stephen was holding. "He said that he'd decided at the last minute to add the shellfish which came in with the latest shipment, because he thought it would give richness and flavor to the soup."

"The latest shipment? Doesn't Michael Fodor buy his food locally?"

"I wondered about that too, but I'm sure that's what Istvan said. Maybe he likes to have certain specialties shipped in."

"I'll bet he does." I picked up on Stephen's tone of voice, but Christina didn't seem to notice the irony underlying his words. All she said was, "Michael insists on nothing but the finest ingredients."

I decided I'd better get into this conversation before Stephen asked any more questions. "Thanks so much for getting the recipe, Christina. It does explain my reaction. Shellfish was not something I expected in an Austrian soup."

"Of course it wasn't dear." She glanced at her expensive wristwatch. "I'd better be going. I promised Tom I'd have lunch with the students today." She stood and smoothed her skirt. "He was very concerned when I told him about your episode, so I'm sure he'll be relieved to hear how well you're doing." She paused. "Dr. Cameron seems to have taken very good care of you."

While I was considering how or whether to respond to that observation, the doctor she'd just praised rose and followed her to the front hallway. He was helping her into her coat when the buzzer at my front door sounded again. Who could it be this time? I pressed the button, asked who was there, and waited for a voice to come through the speaker.

"Professor Lindstrom. It's Kevin Carlson. I heard that you weren't feeling well and I've brought you something."

I buzzed him in, and tried to think of what to say next. Christina filled the silence.

"Isn't that sweet?' She gave me a hug on her way to the door, and said, "It must be wonderful to have such devoted students. You stay in and rest now Lily. I'll call you tomorrow."

Stephen followed her into the hallway and spoke softly to her as she waited for the elevator to reach my landing. Even though I leaned toward them, I couldn't make out what he was saying, but Christina nodded, then reached out and hugged him just as the elevator came to a shaky stop in front of them. Kevin pulled open the grate and stepped out. He didn't seem to recognize Christina, bundled up as she was in her fur coat and hat, so all he said was, "Excuse me," as he moved aside so that she could take his place. Stephen, however, did not move aside, and Kevin squeezed in next to him outside my door. This was going to be tricky.

I cleared my throat. "Kevin. What a surprise."

He stood facing me, a tall lanky Minnesotan dressed sensibly in a knit cap, parka, gloves and boots. His face was red from the snow and the cold, and he was clutching a shopping bag.

"You'd better come in." He moved forward, followed closely by Stephen, and came to a stop just inside my door. Stephen closed it, and then stood silently in front of it, arms crossed. Kevin ignored him, but then I hadn't introduced them yet. His eyes went to the roses he'd left with Frau Frassl.

"I see that you got the roses."

"Oh. Yes, I did. Thank-you, Kevin. They're quite lovely."

"Not nearly as lovely as you, Professor Lindstrom." He pulled off his knit cap, revealing neatly cut dark blonde hair. "Do you think I could call you Lily now?"

"Call me Lily?" My usually well modulated voice came out in a high pitched squeak. I threw a desperate glance at Stephen, who just shrugged. Big help he was. Kevin put down his shopping bag, unzipped his parka, and pulled it off while I was trying to come up with an adequate response.

"Is there someplace I can put this?"

"Oh. Sure. There's a hook behind you."

He turned to hang it up, and when he did, he faced Stephen. Neither of them said a word, so I had to perform the introductions. "Stephen, I'd like you to meet one of my students, Kevin Carlson. Kevin, this is Dr. Stephen Cameron."

They shook hands and then Kevin said, "I'm so glad that Lily found a doctor to take care of her."

"Yes, well, I do what I can." Stephen's smile sent a private message to me, and I was starting to worry about what he might say next, when he surprised me. "It was good to meet you Kevin. Now, I think I'll run a quick errand while you two chat. See you later, Lily." And with that, he grabbed his coat and left before I had a chance to stop him, or even slow him down.

I was still listening to his footsteps when Kevin said, "Is there a place where I can sit down to take off my boots?"

I led him to the kitchen, pointed to a chair and started to brew another pot of coffee. By the time I sat down across from him, ready at last with the speech I needed to deliver, he was unpacking his shopping bag.

"I'm not sure that you should be drinking coffee," he said. "I've brought you some herbal tea and a box of crackers." He looked quite pleased with himself. "And I'll be glad to spend the rest of the day with you while you rest and recover." Next he pulled a biography of Schubert from his bag. "I've brought this along to read, so that I'll be ready for next week's work."

It was apparent that I was going to have to be quick and firm with him. I'd had admiring students before, but their overtures had been limited to compliments after class and shy invitations to join them for coffee at the student union. No one had ever sent me roses or come to my apartment. Vienna must be having an unfortunate effect on Kevin.

I cleared my throat and sat up as straight as I could. "We need to talk about the roses, Kevin, and about your coming here today."

He sat across from me smiling as if I were about to say something wonderful to him. I hated to hurt him, but truthfully, he was starting to irritate me.

"Kevin. I'm your professor. You may not call me by my first name, and you may not send me roses again, not ever. I appreciate your thoughtfulness, but there is no possibility that we will ever have anything other than a student/teacher relationship. You are here to study and to absorb everything Vienna has to offer, not to pursue a liaison with me."

There, I thought that was pretty well said. Kevin, however, didn't seem convinced. "But Professor Lindstrom, I heard you whisper, 'I love you' the other night, at the opera." He looked at me with bruised eyes. "You were quite clear."

Oh dear. It was that unconscious brain to mouth connection again. It happens when the music inundates my senses. I knew that I had hummed along that night, but I honestly didn't remember saying those words. What a disaster. Now I'd have to apologize and hope that he recovered before classes next week.

"Kevin, I'm so sorry. If you really heard me say that, I was talking to Mozart, or possibly to Tamino, or even Papageno. Sometimes, words just slip out of my mouth without my knowing it when I'm overcome by the music. I wasn't talking to you, Kevin. Believe me, I wasn't talking to you."

He stood, shoved his chair back, picked up his book and stumbled from the kitchen. He had untied his boots, but not removed them. He stopped, bent over, retied them, and then reached for his coat. Now I did feel awful about the poor boy, who seemed to be in a race to get away from me.

"I won't bother you again, professor." He pulled open the door and dashed out into the hallway and down the stone steps.

Stephen pulled himself away from the wall outside my doorway. "I guess your little chat went well." He came in and shut the door.

I didn't say anything. I was not in the mood for irony; I was so mortified by what I had done to Kevin that I did the one thing I knew would help me work through my feelings. I headed to the piano. He followed me, and slid onto the bench beside me. He didn't say anything else about Kevin, but instead asked, gently, I admit, "Do you have any duets, Lily?"

I wasn't sure whether I wanted to share the keyboard with him at that moment, when what I longed to do was lose myself in the music, but I nodded and reached for the stack of books beside me. Maybe it wouldn't hurt to double the vibrations. What I set in front of him was the only volume of duets I could find, "Selected Piano Works for Four Hands," by Franz Schubert.

"I might have known." He opened the thick volume, scanned the table of contents, and then turned to a group of *Ländler*. "Country Waltzes. These don't look too bad. Maybe they'll cheer you up."

"Do you really think that playing a light hearted waltz is going to make me feel better about hurting that boy?" I'd been intending to play something much more serious and gloomy.

"Of course not, but it's better than brooding alone, isn't it?"

It turned out that he was right. The gentle dances were lovely, Schubert at his most light hearted and tender, and playing elbow to elbow with Stephen ended up feeling almost as good as kissing him.

At this point I should have remembered my mother's warning about what can happen when two people share a piano bench. Our bodies were touching from shoulder to hip; I could feel his breath moving in and out with the music. Our fingers glided rhythmically over the keys; the melody flowed with gentle elegance; it made me want to dance, as Schubert had intended. Maybe it would be more accurate to say that it made me want to make love. Freud could say what he wanted about sublimation; making music with Stephen felt like foreplay. There's a reason the Viennese feel a whole lot more affection for Schubert than for Freud. By the time we had played all four of the *Ländler*, I was feeling pretty affectionate myself.

I leaned into him, exhaled and said, "Thanks."

He put one arm around me, pulled me closer, and responded with a simple, "You're welcome."

"That was you playing the Bagatelle this morning, wasn't it? I thought maybe I had dreamed it."

"I wasn't kidding about my mom being a piano teacher." He laughed softly. "I didn't always thank her for making me practice, but right now I'm feeling pretty grateful."

"You're not the only one." And then we moved to the couch and picked up where we'd left off when Christina had interrupted us earlier. I was breathless and mindless and in no mood to stop what we were doing when Stephen pulled away from me.

"Don't stop."

"Lily, I have to stop."

'No you don't."

Those blue eyes met mine and held my gaze while he pulled me up from where I lay in a state of rumpled bliss. He smoothed my hair, soothed me with his gentle touch.

"Well, it happens that I have to leave in a few minutes, but we may want to save some of this for another time anyway."

I reached out to him, rubbed my hand along his cheek, ran my fingers gently over his lips. "Another time?"

"Yes." He stood up, turned, and held his hand out to me. I took it, rose to meet him and leaned into his embrace.

"Ah, Lily. I didn't expect this. It complicates things."

Not exactly words of passion. Where did he find such self-control? I sighed, a deep heartfelt Mozartian kind of exhalation, with its own soft melody. He kissed me once more and then turned toward the door.

"I'll call you." I watched him pull on his coat, hat and gloves, pick up the small leather duffle bag Janos must have brought while I was sleeping, and open the door. I might have followed him to the hallway, or called out something more eloquent than "Good-bye," if I hadn't seen who was standing there.

It was Mitzi, and she was dressed to go out, in her boots and coat and hat. She murmured something to Stephen, who leaned much closer to her than he needed to, at least from my viewpoint, and handed him a folded sheet of paper. He tucked it into his pocket, kissed her on both cheeks, and then hurried down the steps without looking back.

Mitzi stepped across the threshold into my front hall, sent a dazzling smile toward me, and said, "Good work, Lily. He's already spent the night with you." She leaned down to smell Kevin's roses. "And he brought red roses too."

"It's not what you think." I took a step toward her. "I can explain."

"What is there to explain?" She lowered her voice. "He's a very attractive man. I can see why you wasted no time."

There seemed to be no reason to disillusion her, if she wanted to compliment me, so I just said, "I never waste time, if I can help it." That was the truth about my life, and even though I wasn't talking about my relationship with Stephen, it did seem to apply to that as well, at least from Mitzi's perspective.

"Well, you can rest assured that I won't try to add him to my client list." She spoke with conviction and looked me right in the eye. "I would never do that to you, Lily."

"Of course you wouldn't." The rest of that thought, the part I left unsaid, had to do with what I felt capable of doing to both of them, if such a thing were to happen. I was surprised at my own powerful reaction. She must have seen something in my expression, because she took a step backward.

"Don't worry, Lily. I really didn't even need to mention it to you, or to make that promise; I can tell that he isn't interested in me, not in that way. He's not a man who would want a woman like me."

And with that, she turned and started down the stairs. I listened to her footsteps echo in the stone enclosed space, and then I closed and locked my door. I needed a nap.

CHAPTER THIRTEEN

It had stopped snowing during the night, and Sunday morning dawned bright and clear. I know that, because I had spent so much time resting and recovering on Saturday that I woke up earlier than usual on Sunday. It was January 31st, Schubert's birthday, and the Lichtental Church, his church, was honoring him with a performance of his Mass in E Flat, written in 1828, shortly before his death. I loved this mass more than any of his others, loved its poignant melancholy, its bittersweet beauty.

I ate a big breakfast, dressed in warm layers, and then pulled on my wool hat, lined leather gloves and sensible walking boots. There was no one else on the stairs today, no one in the elevator, and no one on the sidewalk in front of my building, not even Frau Frassl, who didn't open her shop on Sundays. The street had been plowed during the night, and the snow was piled up at the curb. The sidewalk had been cleared too, but it was still slippery in places, and I had to be careful as I made my way up my street, Sobiskiegasse, to Schubertgasse and then onward to Nussdorferstrasse. I crossed this wide street, walked past the Schubert Museum, and turned left just beyond it into the passage leading to the Himmelfortstiege, "The Heaven's Gate Stairway." It got its name from an old Vienna cloister, no longer in existence, which used to own it. In fact it used to be called simply "The Big Stairway," an appropriate name, and it was the same route to church the Schubert family had used more than two hundred years ago.

Underneath the layer of snow, uneven cobblestones alternated with smooth sections of asphalt to form the walkway leading to the stairs. There were lights on in some of the windows of the apartments lining the walkway, but there were only a few people ahead of me on the steps leading down to Liechtensteinstrasse. I held onto the iron railing, placed my feet cautiously on the concrete steps. They turn at right angles, one section after another, just like the switchbacks on a mountain road. The bells of Schubert's church had begun their rhythmic pealing by the time I reached the bottom. I was only a block and a half from the church now; it stood at the corner of Marktgasse and Lichtentalgasse where it had stood since the early seventeen hundreds.

It's a sturdy Baroque church, with a pale yellow façade and twin towers. It's been restored inside and out, and the result is lovely to look at on any day, but today, with the winter sun shining on its snow covered roof and its towers reaching into the bright blue sky, it was truly beautiful. I followed an elderly couple up the steps to the front entrance; they were both wearing grey wool jackets with green trim and matching hats and looked as if they could have come in from a mountain village for the day. In truth, Vienna itself is a city made up of many village like neighborhoods; they are called districts, and each one has its own name and number. The ninth district, where I live this winter and where the Schubert family once lived, is called the Alsergrund district. It's situated northwest of the heart of the city, and is itself divided into several sections, each with its own moniker.

Schubert's parents were not native Viennese; they had both moved to this city from Silesia. His father was a schoolmaster, and the school was located in his home, in the Schubert Garage I walked by almost every day. He taught Franz and his other children, and they, in turn, became his assistants once they were grown. Franz, though, had the extra advantage of winning a place in the choir of the Imperial Court Chapel, the famous Vienna Choirboys, and attending their school. He received one of the finest educations to be had in Vienna at that time, and he repaid that gift many times over with his music. There is a strong love and devotion to Franz Schubert in his city, particularly here at the church where his parents were married, where he was baptized, and where he sang in the choir. He wrote some of his best known church music for this parish, including the beloved Mass in G Major. It's much more popular than the more somber and complex one being performed today; in fact, it's a favorite of church choirs where I come from.

The sweetly smiling woman who handed me the program reminded me of the ladies of the Altar Guild at the Lutheran church where I'd grown up. "It's our Franzl's birthday today," she said to me and to everyone she greeted. Then she added, "Please feel welcome to join a tour of the church later, and to see the organ he played." She was glowing with pride, as if she were talking about a favorite grandchild.

From the organ pipes in the choir loft came the notes of the only piece this son of the Lichtental Church had ever written for organ, at least as far as I know. It's the Fugue in E Minor; I recognized it not because it's famous. It's not. When we think of great organ music, we don't usually think of Schubert. I knew it because it's also arranged for piano duet, and I had played it. Stephen hadn't chosen it yesterday, but it's in my book, along with the *Ländler*. It's a perfectly nice piece, even if it's not well known, and it provided a steady beat for my feet as I entered the church and walked up the center aisle.

The interior of the church was bathed in the same strong sunlight which glistened on the snow outside. Everything, from the crystal chandeliers, to the bright stone walls and arches, to the highly detailed Baroque paintings on the walls and the ceiling, shone as if in celebration of its favorite son. I found a spot in one of the polished wooden pews and scooted across the fabric covered seat toward the middle, as I'd been trained to do my entire life, to leave room for latecomers. All around me were parishioners bundled in fur trimmed wool coats and hats, worshippers who knelt and crossed themselves before settling into their seats. I felt very young and Lutheran in comparison, and hoped that some of my fellow Minnesotans would show up soon. I'd spoken to Tom Thornquist yesterday about Kevin, and he'd promised to accompany any of the students who chose to come today.

It wasn't Tom or any of the students who sat down beside me a moment later though, but my friend Kurt, the Schubert loving librarian. I'd called him yesterday too, and we'd arranged to meet at the church this morning. He nodded and smiled his greeting, but he had turned around, and his attention was now focused on the small orchestra seated in the balcony. They were bundled up in thick sweaters; a few even wore hats. The church did not have a central heating system. The seats of the pews were heated now, just like the seats in some cars, but that wouldn't help the musicians keep their arms and fingers warm.

From this distance, they looked as if they could be our neighbors. There was nothing glamorous about them, or about any of the choir members, who filed in and clustered around the orchestra. They looked like typical middle class Viennese, like church choirs anywhere in the world. They didn't sound like them though. As soon as the horns and strings sent forth their first mellow notes and the choir joined them in the opening *"Kyrie,"* the vibrations filling Schubert's church were nothing short of heavenly. I know, it sounds like a cliché, but there's no other way to describe it. I closed my eyes as the harmonies resonated along my nerve endings, traveled from my ears to my heart. The voices blended together in a melodious mélange; the horns were strong and smooth; the strings, with their warm velvety Viennese tone, were simply exquisite. Schubert's tenderness and passion enveloped me with each chord and held me until the reverberations had faded into silence. Then I heard the voice of the priest, a reminder that this was not a concert performance, but a high mass.

I opened my eyes and joined the rest of the congregation as we were led through the age old service. Across the aisle and a couple of rows ahead I saw a familiar profile; it was Trudi Vogl, and beside her was Helmut, pale but alive, on his knees next to his wife as the priest led everyone in prayer. They must have come in while I had my eyes closed. There was a creaking and rustling as everybody settled back into their seats and the priest moved to the pulpit. Usually I tune out during sermons, plan lectures or make shopping lists, but this priest grabbed my attention with his first words.

He spoke about Schubert, his life and his music. He was thoughtful; he was poetic; he paid tribute to the man and his work. Ordinarily, it's the power of a melody which touches my heart, but I was moved by this priest's elegy to the son of this city, this neighborhood, this church. He must have known, surely, that Schubert did not remain a devout Catholic, that he distanced himself from the teachings of the church and felt more comfortable with the philosophy of pantheism. I understood Schubert's point of view; it wasn't the dogma which attracted me to these services, but the ritual and the music. However, the priest put into words the most important thing about Schubert, his ability to express life's joys and sorrows, its heart stopping beauty, in perfect harmony.

I closed my eyes as the music flowed through the space again. First the cellos and then the solo voices intertwined in the lovely melody of the *"Et incarnatus est."* That means "and became flesh," and it's part of the creed. Schubert had written it as a *Siciliano*, a dance in six eight time, and it was all I could do not to sway from side to side with the seductive rhythm. It felt more like a love song than a statement of belief. It was purely gorgeous. By the time the mass had wound down to the *"Dona Nobis Pacem,"* I had all but melted into the pew. Kurt squeezed my hand and gave it a little tug. I stood up beside him for the priest's blessing and dismissal, and then turned toward the aisle.

Above us, in the balcony to the rear, the organist sounded the first notes of the postlude, and the congregation began to file out. I looked for Trudi and Helmut Vogl, but saw only their backs as they slipped out a side door. Someone tapped my shoulder and I turned to find Tom and a row of students behind me. Kevin Carlson was at the far end of the pew, pointedly looking in the other direction. I introduced Tom and Kurt, and then we joined the line of worshippers exiting the church.

"I'm glad to see you here, Lily. We've been worried about you." That was Tom speaking. Kurt lifted one questioning eyebrow and I whispered, "I'll explain later." I hadn't told him about my unfortunate reaction to Michael Fodor's soup. Meanwhile, Tom kept talking. "Do you want to take the students up to see the organ, or do you want me to do it?" Apparently he was still concerned about my health. That was fine; I'd been to the balcony several times, and was more interested in having a word with that eloquent priest than in going up there again.

Like most Midwesterners, I rarely communicated with anything other than absolute forthrightness and occasionally brutal honesty. However, from the Viennese I'd learned the power of charm, and I used it now, fixing Tom with what I thought to be my wide-eyed, vulnerable gaze and speaking softly. "Oh, if you'd take them up, that would be wonderful, Tom."

"Sure, Lily. You take care of yourself now." And with that he ushered my students toward the back stairway leading to the choir loft, where the sweet lady who'd been handing out programs was waiting. I stayed in the line moving toward the main door, where the priest stood shaking hands, as if he were a Lutheran pastor recruiting new members. Was this one of the reforms the Roman Catholic Church had adopted, or was this priest as unusual as his poetic tribute to Schubert had indicated? I watched him as I approached, watched his friendly interaction with his parishioners, and couldn't help but notice that he was even better looking up close than he'd appeared in the pulpit. What could have led such a handsome and intelligent man to the priesthood?

Kurt was right behind me, and when there was only one person between me and the priest, he whispered, "I have to call my wife. I'll see you outside." His wife was expecting their first baby in a few weeks and had decided, very sensibly, to stay at home on this cold winter day.

The priest was reaching out his hand to me now, and I found myself drawn into his warmth. I told him how much I'd appreciated his words about Schubert, and when I asked about getting a copy of his sermon, he smiled and said, "Of course. Come by on Wednesday morning after mass and I'll have one for you." I thanked him, said "Good-bye," and stepped out into sunshine so brilliant that I was momentarily blinded. When I felt a firm hand on my elbow, I assumed at first that it was Kurt. I should have known better; I should have recognized that touch by now, but in my defense I need to say that there were layers of wool and leather separating us. It was Stephen, of course.

"I was hoping you'd be here. I called, but you didn't answer."

I blinked, tried to focus on the contours of his face, outlined against the bright façade of the church. He pulled me off to the side, away from the people clustered around the steps, pulled me right into the circle of his arms. I tipped my face toward his, watched his lips approaching mine, but all I got was a whisper from those lips.

"Not here, Lily." Of course not. What was I thinking? I pulled back a little and lifted my eyes to his, tried to read what was in them, but he was looking at something over my shoulder.

"Is this man with you, Lily?" He kept me within the circle of his arms, but turned me slightly, so that I could see Kurt hovering behind us. Both of his eyebrows were raised now. I introduced the two men. Stephen removed his arm from my shoulders long enough to shake Kurt's hand, but then put it right back where it had been, and, amazingly, pulled me a bit closer. So much for the "not here" statement; he seemed to be making a proclamation with his body.

Kurt, who was nothing if not astute, held up his phone as if it were a talisman. "Marta's parents are with her, so we can go on to the cemetery, Lily." He spoke directly to Stephen then. "Marta is my wife and she wasn't able to accompany me today." When he went on to explain about the expected baby, Stephen's grip on me loosened slightly.

He congratulated Kurt, but then asked, "Which cemetery, and why do you have to go today?"

"It's Schubert's birthday!" Kurt and I shouted it at the same time.

Unmoved, Stephen responded, "And?"

"And we're going to pay our respects at the Zentralfriedhof, of course." That's the Central Cemetery, and it's the biggest and best known in Vienna. I spoke very distinctly, as if I were explaining this to an exceptionally slow student. Stephen is not a bit slow, but something seemed to be bothering him; his eyes narrowed as he looked first at Kurt and then at me.

"Okay then. We can drop you off; it's on our way." As he spoke, he gestured toward the street where the little grey Skoda idled.

That's how I found myself once more greeting Janos and then sliding into the back seat of the Skoda, with Stephen close beside me. Kurt, after a quick glance at me to get some signal that this was okay, got into the front next to Janos. Skilled driver that he was, he shifted gears, pulled away from the curb, drove expertly through the narrow streets of the Lichtental neighborhood, and then turned left on Alserbachstrasse. When we reached the Danube Canal, he turned right on the street running beside it, a street which eventually merges into the Ringstrasse.

Because I was watching Janos' route through the streets of Vienna, and then listening to his conversation with Kurt about, of all things, Friday night's hockey game, I didn't notice for a moment that Stephen had extracted my cell phone from my purse.

"What are you doing?"

"Programming my number in here, of course. It was sheer luck that you had that piece of paper with you the other night."

Before I could even question how this man had inserted himself so deeply into my life during the past week that he was adding himself to my contact list, he went even farther.

"And I'm adding two more numbers. The first one is that of a reliable doctor you can call if you can't reach me. You don't have one in Vienna, right?" Without waiting for an answer, he went on. "The second one is for a colleague of mine you can call if anything . . ." He paused and made sure he had my full attention, then repeated that word, with strong emphasis. "Anything at all happens to worry or frighten you."

He did have my attention now, totally. "Why wouldn't I be able to reach you? And what do you think could possibly worry or frighten me?"

"Janos and I are headed out of town for a day or two, and I may not be able to answer my phone or return calls immediately." I had my mouth open to ask exactly where they were going, but Stephen put his finger over my lips and shook his head. "And I hope that nothing will happen to frighten you, but you have shown an uncanny ability to land in the middle of a drug smuggling operation run by people who, believe me, would not hesitate to remove anyone who got between them and their profits."

"Remove?" I did manage to get that word out before he replaced his finger with his lips. It had been years since I'd done what Stephen and I were doing in the back seat of a car. We were both so absorbed in each other, in the heat and pleasure we were sharing back there, that I have no idea how long Kurt and Janos had been clearing their throats and trying to get our attention. When we finally managed to pull ourselves a few inches apart and to focus on something besides each other, we discovered two faces grinning back at us.

"We're here," said Kurt.

"Have been for at least five minutes," added Janos.

"Yes, well." Stephen disentangled his arms and legs from mine. I have to admit that it felt good to see him finally looking as dazed as I felt. He opened the door on his side, stepped out, and held his hand out to me. I scooted over, put my hand in his, and stood up facing him, nose to nose.

"I'll see you in a few days. Take care, Lily." His voice was soft and strained, as if he had trouble getting those few words past his lips.

"You take care too," I whispered back.

He gave me one last kiss and then took Kurt's place in the front seat. Janos wasted no time, but pulled directly into the stream of traffic on the Simmeringhauptstrasse, heading out of Vienna. I watched until the Skoda disappeared from sight, then turned to Kurt. He was grinning at me.

"Well, well, Lily. I can't say that I've ever seen this side of you before." It was apparent that Kurt was stifling an urge to laugh. I frowned at him, and he took a deep breath before he continued. "Who is this guy anyway?"

I took a step toward the main gate of the cemetery, tried to pull my scattered wits together enough to speak coherently, or at least in complete sentences.

"He's a fellow American on a special assignment from the Centers for Disease Control." I went on to elaborate on Stephen's credentials, including his double doctorate, but Kurt was still focused on our back seat behavior.

"Sure, Lily. Special assignment. Likely story. What's he studying, the mating habits of musicologists?"

I hoped that my cheeks were rosy enough from the cold that Kurt wouldn't think I was blushing. "Don't be silly. He'd have to be an anthropologist to do that. As a matter of fact, he's interested in pharmaceuticals."

I had stopped at a flower stall outside the gate and was digging into my purse for enough coins to pay for the bouquet of flowers I wanted to leave on Schubert's grave. I chose lilies of course, white ones, and buried my face in their subtle fragrance.

Kurt smiled his approval. "Lovely gesture, Lily. You act so Viennese, it's hard sometimes to remember that you're not a native."

I was truly touched by this statement and stopped to thank Kurt. "I may be from Minnesota, Kurt, but in my heart I am Viennese." Then I surprised myself by leaning in to hug him.

He hugged me back and then said, "Of course you are, Lily."

CHAPTER FOURTEEN

We walked through the main gate of the cemetery, which is so impressive that it looks like the entrance to a city. In fact, the Zentralfriedhof has a bigger population than Vienna does, and like Vienna, it's divided into sections. We were headed toward the area reserved for *Ehrengräber*, Honor Graves. To be a given a burial place in this section is one of the highest tributes the city can bestow on its citizens. Straight ahead of us was the broad, tree lined avenue leading to the magnificent green domed church named for Dr. Karl Lueger, a former mayor of Vienna. Its creamy stone walls rose in stately symmetry out of the snow which surrounded it today and coated the area directly in front of the church which is reserved for former Austrian presidents.

Viennese cemeteries feel like beautiful parks, and on Sundays, even in winter, are full of people from all walks of life, coming to visit the resting places of their own family members, or, as we were doing, visiting the graves of famous artists and musicians, poets and writers, soldiers and statesmen. Ahead of us on the broad central avenue were several others, bundled up against the cold, just as we were, carrying flowers along with their memories.

The section reserved for musicians is on the left, about halfway down the avenue leading to the church. We turned off there and followed the path which led us to Vienna's most honored composers. The musicians' graves were covered with snow, and the tall evergreens behind them looked as if they'd been frosted with dollops of whipped cream dropped from a spoon. Schubert's grave lies next to Beethoven's, and in a place of honor in the middle of the walkway in front of their graves is a memorial to Mozart, who is actually buried in an unmarked pauper's grave in St. Mark's Cemetery in Vienna's Third District. Because it is a mass grave, they weren't able to move him to the Zentralfriedhof.

I walked around the memorial to Mozart, stopped in front of Schubert's grave, leaned down to brush away some snow from the flat stone in front of the tall monument, and placed my lilies there beside flowers already left by other mourners. Then I stepped back next to Kurt, who reached for my hand, and spoke quietly.

"The art of music here entombed a rich possession but even fairer hopes."

Of course Kurt would know that phrase. He was quoting the words of the poet Grillparzer, from Schubert's original gravestone in the Währinger Cemetery. Both Schubert and Beethoven had been moved from that more humble place to this one in the late eighteen hundreds. Schubert's family had originally buried him close to Beethoven in that small cemetery, responding to words Franz had whispered while he was near death. Schubert had been a torch bearer at Beethoven's funeral in 1827.

The Währinger Cemetary is no longer a cemetery. It's now a park, called the Schubert Park, and it's on the list of places I want my students to visit. It's a list I have to be careful with, because there are so many locations in Vienna where composers have lived, or eaten, or died, or been buried, that a diligent student could spend weeks trying to see them all. It was up to me to choose the most important ones.

We had been standing in front of Schubert's grave for at least five minutes by now, long enough so that the cold from the snowy ground was seeping up from my toes to the rest of my body. I shivered, and Kurt spoke again.

"Do you need to do anything else here, Lily, or should we move on?"

"We'd better start back. I'm freezing."

We turned around and headed back toward the main gate, then walked down the wide, tree lined path, through the exit and to the streetcar stop where we would wait for the number seventy-one, sometimes called "The Widow's Express," by the Viennese, who have a fondness for dark humor. There was a cluster of people already waiting there, and we joined them, all of us huddling close together to try to stay warm. When the red and cream tram glided to stop in front of us, we followed the others up the stairs and into the welcome heat. There were enough seats for all of us, and I sat down next to Kurt as the streetcar pulled away from the cemetery.

"We haven't talked about the lost songs yet." I had been focused on Schubert's Mass, and then on Stephen, and finally on our visit to the grave, but I hadn't forgotten why Kurt had offered to meet with me. "Do you know something specific?"

Kurt had removed his gloves and was rubbing his hands together.

"I don't have proof, but I have heard hints."

"Hints?"

He turned toward me, removed his glasses, which had steamed up in the heat of the streetcar, and wiped them with a handkerchief he produced from one of his pockets. Only after he had settled them back on the bridge of his nose did he proceed to tell me what he knew.

"Well, you know already that he wrote more than one draft of his compositions, in fact, often as many as four sketches for any given song, and more than that for more complicated works.'

"Sure, I know that."

"Then I'm confident that you also know that there were times in his life when he economized by using up half-empty sheets of music paper on which he had written other compositions, or parts of compositions."

"Yes, and that complicates things for anyone who tries to study his works or to catalogue them."

"So, my point would be that people are continuing to find previously unknown songs, or fragments of songs, written by Schubert, and they're finding them on library shelves in Vienna, in collections of old music, in family papers and archives."

None of this was news to me, and I was still waiting for whatever tantalizing hints Kurt had wanted to share with me. I didn't have to wait long. He leaned in so close to me that our noses were almost touching, and he whispered. "Lily, the word in research circles is that there are descendents of his closest friends right here in Vienna who possess some of these songs."

When I didn't respond, he frowned and shook his head. "Think, Lily. Think of the names of his friends, and then think of the people in Vienna with those names, people who are well known and devoted Schubert lovers, people who might have these songs in their possession."

"But Kurt, why wouldn't they have come forward by now? Why would they want to keep such important treasures to themselves?"

"Now you have the right question, Lily. Why indeed?"

He pulled away from me, looked out the window to see where we were, and then pulled his cell phone from his pocket.

"I'd better check with Marta."

While Kurt phoned home, I contemplated his hints, looked out at the nondescript apartment blocks along our route into town, and scrolled through the list in my brain of the people with whom Schubert had spent most of his time. I was ready with my question when he finished his call.

"Did you have anyone in particular in mind when you mentioned descendents of Schubert's friends, Kurt?"

"I have a couple of ideas, Lily, but it might be better for you to come up with your own possibilities. I don't want to influence you too much, because you could very well think of something I hadn't considered."

He was pulling on his gloves now as we glided past the Belvedere Palace on our left. We were approaching the Schwarzenburgplatz, where we both had to get off and change to other streetcars.

"Why don't you call me after you've done a little research, and we can talk some more." He stood up then and pushed the button which opened the exit doors. I followed him down the steps and onto the pavement. "I have to get back home now. Marta and her parents are waiting for me." He waved and hurried away from me, and I walked on alone toward the line of people waiting for the streetcar which would take me around the Ringstrasse.

I had just settled into my seat when I heard the opening notes of "The Radetsky March" coming from deep inside my shoulder bag. It was my cell phone, and I plunged my hand into the bag to search for it.

"Hello!"

"Oh. There you are. I was about to give up. I've been trying to reach you all morning." My phone had been turned off at the church;

Stephen must have turned it back on when he entered those numbers in my contact list.

It was Christina Anderson. "Have you eaten yet?'

It had been a long time since breakfast, so of course I said, "Not yet."

"Oh good. I know it's a spur of the moment invitation, but I'm hoping you can join me. I'm on my way to a charming old restaurant on the Singerstrasse, in the first district. It's called *"Zu den Drei Hacken."* Are you familiar with it?"

Of course I was familiar with it; it's one of Schubert's old haunts. I assured Christina that I knew the restaurant and that I could join her there. "I'm on a streetcar on the Kärntnerring right now. I can get off at the next stop and walk over."

"I'm so glad I reached you. See you soon."

I stood up and made my way to the rear exit, just as the streetcar came to a stop at the corner of the Ring and Kärtnerstrasse, across from the Opera. I stepped off, maneuvered around the group standing on the sidewalk waiting to board, and started walking through the first district, the old town. Just as they had been in the Zentralfriedhof, the Viennese were out strolling, even on a cold winter's day. There were well dressed women walking dogs on leashes, mothers pushing bundled up babies in strollers, couples ambling arm in arm along Vienna's favorite pedestrian thoroughfare.

I threaded my way through the crowds, walked past shop windows full of souvenirs, lovely clothing, and handmade Austrian ceramics and linens. I could have kept going all the way to Stephansplatz, the large square in front of St. Stephen's Cathedral, but instead I turned right on Himmelpfortgasse and cut through narrow back streets lined with so many architectural treasures that you could only take them in if you walked very slowly looking up at the facades as you passed by them, a hard thing to do when there are other people on the sidewalk. From Himmelpfortgasse I turned left onto Rauhensteingasse, paused at the site of the house where Mozart had died, and then turned right into Ballgasse, a winding medieval street which feels more like an alley. I love shortcuts like this, routes which take me down paths walked by my favorite composers. Beethoven had once lived at Ballgasse Four; of course, he had lived in several different places in Vienna. You could spend a lot of time visiting all of them.

I didn't plan to do that, especially not today. When I came to the end of Ballgasse, I crossed Weihburggasse and walked through the Franziskanerplatz, a lovely small square formed by the Franziskaner Church and its cloisters. Finally I turned onto Singerstrasse, made my way to number twenty-eight, and stopped in front of the dark green double doors leading into the restaurant. It stands where it has stood for centuries, and the sign above those doors, with their large glass panes, reads *"Gastwirtschaft zu den Drei Hacken."* In English it would be called "Restaurant at the Sign of the Three Axes," and it had once been a favorite meeting place not only for Schubert and his friends, but for Viennese of all professions, including playwrights and poets, artists and musicians.

I stomped the snow off my boots, reached for the door, and entered the cozy warmth of the restaurant. Christina was waiting just inside the tiny vestibule; we hugged each other and gave each other a kiss on each cheek. "I'm so glad you could make it! We're lucky they're open. They're usually closed on Sundays, but they made an exception today, since it's Schubert's birthday. I just knew you'd want to eat where he had eaten, today of all days. I already have a table, and a surprise."

I followed her through the restaurant, past other diners sitting at rectangular tables covered with crisp white cloths. The floors were dark wood, and on the white walls were pictures of some of the famous people who had eaten here. Like many old Viennese restaurants, this one has more than one room, and Christina led me directly to the *Schubertstuberl,* the Schubert chamber. It's a tiny room with benches for seating on two of its walls, and only three tables, one of them so small it can barely seat one person. It has a bust of Schubert above the tiny table, plus several pictures of him, though not of the friends who used to join him here, including Franz von Schober, a writer and actor, and Moritz von Schwind and Leopold Kuppelweiser, both painters. Those were a few of the names on the list Kurt had suggested I investigate.

Ordinarily I would have been looking at the pictures on the walls and at the sculpted likeness of Franz Schubert, but today my eyes went straight to the man sitting directly in front of us, a man I thought was spending the winter in Minnesota. What in the world was he doing here?

"Arthur! What a surprise!" That was an understatement. There was Arthur Larson, looking even more pale and unhealthy than usual, probably as a result of flying over the ocean and missing a night's sleep. He scooted off the bench and stood to greet me, while I stepped close enough to give him a very careful hug. Really, the man looked as if he could collapse at any moment.

"Please, Arthur, sit down." He did, and I took the chair across from him, with Christina in between. "Now, tell me what brought you here in January. I thought that you were going to come during spring break."

Arthur met my eyes. His own pale blue ones looked dull and tired behind his wire framed glasses, and the skin on his face was pasty and colorless. His hair, a light blonde so faded that it appeared almost white, was thinning; he had combed what was left of it away from his forehead. The effect was not flattering.

He coughed, then cleared his throat. His voice came out sounding rather raspy. "I wanted to surprise you on Schubert's birthday."

"Isn't that the sweetest thing, Lily? When he called to tell me, I told him I'd pick him up at the airport and take care of everything. I was so touched."

Yes, well. I was touched too, but probably not in the same way. Christina was gazing at him as fondly as if he were a favorite pet. My feelings toward Arthur were not nearly as tender at the moment as hers appeared to be; I hoped that they didn't show on my face or in my eyes. I was remembering this day a year ago, when, after having a few too many beers, Arthur had made a very clumsy attempt to seduce me, followed by an even clumsier proposal of marriage. It was not a good memory.

They were both looking at me as if expecting me to congratulate them. Fortunately, I was saved from having to do so by the waitress, who chose that moment to appear. I ordered a glass of my favorite beer and a dinner of roast pork with dumplings and sauerkraut, a totally Austrian meal. I was starving after all that walking around in the cold and snow.

"Arthur just arrived this morning, Lily, and the first thing he wanted to do was see you." Christina actually patted his hand. "Of course, I insisted on taking him out to the Villa to shower and take a short nap while I tried to reach you."

"He's staying at the Villa? Villa Christina? With the students? I thought there was no space left."

"It's true that there's nothing suitable for you, Lily; that's why I rented that apartment for you. Luckily, one of the boys has an extra bed in his room. It's a perfect solution, don't you think? Now Arthur can be close at hand to help out with your classes or do anything else you need him to do."

I wouldn't call this perfect, but it wasn't even the beginning of the story, as it turned out. It's good that l had already started on my beer when Arthur told me the rest of it.

"Yes, Lily. You won't believe it. The new graduate assistant this term is so good that I felt perfectly at ease leaving him in charge all week. I don't have to fly home until next Sunday."

This time I did manage to say something. "How fortunate for you, Arthur." Apparently, he didn't pick up any hint of sarcasm in my tone, because he kept on talking about his plans.

"And I haven't even told you the best news yet, Lily."

I cut into my pork and took a bite of the perfectly cooked, juicy meat, while he continued. He was so excited that he had lost a bit of his pallor; he leaned across the table toward me.

"Dürnstein, Lily! We can go there! Tomorrow!"

"We? As in you and me? Tomorrow? How? I have a class to teach, and I have no car. Surely you don't want to take a train and a bus?" Arthur was not fond of public transportation. At home in Minnesota, he drove around in an old green Volvo his father had passed down to him.

"No problem, Lily. I took the liberty of moving your class to Tuesday, and Christina has been kind enough to offer us the use of her car."

"Oh my. How generous." I took a deep breath, followed by a sip of beer, and then spoke to Christina. "Are you planning to join us then?"

She shook her head. "Oh, no. Sorry. I already have plans for tomorrow, but I trust you to drive my car, Lily."

Arthur was clearing his throat and trying to get her attention, but she seemed not to notice, intent as she was on her schedule. "I can stop by in the morning to pick you up and then drive on to the Villa. Tom and Eva have asked me to spend the day with them."

She motioned to the waitress then, and asked, "Dessert, anyone?"

The waitress, dressed in a tailored white blouse and black skirt, cleared our dinner plates and took our dessert orders. Arthur's complexion was fading again, and he was slumping in his chair. He revived only slightly when his coffee and apple strudel were placed in front of him. I had ordered *palatschinken* with chocolate; that's a wonderful crepe like delicacy, and it was melting in my mouth when Arthur finally spoke again.

"Christina has been telling me what happened to you, Lily. Are you sure you'll be up to driving tomorrow?"

I stirred the whipped cream into my coffee, added a cube of sugar, and took a swallow of the strong, sweet concoction. Arthur loved to drive, but he was terrible at it. Christina must have known this. She caught my eye and sent a strong message my way.

"I'm fine, Arthur, fully recovered, thanks. Besides, I know the way, and I'm used to the roads around here."

Christina patted his hand. "It's better this way, Arthur. You'll be able to enjoy the scenery more if Lily's at the wheel."

He brightened up at that. "Good point, Christina. I may want to take pictures along the way too."

"Exactly." She called for the check. "Now, we'd better get you back to the Villa. You'll need to rest and recover from your trip before tomorrow."

He wasn't the only one who needed to rest. I was only too glad to ride back home in Christina's dark blue BMW, instead of on a Vienna streetcar. It almost made up for the fact that I was going to have to spend the next day with Arthur, listening to him talk about Richard the Lion Hearted and Blondel de Nesle. Almost, but not quite.

CHAPTER FIFTEEN

The sky was cloudy the next morning, but at least it wasn't snowing. Not yet. I was dressed in my warmest sweater and slacks, and on my feet I wore thick woolen socks inside my sturdy hiking boots. I was standing at the counter waiting for Frau Frassl to hand me my morning papers, plus enough chocolate to get me through the day. Willie Nelson was singing, "Forgiving you was easy, but forgetting seems to take the longest time." Frau Frassl's hair formed a bright red cloud around her head, which swayed along with her as she moved to the music. Her eyes were half closed, and her lips were slightly parted, as if she were about to whisper something sweetly seductive to Willie. I hated to interrupt her fantasy, but Christina had just pulled up, and I needed to get moving.

"Frau Frassl. Frau Frassl. Please. I have to go."

Her eyes opened slowly, and she looked at me as if she'd never seen me before.

"Newspapers. Chocolate. Remember?"

Finally she focused on me, pulled her swaying body toward the counter, and reached across it to hand me my papers and chocolate bars. I thanked her, opened the shop door, and hurried outside.

The BMW sat purring at the curb, as elegant as its driver. Christina greeted me, waited a moment for me to fasten my seat belt, then pulled smoothly into the street. She was dressed all in wool too, but hers looked as if it had been bought in Scotland, rather than in Minneapolis. Lars must have done very well with his business. I busied myself tucking my newspapers and chocolate into my backpack while Christina drove through my neighborhood, then turned left onto Nussdorferstrasse and headed out to the Villa in Döbling.

We had exchanged greetings, but hadn't conversed beyond that until she said, "I hope that Arthur's fondness for you isn't too awkward, Lily."

Fondness. That was one word for his obsession. What could I say, without maligning the man who was, after all, my boss. "I'm used to it, Christina. I can handle him. I just wish that he'd give up on me and find someone else."

She laughed. "That's about as likely as abandoning his obsession for troubadours." She reached for the gear shift and continued talking while she brought the car to a smooth stop at a red light. "His mother has almost lost hope for him. I know her, because she's married to a distant cousin."

The light changed, and Christina drove on across the wide thoroughfare called the *Gürtel*. It means just what it sounds like it means, and it forms a wide circle around Vienna, parallel to the Ring, but farther out.

"If I could think of someone to fix him up with, believe me I'd do it, but who would want to date Arthur. Really, it's difficult."

I had to agree, but I couldn't help offering her a ray of hope. "You know, Christina, there are other professors at the college who love the Middle Ages as much as Arthur does." I had one specific professor in mind, a Beowulf specialist. She was very shy and spent most of her time in the library, but I had spoken to her a few times, and had found her a very appealing, gentle person.

"That's interesting. Tell me more." So I did, and by the time we had parked in front of the Villa, we were both feeling much better about Arthur's prospects. That feeling lasted until he emerged from the front gate, dressed as if he were headed for an expedition in the Alps. Where had he found this outfit, all quilted and red, except for the reflective stripes running down his sleeves and the legs of his slacks? Even his stocking cap was bright red. At least I'd be able to find him if he wandered off.

While he busied himself stowing his backpack, Christina showed me the controls of the BMW, including the switch for the heated leather seats. This was quite a step up from the ten year old Toyota I drove in Minnesota, reliable as it was. I slid into the driver's seat, selected a CD from her collection, an assortment of Strauss Waltzes to accompany our drive through the Austrian countryside.

Arthur settled himself in the passenger seat in the front, fastened his seat belt, and began fiddling with the controls to the stereo system. By the time I'd navigated the streets of Döbling, crossed the Danube and merged onto the autobahn which runs along its banks, it sounded as if the orchestra was playing in the back seat. Arthur seemed quite pleased with himself as he hummed along to the music.

It was a beautiful drive, with the Vienna woods off to our left, and the terraced vineyards and orchards of the Wachau region appearing to our right. "The Blue Danube Waltz" was playing now, but the river itself was a churning brown waterway beside us, a thoroughfare for barges and river boats. As many times as I've seen this legendary river, it's never looked blue. Maybe it was that color back when Strauss wrote the waltz, but that was a long time ago.

We had turned off onto a smaller road in Krems, a lovely old town worth exploring, if only Arthur weren't in such a hurry to get to Dürnstein. He had been snapping pictures almost constantly since we'd left Vienna, and exclaiming over the picturesque villages and Baroque churches we'd passed along the way. By the time I pulled into a parking space outside the walls of Dürnstein, he was in a state approaching euphoria. He grabbed his backpack, leaped from the car, and hopped from one booted foot to the other while he waited for me.

"Lily, look! There it is!" He was pointing up the hill to the ruins of the castle where Richard the Lionhearted had been imprisoned back in 1192. That part of the story at least is true. Richard had offended Duke Leopold the Fifth of Austria during the Third Crusade, with the result that the Duke captured Richard as he was traveling back home and imprisoned him in the castle above Dürnstein. A ransom was paid by the English, which provided money for building projects in medieval Vienna; Richard was freed: and Leopold was excommunicated for his role in the kidnapping.

That isn't the story which inspires Arthur's enthusiasm though. He loves the legend of the minstrel Blondel, who supposedly went from castle to castle searching for Richard, singing a song which both of them knew. Richard himself was said to be not only a patron of the traveling singers known variously as troubadours, trouvères, minnesingers, or minstrels, depending upon where they were from, but also one of those musicians himself. Not only did he hear and recognize the song, so the story goes, but sang a verse of it back to Blondel, thereby revealing his location.

It is a lovely story, but really, I wished that Arthur would get a grip. He had pulled a version of the famous song from his backpack and was holding it out to me.

"Here it is, Lily. Once we get up there, you can be Blondel and sing a verse from outside the walls, and I'll be Richard and sing back from the dungeon."

To say that I had reservations about this plan is to put it mildly, and those feelings had nothing to do with my singing ability. Those ruins are perched high on the hill above the village, and though there are paths leading up to the top, there was snow on the ground and the paths could easily be icy and treacherous. There was no talking him out of it though, so we made our way through the cobblestone streets of the town and started up the stone stairs which led upward to one of the paths.

The one good thing about Arthur's being so out of shape was that he had to proceed very slowly. That careful pace was probably what allowed us to reach the castle walls, although Arthur was crawling on his hands and knees by the time he finally got there. He managed to turn himself around before he sank down on a large rock, panting so hard that his body was shaking. I sat down next to him, dug into my backpack, pulled out a water bottle and held it out to him.

"Here, Arthur. You'd better drink something. You're not used to so much exertion."

He shook his head and waved his hands at me. He wasn't able to speak. His face was almost as red as his jacket; his glasses were slipping down his nose. His arms were propped on his knees, and he held his drooping head in his hands. Since he seemed to be breathing more slowly now, but showed no sign of wanting my water, I unscrewed the cap and drank half the bottle myself before stopping for breath.

When he finally began to talk, his speech was strained and he had to take a breath between every word, but I figured out that he wanted me to unzip his backpack. There was a bottle of one of those power sports drinks inside; he grabbed it from me, and began gulping the stuff. He finished most of the bottle and then carefully replaced the cap and put the bottle back in his pack. He was able to speak more clearly now.

"Okay then. I'll just find a way around the wall and then you can start singing."

Fortunately, there was a gap in the ruined fortification not far from where we were resting, and he was able to get through to the other side.

"Okay, Lily. I'm ready. You can start now."

What could I do? I stood, faced the wall, and sang the words on the page he'd given me. I can't vouch for accuracy of the melody, but I did my best, and as soon as I'd finished, Arthur's voice came floating back to me. He has a rather nice tenor; I wonder if he sings in the college glee club. While I was thinking about that I heard a strange, high pitched warbling sound coming from the other side of the rock wall.

"Arthur? Is that you? Are you okay?"

I heard the sound once more, and then Arthur shouted. "It's my yodel. How do you like it?"

Before I could think of a polite answer, he came back through the gap in the wall and joined me where I stood looking out over the valley below. There was a spectacular view of the village, the Danube, and the surrounding hills. While I enjoyed just looking at it all, Arthur pulled out his camera and began snapping pictures again, including some of me in front of the castle walls. I can only hope he doesn't post any of them on the Internet. There's no telling how long he would have spent up there, if it hadn't begun to snow.

"Arthur, we need to get back down the hill before the weather gets any worse."

"Yes, yes, sure. I'm almost done here. You can go ahead."

I'm not sure what wisdom made me say, "No, Arthur. I think I'd better follow you," but I'm thankful I did. He started down very slowly, but soon picked up speed on the steep, slippery slope, and by the time he'd reached the end of the path, he was sliding on the seat of his pants. He hit the top of the steps to the village at full speed, and bounced down them as if he were a rubber ball, careening into the narrow walkway below and whizzing past several startled pedestrians before he came to a halt in the doorway of a small gift shop.

By the time I reached him, a small group surrounded his prostrate form, and the shopkeeper was bending over him. Arthur didn't move; he didn't answer the shopkeeper's questions. He didn't even open his eyes. I knelt next to him, whispered his name, stroked his cold cheek, listened to his raspy breathing. At least he was alive.

"We'd better call for an ambulance." That was the shopkeeper speaking, and I had to agree. She pulled out her phone and placed the call, while I stayed beside Arthur, talking to him, hoping for a response. His eyelids had just fluttered open when the ambulance crew arrived, and he seemed to be trying to speak. I leaned in closer.

"Everything hurts," he managed to whisper, before the paramedics moved forward and asked me to get out of the way. They were very efficient and professional, and in just a few moments had placed Arthur on a stretcher and were carrying him down to the waiting ambulance. I picked up Arthur's backpack, thanked the shopkeeper, and hurried to catch up with the crew before they loaded Arthur and pulled away.

The driver wrote down my name and phone number, gave me directions to the hospital in Krems, then gunned the engine and sped away. The distinctive notes of the siren, a perfect fourth, sounded in the distance as I unlocked the BMW and slid into the driver's seat. I started the car and switched on the heated seat before I pulled out of my parking spot and set off behind them. It looked as if I was going to get to spend some time in Krems after all.

Unfortunately, all I saw of Krems that day was the inside of the hospital. I didn't get to walk its lovely old cobbled streets and alleys or admire its medieval and renaissance buildings. By the time I'd reached the hospital and parked the car, they had already whisked Arthur to an examining room. I was left to fill out forms, answer questions, make phone calls, and wait for them to examine Arthur.

I settled myself in a quiet corner, pulled out the newspapers and chocolate bars I'd bought from Frau Frassl that morning, and selected some soothing music on my iPod. I had made my way through the *International Herald Tribune* and started on my Vienna paper when I felt a hand on my arm. A nurse stood in front of me, holding Arthur's hat in her hand.

"Your husband can leave now. We're finished with him."

That was quick work, much faster than it would have been in an emergency room back home. I put the papers and iPod into my pack and stood up.

"He's not my husband, but thank-you."

I took the hat she was holding out to me, and followed her past the admitting desk and around a corner to a small room where Arthur sat slumped in a wheelchair, looking slightly dazed.

"Here are his care instructions and medications." She handed me a small bag and a computer printout. "If you want to bring your car around, we'll help you with him."

They certainly seemed anxious to get him out of there. I was not used to such efficiency, and had to ask her very firmly for more information. I didn't want to leave until I knew the extent of his injuries and what they had done for him.

The nurse heaved a great sigh, as if I were asking too much of her. Then she glanced pointedly at her watch, said, "My shift is ending. My colleague will have to talk to you," and walked away.

Arthur was humming Blondel's song softly under his breath and leaning so far forward in the wheelchair that I had to grab his shoulders and push him against the backrest. He looked at me, but didn't seem to recognize me and didn't stop humming. I dragged a chair from across the room, sat down right in front of him, and started to read the instructions the nurse had given me. Who knew when her colleague might appear to talk to me. I had gotten to the words "Fractured coccyx," when another nurse appeared in the doorway.

"You have questions?" I did, and I got answers, complete with details on the physical examination, blood work, and x-rays they'd done. It was actually more than I wanted to know, but at least now I felt better about Arthur's prognosis. A fractured tailbone is certainly painful, but not life threatening, and is a much less serious injury than he could have sustained during his speedy downhill slide. Nevertheless, by the time they'd deposited Arthur into the car on top of his icepack and his donut cushion, I was on the phone to Tom again, to let him know that I was on the way, and to tell him that I'd need help getting Arthur into the Villa.

It was still snowing as I followed the autobahn along the Danube and back into Vienna, but the road crews had been out, and the BMW had good tires. It would have been an uneventful trip, if Arthur hadn't progressed from humming softly to singing at the top of his lungs and calling out to an imaginary Blondel.

"I'm here! I'm here! In the dungeon! Can't you hear me?"

Whatever they'd given him for pain seemed to have gone to his head. He was not only stuck back in Dürnstein, he was stuck in 1192. He started waving his arms and calling out more strongly, and finally I had to shout at him.

"Arthur! Arthur! Stop!"

He sang another verse, as if he hadn't heard me, and his voice rose from its usual tenor to a shrill counter tenor range. I decided that if his own name hadn't worked, I'd have to go back in history.

"Richard," I shouted. "Most honored liege lord," I added for good measure, and then I started to sing my verse again, at least what I could remember of it. It worked. He stopped singing, dropped arms to his sides, and leaned his head back against the seat.

"Thank God, Blondel. I thought you'd never come. You've got to get me out of here."

"I will sire. Just rest now, while I get reinforcements."

Within minutes, he had started to snore, and I could focus on getting us back into Vienna. He was still asleep when I pulled up in front of the Villa, his head tipped to one side and drool dripping out of his open mouth. I decided I'd better not leave him alone, since I wasn't sure whether he'd be Arthur Larson or Richard the Lionhearted when he woke up, so I used my phone to let Tom know we were out here.

It wasn't Tom who answered, but Helga the receptionist, and she said, "Oh, Dr. Lindstrom, I'm so sorry, but Professor Thornquist had to go out. I'll send some students to help you."

It was Kevin Carlson who came out a few minutes later, with two other young men behind him. He didn't speak to me, but nodded when I opened the car door and gave a very short explanation of Arthur's condition. He was still asleep, so I leaned over him to unfasten his seat belt and shook him gently.

"Arthur, wake up. We're back."

I had no warning whatsoever before his arms flew up and locked me in a tight hug, and his lips fastened themselves to mine. It was not a pleasant kiss, not only because of the drool still draining out of his mouth, but also because of what I can only call terrible technique. Apparently Arthur had not had much practice at this. I pulled; I struggled; I grunted. Nothing worked until I smacked him on the side of his head.

"Ow! Help!"

"Dr. Lindstrom! What are you doing?"

That, of course, was Kevin. Big help he was. He probably thought I was simultaneously seducing Arthur and breaking his heart. Arthur's plaintive wail didn't help.

"Lily, Lily. You know I've always loved you."

It might have been easier if he'd thought that he was Richard the Lion Hearted. As it was, all I could do was back out of the car, turn to my students and say, "He's having a bad reaction to his pain medication. He doesn't know what he's doing." I certainly hoped that was true. He had stopped calling my name now, but had put his head in his hands and was weeping loudly.

Kevin stepped forward, brushed past me, and said, "I'll help him." To his credit, he did well. He reached into the car, put his arms around Arthur, and pulled him out gently. Arthur groaned with pain, leaned on Kevin, and shuffled forward far enough that the other students could help support him, one on each side. I got our backpacks, along with Arthur's icepack and donut cushion, locked the car, and followed them up the steps and into the Villa.

Helga met us at the door, and held it open while the students guided Arthur into the entrance hall. She took one look at Arthur, who was still weeping, and said, "You'd better help him up the stairs and into bed while I talk to Professor Lindstrom."

I hung up my jacket, sank into a chair opposite her desk, and pulled Arthur's medications and instruction sheets from my backpack.

Helga, meanwhile, hurried to the kitchen and returned a few minutes later with a tray full of small sandwiches and a cup of coffee.

"Thank-you, Helga. How did you know I was hungry?'

She smiled. "You're always hungry, Professor Lindstrom."

I would have answered her if my mouth hadn't been full. All I could do was meet her eyes and nod my head. She watched and waited, and finally, when I had finished eating, I began to tell her everything that had happened, up to and including Arthur's kiss and his subsequent bout of weeping.

"I'm sure that he's having a reaction to whatever painkillers they gave him, but I don't know what to do about it. He's due for another dose soon."

Helga held out her hand, and I passed the prescription and the information sheets over to her. She scanned everything, double checked the dosage on the pill bottle, and then picked up her phone.

"I'm calling the doctor we use for the students to see if he can tell us what to do."

While she was on the phone, the door to the Villa opened and closed and then Tom appeared, with Christina at his side. In his hand was Jack's favorite teddy bear, looking a bit damp and dirty.

"Lily, you're back. I'm so sorry not to have been here when you arrived. Jack dropped his bear while we were out walking and I had to go look for it."

"It was under a bush beside the sidewalk." Christina took it from him. "I'll take it up to Eva."

She headed for the stairway. Tom sat down beside me, and I told the story all over again. To his credit, he didn't laugh out loud, though his lips did twitch a bit during the Richard the Lion Hearted segment. However, when I got to the kiss and my reaction, he began to shake, and finally burst into loud guffaws.

"It's really not that funny, Tom." In fact, I was starting to feel more than a little irritated. "What if he does it again?"

That sent him off into another round of laughter. Only Eva's entrance into the room with her finger to her lips dampened his hilarity. He took a deep breath and looked at his wife.

"Well then." He stood up. "I'd better go up and see if the guys need any help with him."

"Fine idea. He may need these." I handed Arthur's ice pack and donut cushion to Tom, along with his backpack. He headed for the stairs, just as Christina followed Eva into the room.

"What was that all about?"

"It's a long story."

Helga, who had brought in a carafe of coffee, refilled my cup, and I told it once more. The women, bless them, didn't laugh once.

Helga, in fact, bundled herself into her coat and hat and said, "I'm going to pick up a different medication for him."

Eva said, "I'll have Tom keep an eye on him. I'm not sure it's a good thing for him to be rooming with Kevin, all things considered."

"Meanwhile," Christina continued. "Lily shouldn't be left alone with either of them, if they can't control their fantasies." She turned to me then. "Where is Dr. Cameron these days, Lily?"

"I wish I knew." That was certainly the truth.

"They need to see you with him. That will give them a dose of reality."

Maybe so, but I had no idea when, or even if, they would have that opportunity.

CHAPTER SIXTEEN

I had hoped that Arthur would still be resting in bed the next day, but there he was sitting in my classroom, right next to Kevin Carlson. I wouldn't say that he looked good; Arthur never really looks good. He did, however, seem to be much more alert and aware of his surroundings than he had been the last time I had seen him. I wondered if he remembered anything that had happened the day before, after his slide down the hill. I hoped not, but I wondered, because when I said "Good Morning" to him, his cheeks turned bright red and he began to flip through the pages of the book in front of him as if he were looking for a very important fact.

I pulled my notes from my bag and launched into an overview of Schubert, starting with his life story and proceeding to the most notable characteristics of his music. Most of the students seemed to be attentive and interested, though a couple of the girls were gazing out the window, as if they had other things on their minds, and Kevin was frowning at a spot on the wall behind me. At least that's what I hoped he was frowning at. Arthur was still studying his book and had yet to meet my eyes.

When I asked for questions and discussion, a couple of the students made very perceptive comments about the mass they'd heard on Sunday, and one girl, a music major, brought up the distinctive way Schubert had of combining the major and minor tonalities in his writing. That's when Arthur snapped to attention, as if someone had pushed a button. He looked up and began to speak in his most professorial manor.

"Yes," he said. "She's made an important point about Schubert, about the way he expresses joy and sadness as two parts of the same whole, about the way he weaves together the major and minor modes to form one perfect harmonic unity." He looked around at all of us as he spoke, and I began to feel uneasy when I noticed that his eyes looked as if they had tears in them. I hoped he would stop, but he didn't. "It's exactly like life," he continued, and his voice had begun to quiver slightly, "when our greatest hope and happiness gives way to the most profound sorrow." He sniffed and stopped suddenly, and the room was abruptly silent except for the loud ticking of the clock on the wall and the nervous tapping of a pencil on the table.

I cleared my throat. "Yes. Well said, Professor Larson. Thank-you." With those words, I brought the class to a close and reminded the students of the scheduled visits to the Schubert Park and the Schubert Museum.

Arthur had shut his book, a biography of Schubert, and was pulling himself to his feet, with Kevin's help. He leaned forward and shuffled slowly toward the door, without even glancing at me or saying a word. I felt guilty, a response I have yet to be able to control, even when I have nothing to feel guilty about.

"Arthur, please wait." He paused, but didn't stop. "I want to say something." What did I want to say? Many things, but most of them I couldn't express when Kevin was standing right there staring at me. I tried though, I really did. "I'm sorry, Arthur, sorry about your pain." I didn't mention whether I meant emotional or physical pain.

He lifted his head and looked at me; his eyes were still damp. He tried to speak, but he choked up and couldn't get any words out. Kevin was more than capable though.

"Can't you leave well enough alone, Professor Lindstrom?'

Then he put his arm around Arthur and helped him through the door. I admit that I was feeling less than good about that remark, but I gathered my papers together and stuffed them into my bag without a word. I heard a few words behind me though, and they lifted my spirits.

"Pitiful, aren't they?" Eva stood in the doorway, composed and calm, as always. "Don't you wonder why they always seem to blame the object of their unsolicited, unwanted affections, rather than examine themselves and their own shortcomings?"

I had an answer on the tip of my tongue, but I didn't need it, because she wasn't finished yet. "I mean, what can they be thinking? You, Lily, have never done anything except behave like a fine teacher and scholar. I have never seen you act even a little bit seductive, and I've watched carefully, believe me."

"You've been watching me?"

"Of course I've been watching you. My husband works closely with you, and he is as susceptible to a beautiful woman as any man on the planet."

"You think I'm a beautiful woman?"

"Have you looked in a mirror lately, Lily? Of course you're a beautiful woman. That blonde hair, those eyes, that lovely body. Have you not noticed?"

"Eva. Be serious. I look exactly like at least half the women back home in Minnesota, women descended from the same Scandinavian ancestors I have."

Eva shrugged. "It's lovely that you're so self-effacing, Lily, but I think you may not have an accurate vision of yourself."

"Blame my brothers for that," I muttered. "They've devoted their lives to keeping me humble."

Eva smiled. "Well, they've succeeded." She held out her hand to me then; in it was a small piece of paper. "I almost forgot. Helga asked me to give you this message."

"Thanks, Eva." I took the message and hugged her. "Thanks for everything."

"You're welcome, Lily." She headed for the dining room. "I'll see what I can do to divert Arthur and Kevin."

The message was written in Helga's almost illegible writing, but I was able to make out the words "Trudi Vogl, driver, noon." I looked at my watch. It was a quarter to twelve now, or three quarters twelve, as the Austrians would say. I had just enough time to freshen up, have a word with Tom, and get myself out the door.

I stepped through the front gate just as the black Mercedes pulled up to the curb. The uniformed driver came around to open the car door for me. I looked closely to see whether it was the same man who had helped Helmut Vogl the night he'd been stricken in Mitzi's apartment; I was pretty sure that it was. He had the same solid build, the strong nose and jutting eyebrows I remembered. He gave no indication that he recognized me, but how could he? It had been Helmut Vogl who'd helped me up from the sidewalk that night, and later on, I'd watched from the doorway while Stephen and the driver had assisted the Minister of Interior.

I thanked the man; he returned to the driver's seat and put the car into motion, while I contemplated the odd sequence of events which had brought me to this particular back seat. Who would ever believe the circumstances under which I'd met the Minister of Interior of Austria, not that I'd ever talk about that incident publicly? And who would think that I'd meet and like his wife? As my mother would say, life was one surprise after another, some of them better than others. When Trudi Vogl had called over the week-end to see how I was doing and to invite me to lunch, I had considered her invitation to be one of the better surprises.

Now, as the driver pulled up in front of the Vogl Villa in Döbling, I wasn't so sure of that. I was so nervous that my hands actually shook as I followed him up the walk to the front door. When Trudi opened that door herself, and greeted me with Viennese warmth and charm, I began to feel somewhat better. She took my coat, hat and bag and ushered me into a lovely, high ceilinged sitting room. There, in a Biedermeier chair, sat Helmut Vogl. I met his eyes, wondered if he would remember me, saw the flicker of recognition in them, followed by an almost imperceptible shake of his head. His skin was pale, and his cheekbones stood out more strongly than I remembered. Trudi introduced us, and he spoke in that low, gravelly voice I remembered.

"Please forgive me for not rising to greet you," he said, and gestured to a chair across from him. "Do sit down."

I did, and so did Trudi, who settled herself in a chair next to her husband, and then passed a small dish of mixed nuts to me.

"May I offer you a glass of wine before we eat?"

I declined and asked instead for a glass of mineral water. Austrians often eat the biggest meal of the day, called *Mittagessen*, at noon. While I was looking forward to the food, I wasn't ready for alcohol, at least not yet.

"I've been telling Helmut about your interest in Schubert and your current research, Lily." Trudi took a sip of her wine and smiled fondly at her husband. He smiled back at her and reached for her hand.

They certainly looked like a contented couple. I tried not to think about Helmut and Mitzi, but the picture if him in her bedroom kept flashing through my brain. He looked at me, lifted his bushy white eyebrows, and seemed to challenge me to erase that memory. I tried.

"My wife tells me that you're hoping to discover some lost songs, Dr. Lindstrom."

"Please, you can call me Lily." After all I've seen you without your clothes on, I added, not out loud, of course. "Yes, the word in research circles is that there may be some unpublished manuscripts in private collections here in Vienna." I went on to repeat most of what Kurt had told me, including Schubert's habit of writing more than one sketch for each of his songs.

Helmut Vogl nodded, and the sunlight streaming through the tall windows of the room caused his silver hair to glisten.

"Yes, I know all of these things." He paused, cleared his throat. "What I'm not sure of is how, exactly, you propose to gain access to any of these hypothetical private collections?"

"That's the question, isn't it?" And then I shared with him my plan of looking up descendents of Schubert's closest circle of friends and of approaching them, with the hope that at least one of them might have something to show me. He nodded again, and it seemed as if he might have said more, if Trudi hadn't stood up at that moment and announced that it was time to eat. She stayed close to Helmut while he rose slowly from his chair, and then she took his arm and led the way to the dining room.

The meal was delightful, as was the conversation. We started with a delicious dumpling soup, followed by schnitzel with potatoes and vegetables, and ended with chocolate torte and coffee. Trudi steered us away from our discussion of Schubert, at least for a while, and instead talked about the time they'd spent in Minneapolis, at the Center for Austrian Studies of the University of Minnesota.

"Helmut was lecturing on Austrian politics, and I came along to visit old friends. I'm so glad that I did, because that's how I met Christina. We've stayed in touch ever since."

Aha. That explained their friendship. We talked a bit more about their time in Minnesota, and then Helmut looked directly at his wife, and said, "Trudi, my love, would you mind if I spirited Lily off to the library for a little while to discuss Schubert?" He reached over to squeeze her hand. "I'm starting to feel tired, and I want to make sure that I have time to tell her what I know."

"Of course, Helmut. You go ahead. I'll bring more coffee and then leave you two alone for a little while."

She smiled at me and gestured toward the double doors at the end of the room. I followed her husband into the book lined room and sat in a chair facing his desk. On it was a leather portfolio. He stroked it gently as Trudi poured our coffee and then left the room, closing the doors behind her.

He waited a moment before he spoke, and when he did, it was not of Franz.

"I appreciate your discretion, Lily, your consideration for my wife's feelings." His voice was low, almost a whisper, and his eyes were full of shrewd intelligence." I realize that we met under unusual circumstances." He paused and seemed to consider his next words carefully. "I could tell you all the reasons for my relationship with your neighbor, but you don't need to know the details." He took a deep breath and then continued. "What you do need to know is that I value my marriage, and that I have ended my liaison with Miss Tauber."

I didn't say anything in response, and he didn't seem to expect me to talk, so I sat silently and continued to look at Helmut Vogl. His eyes revealed more than just intelligence; there was a vulnerability in them, a gentleness.

"Perhaps it has to do with coming so close to death that night, with feeling that I've been given a second chance, but I'd like to do something for you. Your friend Dr. Cameron refused to let me pay him for his help, and I would never offer you money in exchange for your thoughtfulness in keeping that episode to yourself. You've already proven that you are a young woman of exceptional sensitivity."

Uh-oh. I'd have to caution Sophie to keep quiet, although, if I remembered correctly, she had already sworn to do so. In the meantime, I nodded and kept listening.

"The interesting thing is that when Trudi came to me and asked me to consider sharing what's in this portfolio with you, I had no idea that the young woman she spoke so highly of was the same young woman I'd met so recently." His mouth lifted slightly, and he directed a somewhat rueful smile toward me. "I didn't realize that fact until you walked into my sitting room today." At this point, he actually did chuckle. "You can imagine my surprise."

I certainly could, and once more I nodded, but kept silent, since he seemed to have more to say.

"I trust Trudi's instincts, but when she and Christina both urged me to consider showing you what's been safeguarded by my family for many years, I admit that I felt some reluctance." He stroked the leather portfolio again while he spoke. "However, after checking your background and credentials very thoroughly, I decided that you could indeed be the perfect person to deal with what I'm about to show you."

At this point, Helmut Vogl picked up the portfolio in front of him and handed it to me. I took it from him, opened it and stared at what was inside. To my credit, I did not drop the treasure he'd just placed in my hands, but I did gasp.

It contained several clear archival document protectors and inside each one was a piece of paper, faded from age and a bit ragged around the edges, but otherwise intact. The first one was a piece of music manuscript paper, and at the top were Franz Schubert's signature, along with the date. He always did that, dated his manuscripts. It was a song, and the title, written in his familiar handwriting, was, *"Unser Geheimnis,"* "Our Secret."

"Oh my." That was about all the speech I could manage as I scanned the words. The poetry was not familiar to me; it didn't sound like Grillparzer or Heine or Goethe, or any of the other poets Schubert favored for his song texts. I turned to the next sheet and continued to study the text. "Who could have written this?"

"Turn to the letter at the end and you'll find out."

I did what he asked, and what I saw was like nothing I'd ever seen, at least nothing written by Franz Schubert. It was a love letter. As you might expect, it was full of tenderness and adoration for the object of his love. What you might not expect, unless you'd been keeping up with the music journals and scholastic essays of the last couple of decades, was that it was written to a man. That man, however, was not the one most often mentioned in connection with the discussions of Schubert's sexual preferences, Franz von Schober. Schober was one of Schubert's dearest friends, and Franz lived with him for quite a long period of time; it's pretty well documented that Schober surrounded himself, and thus Schubert, with a close circle of artists for whom homosexuality was a common and accepted lifestyle. If you go to any symposium on Schubert anymore, you can pretty much expect an emotional discussion on this topic.

For me, however, it's not a significant subject. I don't think it matters whether he loved men, or women, or both. What's important is the beautiful music he wrote, the legacy he left in his melodies. I said as much to Helmut Vogl, when I finally looked up from the letter, which was addressed simply to Anton, a common enough name in Austria.

"I agree, but as you know, not everyone in Austria, or the rest of the world for that matter, shares our viewpoint." He took a sip of his coffee and then continued. "I haven't been able to find out Anton's last name. I can only assume that my relative, Michael Vogl, had this song in his possession because Schubert asked him to sing it. The family has kept it in our possession for all of these years without making it available for study and publication, not just because of who Schubert dedicated it to, but also because . . ." Helmut Vogl stopped and cleared his throat. "Because, as you have surely noticed, neither the poetry, apparently written by Schubert himself, nor the music, is among his finest endeavors. We felt that we were protecting Schubert's artistic reputation above everything else."

I nodded and agreed that at first glance this song didn't appear to be one of Schubert's finest, though I admit that I longed to get to a piano to play it for myself.

First, though, I had to ask the question foremost in my mind. "Why are you showing it to me now? Have you changed your mind about protecting Franz Schubert?"

He leaned his head back and ran his fingers through that thick silver hair. "Actually, I've changed my mind about many things lately. This is just one small detail among many matters I'm dealing with."

I could certainly believe that, and said so, before I asked my next question. "What do you want me to do with this song and letter?"

"I think that you should write an article about this discovery for an academic journal, and then, after it's published, we can donate the manuscript and the letter to the Stadtbibliothek for their collection. I have already spoken with your friend Dr. Baumgartner about authenticating the manuscript and the letter. He agrees that if we do this carefully and correctly, everyone can benefit. You will receive recognition for your find, and the library will add an important piece of Schubert history to their archives."

He paused at this point and focused his intelligent eyes on mine. "However, none of us should underestimate the possible response to this apparent proof of what has been, until now, only conjecture. We will surely hear from people who don't want to believe this of Schubert, and who have strong, and not necessarily rational, feelings about what is contained in the letter. It could be unpleasant for all of us."

He had certainly thought carefully about this, and although I couldn't disagree with anything he had said, this seemed like something I couldn't turn down, and I told him so.

"I agree that there will be some people who will not like what is revealed in this song and letter, but I still think it's a significant addition to the research into his life and work. I'm honored that you've chosen me."

He smiled. "You have my wife and her friend Christina to thank for that." Then he rose, and said, "Now, if you'll excuse me, I need to rest."

CHAPTER SEVENTEEN

The first thing I did after the Vogl's driver deposited me at my doorstep that afternoon was call Kurt. He was not surprised to hear from me.

"Lily! I've been expecting your call. I heard from Helmut Vogl yesterday. How in the world did you manage such an incredible discovery so soon after our conversation?"

That was a good question. "I can't explain it, Kurt. It was a totally unexpected gesture from the Vogl family." I proceeded to tell him about the connection between Christina Anderson and Trudi Vogl, and their sudden and somewhat puzzling interest in me. He, in turn, filled me in on his schedule for authenticating and studying the manuscript and letter.

"Dr. Vogl indicated to me that he wants you to be kept informed at every step of the process and to be the first scholar to publish this news, if, in fact, it all turns out to be genuine, as we expect. Oh, and by the way, Lily," he finished. "It's not at all puzzling that these people would trust you. Has it ever occurred to you that you underestimate yourself?"

I didn't answer that last question, because it would probably require several sessions of therapy for me to begin to deal with it. Instead, we talked some more about the timing, and he promised to let me know as soon as he had confirmation of authenticity, so that I could proceed with my article. The wheels of academia move slowly, and the earliest I could possibly expect to have an article published would probably be spring. Nevertheless, I couldn't keep myself from shouting for joy as soon as Kurt hung up.

"Yes! Yes! Yes!"

Even Arthur would have to be impressed by this, though I didn't plan to tell him until I knew for certain that everything was in order. In the meantime, I called Sophie. As I might have expected, she was insulted that I would think for a minute that she would ever divulge what I had told her about Helmut Vogl and Mitzi.

"First of all, I'm your friend. You can trust me. You know I'd never betray your confidence." I agreed, though I admit to a feeling of relief when I heard her say so out loud. "Secondly, keep in mind that this is Europe, not the United States. Not only is no one likely to care about whether a man seeks sexual fulfillment outside his marriage, but really, they'd only be worried if matters of national security were involved, that is, if your neighbor were a secret operative or something like that."

"I'll have to ask her."

Sophie apparently didn't pick up on my sarcasm, because she just kept on talking. "Thirdly, and most importantly, it occurred to me that all of this might be simply a delusion on your part, brought on by your sudden infatuation with the American doctor you brought to lunch last week. How is he, by the way?"

"Delusion?" Now I was the one feeling insulted. "You think I imagined it all?"

"Now Lily. You know what a romantic you are. I just thought that you might be seeing love where there wasn't any. That's all."

"Oh."

"Now, are you going to answer my question?"

"Which one?"

"How is he?"

"Well." I didn't want to admit that I not only had no idea how Stephen was, but where he was, but Sophie was insistent.

"He's gone, isn't he?"

"Don't be such a cynic, Sophie. He's just out of town for a few days. On business," I added, to help convince her, and myself.

"Right. You let me know when, or if, he ever returns."

"If you weren't such a dear friend, I'd hang up on you."

"I know. Just let me know if you need a shoulder to cry on."

With those words she ended the call, and I poured myself a glass of wine. I hadn't been ready for alcohol earlier, but I was now. What if Sophie was right about Stephen? What if he'd disappeared from my life just as smoothly as he'd entered it?

I tried not to brood about that possibility as I went about my work that afternoon. I tried not to imagine that it could be true as I tossed and turned all night, plagued by dreams of Arthur dressed as a knight, singing songs with troubadours, of Kevin Carlson pelting me with wilted roses, of Hungarians chasing me through the narrow streets and sidewalks of Vienna.

It's no wonder that I was groggy and out of sorts the next morning as I made my way down the Himmelpfortstiege again, on my way to Schubert's church. It was still cold, but the sun was shining, and the sky above the Lichtental Church was a brilliant blue. Those who had attended this morning's mass were filing out the door as I approached it, and I waited on the sidewalk until the last parishioner had stepped out.

Inside, the narthex was quiet and empty, except for one small, white haired woman busily straightening the pamphlets on a small table near the door. She greeted me and told me that she was so sorry, but I had just missed morning mass. Then she handed me a church newsletter, with a schedule of services and special events, apparently so that I could be on time for the next one. I thanked her, explained why I had come, and then watched in amazement as a huge smile transformed her wrinkled face.

"Oh, you're the one who asked for his sermon! He told me you'd be coming." She grabbed my hands and squeezed them so hard that I winced. "Father Spohr is wonderful with words, isn't he? I'm so glad you appreciated what he said." She let go of me at last, stepped back to the table, and picked up a large envelope. I rubbed my hands together, tried to ease the pain caused by her strong grip.

"Here it is." She handed me the envelope. "He had it printed up for the Schubert Society meeting this week, but this extra copy is especially for you."

I thanked her profusely, placed the envelope in my bag, and turned around to leave the church. I stopped when I heard the first notes of a Bach fugue.

"Would it be all right if I stayed to listen?"

She nodded and I started up the center aisle; I wanted to sit far enough toward the front that I could turn around and see the organist up in the balcony. I had just begun to synchronize my steps to the beat, when the counterpoint suddenly stopped in the middle of a phrase, and so did I. The organist must be practicing. I stood still waiting for the music to begin again. What I heard next, however, was not the opening passage of the Bach fugue, but weeping, followed by the murmur of hushed voices coming from somewhere behind me.

I turned around, met the eyes of the woman who'd handed me the sermon moments earlier, held her gaze as she nodded toward a confessional in the back corner of the church. I had just started to retrace my steps, as quietly as possible, and had reached the back of the sanctuary, when I heard a squeak and a creak and then a burst of movement coming from the confessional. As I watched, a woman emerged from it, a woman so distraught that she ran right into me. This was not a stranger; it was Mitzi. I caught her in my arms and held her while tears streamed down her face.

Behind her stood the priest I'd heard on Sunday morning, the one whose words had so moved me that I'd come to pick up a copy of his sermon. Now he stood mute, his face somber, his body absolutely still. He did not move as I held Mitzi and patted her back; in fact, he appeared to be frozen in place, as stunned as I was. There's no telling how long we might have remained there, an unlikely trio held together by an unnamed grief, surrounded by the rich harmonies of the Bach fugue now echoing again throughout the church, if the woman who'd greeted me earlier hadn't called out to him.

"Father Spohr. Do you have a moment?"

He turned without a word and walked away from us.

Mitzi lifted her tear streaked face, stared at me, and whispered my name. I stroked her hair and continued to hold onto her.

"Hush, now. Everything will be all right."

I had no idea if that was true, of course. I was just repeating the words my mother had always used to soothe me in moments of distress. Right now, I wished that she were here, she or anyone more experienced than I was in dealing with the emotionally distraught, someone who might be able to help me with Mitzi and take us home. The priest, however, had made his way to the woman calling out to him, and they had disappeared through a side door. Mitzi and I were left alone there, leaning on each other, inhaling and exhaling together. Her sobs had subsided to soft hiccups, and I concentrated on calming my quivering nervous system. I used the Bach to do so, the supreme orderliness of his composition, the familiar comfort of his cadences. Listening to the music of her favorite composer was as close as I could come to my mother's reassuring presence today, and I felt my balance returning along with my breath. It's a good thing, since it looked as if I were on my own here with Mitzi.

I pulled a tissue from my bag and began to wipe her mascara stained cheeks, to soak up her tears. She held still while I did so, but she looked away from me, over my shoulder, as if searching for the priest who had abandoned us there. I did my best with her face, but there was no hiding her red, puffy eyes, or the pain visible in them.

"Do you have sunglasses, Mitzi?"

She nodded, and reached into the pocket of her leather coat. When she had pulled the dark glasses out and placed them on her face, I put my arm around her and guided her toward the door.

We made our way slowly up Lichtentalgasse, turned right when we reached Liechtensteinstrasse, headed for the steps I'd descended such a short time ago. Mitzi leaned so hard on me that I lurched sideways, caught myself against the handrail, and then had to push against her to regain my balance. By the time we reached the top, I was panting, out of breath. If it hadn't been so cold, I would have rested on the bench at the end of the walkway, but I was afraid that if I allowed Mitzi to sit down, I wouldn't be able to get her back up, so I just kept moving.

By the time we reached our apartment building, my arms ached from the effort of keeping Mitzi upright, and my legs were trembling. I propped her against the wall next to the door while I searched for my key, then put my arms around her once more and eased her over the threshold and into the lift. It shook as it rose through the stairwell, but we made it to the fourth floor, and Mitzi managed to dig her key out of the same pocket which had held her sunglasses.

She stumbled into her apartment, swayed slightly as I helped her out of her coat, steered her through her foyer into her living room, and lowered her onto her couch. She had yet to utter a word, and her eyes, once I'd removed her sunglasses, looked blank and unfocused, as if she were in shock. It reminded me of how one of my brothers had looked after he'd fallen hard and had the breath knocked out of him. I did the only thing I could think of to do; I covered her with a comforter I found on her bed, squeezed in beside her on the couch and held her close, murmuring her name and stroking her back until at last she closed her eyes and drifted off to sleep.

When her breathing deepened and I felt her body warm up and relax, I slipped off the couch and tiptoed from the room. I picked up her key, closed her door as quietly as I could and walked down to my own apartment. It didn't take long to gather up a few books, take off my boots, exchange them for my favorite slippers, and pack up some leftover soup and bread to take back upstairs with me. Nevertheless, I was nervous by the time I unlocked Mitzi's door again, afraid of what I would see when I peeked into her living room.

As it turned out, I needn't have hurried and worried. She slept soundly for another hour, while I sat across from her catching up on my reading. When her eyelids finally fluttered open, it was after noon, and I was stiff from sitting still for so long. We looked at each other for a moment, and then she said, "Lily. What are you doing here?"

Had she forgotten everything? What should I say? I wasn't sure, but I decided to give the simplest explanation I could come up with.

"We ran into each other at the Lichtental Church, and I helped you get home. I didn't want to leave you alone." She didn't respond, so I decided to continue. "Do you remember what happened, Mitzi?"

Her eyes filled with tears again and she sat up, pushing the comforter away. She choked back a sob, and then whispered. "Yes, yes. Of course I remember." Then she drew in a deep shuddering breath, looked at me, and spoke quietly. "Can you stay for a while? I need to talk to someone." She ran her fingers through her hair. "I don't know what to do."

"I can stay." I stood up and stretched. "We should eat something before we talk though. Come to the kitchen with me." Just because she was awake didn't mean that she was all right. I did not intend to let her out of my sight, at least not yet.

I heated up the soup, found some cheese and lunchmeat to go with the bread, poured a glass of mineral water for each of us, and then brewed some herbal tea.

She looked better after eating, but her hands, as she reached for her tea, shook slightly, and the cup rattled against the saucer. I lifted my own cup to my lips, took a sip, inhaled the sweet scent of jasmine, watched her, and waited. Finally she put her cup and saucer back on the table, lifted her eyes to mine, and began to talk.

"Joseph was my first love. We've known each other for years."

"Joseph?"

"Yes, the priest of the Lichtental Church." She hesitated. "Father Spohr."

"Ah."

"We've stayed in touch." She looked out the window now. "Even though we've gone in different directions."

What an understatement. I nodded, but when she continued to gaze at the building across the street, I cleared my throat and said, "Go on."

"He doesn't know about my clients." She did look at me then. "Very few people do. He thinks that my only career is the public one, the one in fashion."

"Fashion?"

"Yes, of course. I'm a model. Didn't you know?"

I shook my head, and she kept talking.

"That's my day job. I got into my other work a few years ago, when one of my colleagues double booked by mistake and asked me if I could possibly take care of one of her clients."

"Oh." I was thinking about just exactly how she might take care of her clients, but I said, "By other work, you mean your work in," I paused, trying to remember the phrase on her card. Finally it came to me. "Human relations?"

Mitzi smiled then. "Yes. Funny, isn't it? It turns out that I have a gift for it, a natural talent, you know, like you and your piano playing. It's not something I had expected to do."

"Umm." I really had no idea what to say, but she didn't seem to notice. I was thinking about all the years of practice and hours of study I'd put in at the piano, and trying to comprehend the comparison she'd just made, but she was still talking.

"So, once I realized that I had this ability to help middle aged men to feel better about themselves, to put them back in touch with their lost youth and their virility, I decided to establish my own business."

"And you printed your cards and set up a regular schedule?" Now this, I could understand. It was like setting up a music studio, almost.

"Exactly!" She was sitting up straighter now, and looking less lost. "I still work as a model, of course, so I have to be very careful with my schedule."

"Of course you do."

"I see only four clients per week; they each have one full evening reserved, except for Fritz, who likes to spend the night. I think you saw him leaving one morning."

"Fritz Gerling. The famous baritone. Oh yes."

"He is so tired after singing an opera."

"I can just imagine. It must be very exhausting."

"That's why he needs the entire night. He's the only one I've made that exception for. I'm able to help the others in just a few hours, or at least I was, until that frightening episode with Helmut. Now that your friend Dr. Cameron has explained the risks of those medications from Hungary I've been offering my clients, I may have to rethink my therapy."

"Your therapy?"

She nodded. "Yes, you know. It's not only their egos which require stroking, although that part of it is very important."

Oh no. How specific was she going to get? I busied myself pouring more tea while she continued.

"Those medications were very helpful physically; they allowed them to maximize their performance, to feel strong and youthful once more."

"Too bad they're not legal."

"It certainly is." She bit her lip. "I guess I should have suspected it, but when my colleague, the one who got me started in this, offered to have her suppliers add me to their customer list, it seemed like a good idea."

When I didn't respond, she continued. "Dr. Cameron did recommend a few things which are legal, and safer too, but it may not matter anyway."

"Not matter?"

Now her eyes grew moist again. Oh dear.

"Yes, you see. Helmut has decided to discontinue our relationship."

She sniffed, and I handed her a tissue.

"I understand his reasons, but I'll miss him."

"Do you have a waiting list?" Once more, I was comparing her second career to a music studio. It seemed to help me cope with what she was telling me.

"No, though I'm sure that I could find someone to take his place, if I wanted to do so. The thing is, I think that I may need to stop seeing clients altogether. Fritz is leaving on a tour soon anyway, and he'll be gone until late spring. The other two, well, I can refer them to a friend. I'll miss the money, of course, and I'll miss feeling that I'm giving them something they need, but . . ."

"But?"

"It's Joseph."

"The priest."

"Yes." She paused, reached for her teacup, which I had refilled.

"I found out yesterday that I'm pregnant." She paused, sipped her tea. "The baby has to be his."

I shoved my chair back from the table and stood up. "I need some slivovitz."

Mitzi followed me back to the living room and sat across from me wiping her eyes, while I poured myself a shot of the soothing plum brandy.

"None for you."

"I know. I'm worried about what I drank before I knew about the baby."

It took me a few minutes and several sips to calm myself. Finally I asked the only question I could think of. "How did this happen?"

She seemed surprised by my question. "Well, in the usual way, of course. How else?"

How else indeed? Certainly not via an immaculate conception, even with a priest. I searched for a diplomatic way to continue, but couldn't find one, so I settled for a direct question.

"Isn't it a fundamental requirement of your work to make sure that you protect yourself from this possibility?"

She had wrapped herself in the comforter I'd brought to the couch earlier, and now she pulled it tightly around herself, as if it were a protective cocoon.

"Sometimes I forget to take my pills." She looked at me as if I must understand this lapse. I said nothing. "And with my clients, well, I take other precautions as well, so it has never been a cause for concern, if you know what I mean." I nodded, as if I did, and she kept talking. "But Joseph is younger, more," her voice softened and she paused, as if looking for the right words to describe him. "Vigorous," is what she said, followed by, "And then, of course, once we ran into each other again, he came to see me quite often."

It could have been the slivovitz, but I had the sudden, awful urge to giggle. I stifled it, and what emerged from my mouth sounded almost like a cough. Mitzi hardly seemed to notice though. In fact, now that she had started to talk about her predicament, she didn't seem to require any more comments from me. She continued without prompting.

"So that's what we were talking about today, the baby."

Now she started to cry again, and it was a few minutes before she could answer my next question.

"What are you going to do?"

"I don't know." She wiped at her eyes. "I thought that he loved me." She took a breath and looked at me. "I never should have believed him." I handed her another tissue and she blew her nose before continuing. "He wants me to have the baby, of course." Her voice started to quiver. "But he doesn't want me to keep it. He thinks that I should give it up for adoption." Her voice had risen to a piercing soprano range. "Our baby! How could he?"

"What makes you think he doesn't love you?" As soon as the words left my mouth, I regretted them. I had thought that the idea that he could indeed love her might be comforting, even though she hated what he wanted her to do.

"If he loved me, he wouldn't ask me to give up the baby. He'd find a way to help us, to be with us."

Yes he would, in an ideal world. That's what I was thinking, but at least I didn't say it this time. Instead, I asked her another question. "Did you ask him to do that?"

Mitzi stared at me for a minute before she responded. "No. No, I didn't. I ran from him as soon as he mentioned adoption. That's when I bumped into you."

"Aha." I poured myself some more slivovitz, just a little, and took another fortifying sip. "I think you need to tell him what you want." I was starting to feel fairly wise, though it could have been a side effect of the slivovitz. "And then you need to make a plan for the next several months, think of where you'd like to live, where you'd like to raise this baby, with or without him." I emptied my glass and licked my lips. "Do you need to keep working in your fashion job, or could you take a break from it?"

She had brightened up a bit. "Oh, I have quite a bit of money saved. Naturally I haven't paid taxes on the income from my clients."

"Naturally." What else could I say?

"Maybe I could go live with my aunt in Villach for awhile, at least until the baby is born." She nodded. "I'm named after her. We're very close. Yes, that's a good idea." Now she actually smiled. "Thank-you, Lily!"

I was pleased that I had been able to help her, but unfortunately, I was starting to feel a bit dizzy from the slivovitz. "You're welcome, Mitzi." I reached across the small table to her, and she took my hand and held onto it tightly. "Tell him though; tell him what you want him to do. You can't expect him to read your mind."

"I will." She leaned back against her sofa cushions again and closed her eyes.

"I'll tell him. I promise I will."

I watched her for a moment. "Call me if you need me."

I swayed slightly when I stood up; the floor seemed to be tilting at an alarming angle. I kept my eyes focused on the painting in Mitzi's foyer and moved very slowly toward it, one small step at a time. What had I been thinking, drinking in the middle of the day? I sat down for a minute in her kitchen, stuffed a piece of bread into my mouth and waited for the room to quit spinning. It took awhile.

By the time I finally let myself out of her apartment and started down the steps to my own, I had sworn off slivovitz for life, probably one of the wiser decisions I've made. I hoped I would remember, once the effects of the liquor wore off.

CHAPTER EIGHTEEN

I almost bumped into Sophie, who had just reached my doorstep. She was out of breath, as if she'd been running. Maybe that was why she grabbed my shoulders and hung onto me.

"Thank God! Where have you been?"

She wheezed the words into my face, and then started to shake me. It didn't feel good, with all that plum brandy inside me.

"Sophie, stop!"

She stopped, but she didn't let go. Finally I had to push her away, so that I could get my key out. I unlocked the door and we tumbled into my foyer. Sophie was leaning forward, hands on her knees, panting. I squeezed past her, walked very carefully toward my kitchen, and sank into a chair. After a few minutes, she followed me and sat down across from me. She was still breathing hard, but she was able to talk more smoothly.

"I've been trying to call you for hours." When I didn't respond, she kept on. "Aren't you going to ask why I've been trying to call you?"

"I figured you'd tell me."

"It's your doctor friend. He's frantic with worry."

"About me?"

"Why else would he call me every twenty minutes and then beg me to come check to see if you're all right?"

I could feel the warm glow spreading from my face throughout the rest of my body. Stephen, from whom I'd heard not a word since Sunday, was thinking of me.

"Aren't you going to say something?"

"Me? Oh, sure."

"Well?"

"I must have left my phone in my bag in the foyer when I went back up to Mitzi's." I paused to consider how much to tell Sophie. "She had a bit of a crisis this morning."

"Lily." Sophie was reaching for my shoulders again. I leaned back out of reach. "Do you have any idea what time it is?"

"Not really."

"It's half past three."

"Oh dear."

"Is that all you can say?"

I cleared my throat. "Yes, I believe so."

Her phone began playing the opening notes of Mahler's First Symphony. She picked it up just as I was beginning to enjoy the melody.

"Yes. I'm with her. She's fine. Of course I'll give her the phone." She mouthed the words, "It's him" as she handed her phone to me.

"Hello." My voice sounded a bit low and throaty to my own ears.

"Lily." That's all he said, but the way he said it was full of meaning. I sat very still, clutching the phone, waiting for what he'd say next. It wasn't exactly what I'd hoped for, which would have been something like, "I haven't been able to get you out of my thoughts. I've longed for you every minute of every day." You get the idea. What he actually said, however, was, "Why haven't you answered your phone? I've been trying to call you all day." He sounded a bit irritated.

"I didn't have it with me."

"But you're okay."

"Yes, I'm okay." I decided not to mention Mitzi, the priest, or the slivovitz. "I just went off without it."

I could hear him breathing, but he didn't say anything for at least thirty seconds. When he did, it was very soft. "Will you call me once Sophie leaves? I'm not back in Vienna yet, but I'm able to talk now."

"Sure. I will. Until later, then."

We said our good-byes, and I handed the phone back to Sophie, who was sitting with her arms crossed and her eyebrows raised.

"I believe you owe me at least a short explanation for all my trouble."

"Sure Sophie. Just wait a minute." I headed for the bathroom, and once I'd finished there I stopped in the front hall to retrieve my phone. When I returned to the kitchen, Sophie had her head in my refrigerator.

"Do you have anything to eat? I'm starving."

"Actually, I'm hungry too."

I pulled some leftover chicken and dumplings out of the refrigerator, placed it in the microwave, and started boiling water for some vegetables to go with it. Sophie was putting together a salad.

"Do you have any beer?"

I opened one for her, but when she started to pour me a glass, I shook my head.

"No thanks, Sophie. Not today."

She let that unusual occurrence go by, but she didn't let anything else get past her.

"How did he get my phone number?"

There was no doubt about who she meant, and I have to admit the same question had crossed my mind. Things like national security surveillance lists and surreptitious sources occurred to me, but I decided that the simplest solution was probably the best. At least I hoped so.

"It must have happened on Sunday, when he added his number to my contact list." I took a bite of chicken before I continued. Fortunately, Sophie's mouth was full too, so she couldn't say anything. "He was worried about being able to reach me, I guess."

"Umm hmmm." She nodded, but kept chewing. I decided to use the opportunity to check my messages. I had my phone to my ear when she asked her next question.

"What's an American doctor doing in Vienna anyway?"

I was busy listening to Stephen's voice, so I shook my head and waved my hand at her. I won't say what lovely thoughts were flashing through my brain, but something must have shown on my face, because when she finished sipping her beer, she repeated the same question, followed by, "Are you ever going to put that phone down and talk to me?"

I would have, if Christina's voice hadn't penetrated my consciousness at that moment. "I have extra tickets to a ball tomorrow night. I've already invited Dr. Cameron and a colleague of his." I wondered if that would be Janos. "Do you have a female friend you could bring, so that we'll all have partners?"

Perfect. I put down the phone and said, "How would you like to go to a ball tomorrow night?" That ought to take her mind off Stephen, at least for a while.

"That depends. Which one? Where is it?"

"Oh, it's one of those big ones at the Hofburg." That's the Imperial Palace in downtown Vienna, the former home of the Habsburgs, who had ruled Vienna for centuries. The grandest balls were held there, by lawyers, doctors, and other professional groups. I hated to admit that I didn't know which particular group was sponsoring this one, but it didn't really matter. What mattered was that Christina had offered us the tickets and that we got to dress up and dance all night. Who could refuse that?

"Wow." Sophie poured herself some more beer. "Do you have a dress?"

"I do, as a matter of fact, a new one. Do you?"

"Of course. Every Viennese woman owns at least one ball gown."

"Well good. I'll call Christina back and accept, shall I?"

Sophie nodded, and I placed the call.

That's why I was dressed in my beautiful deep blue off the shoulder gown the next evening, touching up my make-up and worrying about my hair when the buzzer sounded at my front door. Even though I was expecting him, I felt slightly breathless and flustered as I waited for Stephen to appear. By the time he finally reached the top of the steps and stood in front of me, holding out a lovely bouquet of creamy white roses and lilies, I was a quivering mass of nerves. It was all I could do to say, "Hello."

Fortunately he seemed to be in better command of his body than I was of mine, at least for the moment it took him to enter my apartment and shut the door behind himself. I took the flowers from him and bent my head to inhale their sweet fragrance, then murmured my thanks, before I dared to look at him again. Oh my. To say that he looked even better than I remembered does not begin to do him justice, but then I'd never seen him in formal evening clothes before.

There's no telling how long I might have stood there staring at him, trying to calm my racing heart, if he hadn't stepped forward, placed the flowers on the table in my front hall, and kissed me. He did all of this without saying a word. By the time he lifted his head and whispered my name, I was considering skipping the ball.

"Lily, you're beautiful."

Those blue eyes captured mine and sent shivers throughout my nervous system. I leaned toward him.

"We'd better go, don't you think?"

I wasn't thinking at all, but somehow I managed to nod and reply.

"Just let me put the flowers in a vase first."

I did, and then I picked up the fur evening jacket Mitzi had loaned me, stood still while he smoothed it over my shoulders, barely managed not to sigh out loud at the feel of his hands on my bare arms. To my great pleasure, he did sigh.

"Ah, Lily, I've missed you."

"I've missed you too." I tipped my face up to him and smiled, and for just a heartbeat, I thought he'd kiss me again, but instead he said, "The taxi is waiting," and we headed down the stairs instead.

A cab was idling at the curb in front of my building, another silver Mercedes. I could get used to this; it felt absolutely decadent. It really was the most sensible way to get to a ball at the Hofburg, though, since there would be no parking anywhere nearby.

Stephen opened the rear door for me, and I slid into the leather seat next to Sophie, but it was Sophie as I'd never seen her before. Her dark brown hair, which usually tumbled in uncontrolled curls to her shoulders, was arranged in a stylish knot on top of her head, with only a few spiraling tendrils left around her face. She looked quite glamorous. Beside her, on the other side of the back seat, sat someone I had previously observed mostly from the side or the back and with a knit cap on. Tonight I finally got a full view of his face, and his thick brown hair.

"Hello, Janos. Nice to see you."

He smiled, and he looked amazingly attractive there in the shadowy interior of the cab. No wonder Sophie had such a pleased expression on her face.

"It's good to see you too, Lily." He grinned. "You're looking lovely, as usual."

Stephen had shut the rear door of the taxi and seated himself in the front, next to the driver. I wished that I could have had his warm, solid body next to me, touching me from my shoulders to my toes, but there wasn't room for four in the back seat, especially not when two of us were wearing ball gowns. I had to content myself with a view of his thick, dark hair and try to concentrate on what Sophie was saying. It had to do with fur. I had forgotten about her strong commitment to animal rights when I'd decided to wear Mitzi's jacket. In my defense I have to say that Mitzi had practically forced it on me; she had said that it was the least she could do to thank me.

"Oh, for goodness sake, Sophie. It's probably only rabbit skins. They most likely all lived happily eating lettuce in someone's garden and died peacefully before donating their fur to the noble cause of keeping me warm." I was thinking of what a nuisance they could be back home in Minnesota, and not feeling too much remorse, when Sophie made a sound suspiciously like a muffled snort. I ignored her and continued my defense. "And it doesn't belong to me anyway. I borrowed it."

"That would explain why you don't realize that you're wearing mink, almost certainly raised in inhumane conditions until their brutal and untimely deaths at the hands of greedy and unscrupulous thugs."

I stroked the wonderfully warm and luxurious fur and pushed away my guilt feelings while I waited for Sophie to wind down. "You're right. I'll never borrow it again."

"Good."

While she had been lecturing me, the cab had traveled down Währingerstrasse, and turned right onto Schwarzspanierstrasse, following the same route I'd taken when I'd gone to Michael Fodor's *Schubertiade* last week. We didn't go that far though; instead, the driver turned left on Mariahilferstrasse, then left again on the Ring, then right into the Heldenplatz. The Hofburg was all lit up, and there was a steady stream of taxicabs dropping people off at the entrance. We joined the line as it inched forward until finally we came to a stop, paid the driver and joined the queue moving toward the doorway.

Stephen had his arm around my waist, and we synchronized our steps as we followed Janos and Sophie. He had his head tipped toward her, and was listening to her as if he enjoyed every word she was saying. She had moved on from endangered species to environmentally friendly cleaning products. Either he loved those causes as much as she did or he was a remarkably polite fellow.

I looked away from Sophie and Janos and up at the illuminated columns and arches of the Habsburg's Imperial Palace, resplendent against the night sky. Above us the stars glittered and the full moon shone silvery white. I leaned into Stephen, enjoyed the feeling of his body next to mine, the easy rhythm of his stride. By the time we finally stepped through the outer doorway and into the splendid foyer of the Hofburg, it was easy for me to believe that we'd entered a scene out of a fairy tale, or at least out of another era. I almost expected an Empress to appear on the red carpet of the grand staircase to welcome us along with the beautifully dressed Viennese making their way upward to the ballrooms.

I shared that thought with Sophie, while Stephen and Janos were checking our coats.

"Oh, Lily, you're such a romantic. Don't forget all the downtrodden workers who must have lived terrible lives and died tragic deaths to build all of this for the Habsburgs."

"You're right, of course." I decided to try to divert her attention from past and present social injustice and complimented her on her gown. It was a dark green Grecian style.

"You look amazing, Sophie. Your gown matches your eyes."

Those eyes were presently gazing at someone or something beyond me, and they had an alarmingly dreamy expression in them. She didn't say anything, so I kept talking.

"You know, I do admire your views on animal rights and the environment, as well as your support for laborers, but I'm wondering whether you need to express yourself quite so forcefully to Janos, when you barely know him."

"Oh, I'm certain he agrees with me." Her voice sounded much breathier than usual, even a bit husky. I had an urge to reach out and feel her forehead, to see if she was feverish, but I restrained myself, and just asked her.

"Are you all right, Sophie?"

She whispered her reply. "Isn't he incredible?"

"Who? Janos? I barely know him, and you've just met him." I peered more closely at her. She had an uncharacteristically winsome smile on her face. "Get hold of yourself, Sophie. This isn't like you."

"I know."

Her eyes told me what I hadn't noticed. Janos and Stephen had returned and were standing right behind us. Janos went straight to Sophie, and pulled her hand through his arm. Stephen held his hand out to me, but he was talking to someone on his cell phone and seemed a bit distracted, so I stood still until he finished the call.

He frowned and shook his head at Janos. "That was Christina. She'll look for us upstairs."

Janos raised his eyebrows and sent what I can only describe as a sober look at Stephen, before he turned back to Sophie and started up the stairs.

CHAPTER NINETEEN

Stephen put his cell phone back into his pocket and pulled me close as we followed Janos and Sophie up the gorgeous staircase. The melody of a Strauss waltz floated down to us, and I began to hum along. Stephen laughed softly, and I felt the vibration pass from his body to mine. I glanced over at him. He looked amused.

"We have to wait, Lily. It's not safe to waltz on the stairs."

"Of course. I know that."

We had just passed the bust of Franz Joseph and made the turn at the halfway point. Above us magnificent marble columns rose to the coffered ceiling. A crystal chandelier sparkled overhead, and sconces glittered beside the doorway opening into the ballrooms. The throng ahead of us was moving slowly; we were following them along the red carpeted path. We had just turned to our right and proceeded down a few steps into a room filled with tables at which elegantly garbed people were sipping wine and nibbling hors d'oeuvres when I heard Christina's voice next to me.

"There you are! I've been watching for you."

She was wearing a silver gown, which sparkled when she moved, and there were diamonds dangling from her ears, neck, wrists and fingers. I touched my own modest sapphire necklace and tried not to feel underdressed. She leaned in to brush kisses on my cheeks.

"You look lovely, Lily."

She greeted Stephen then, and he introduced her to Janos and Sophie before he asked about Michael Fodor.

"Oh, he's around here somewhere. He had to talk to someone. I'm sure he'll join us soon." She frowned and seemed to consider her next words. "He is acting terribly distracted and irritable tonight."

Was I imagining things, or did Stephen and Janos exchange a quick glance and an almost imperceptible nod? Sophie, who had her eyes glued to Janos, didn't seem to notice anything. We had entered the grand ballroom now, and the scene before us was enchanting. The crystal chandeliers cast a shimmering glow over the couples swirling in circles around the room; the parquet floors glistened; the ivory walls and golden hued columns shone as if they'd been polished. The orchestra was playing Strauss waltzes; they could do that all night and never run out of music. My feet were tapping in three quarter time, and I must have swayed a bit toward Stephen. Janos had already guided Sophie onto the dance floor, and I longed to join them.

"Soon, Lily, soon." Stephen's eyes when they met mine hinted at more than just a waltz, or so I hoped. He leaned closer to speak softly into my ear. "Let's get something to drink before we dance. We can't leave Christina alone here."

He placed his hand at my waist to guide me, and then turned to Christina. The three of us strolled back through the room full of tables, and then headed to our left into a chamber with a large bar and beyond it, a wall of windows overlooking the Heldenplatz. Stephen asked us what we'd like to drink, and then joined the line at the bar. I watched him walk away, watched how smoothly he moved through the crowd, how perfectly his evening jacket molded itself to his shoulders. Christina must have been watching me while I watched Stephen.

"You'd be a fool to let that one get away."

"I know." I tugged at one of my earrings. I do that when I'm nervous. "It's just that I don't have a very good record when it comes to long term relationships."

She smiled. "Maybe you haven't had a chance with the right man yet." She brushed a strand of silvery blonde hair away from her forehead as she spoke. "Until now." Her hand touched mine, and she gave it a gentle squeeze. "I'm glad that the Vogls and the Heimbergers couldn't use their tickets, glad that you could come tonight." She sighed softly. "There's nothing quite as romantic as a Viennese ball."

Her eyes had a far away look in them, as if she were thinking of another time, another waltz. "I wish . . ." She didn't finish her thought, because Stephen appeared just then holding glasses of champagne for us. We clicked them together in a silent toast, thanked him, began to sip the sparkling liquid. He stood close beside us, scanning the room. His eyes, unlike Christina's, were focused and intent, as if he were watching for someone or something in particular. I followed his gaze to a small group standing in the corner near the windows, a group which included Michael Fodor. He was leaning toward one of the men in his small group, so absorbed in his conversation, that he didn't notice us. Christina noticed him though.

"Oh, there's Michael." She started toward him before Stephen's outstretched hand could hold her back. Before I could even wonder why he'd attempted to stop her, Sophie and Janos joined us. Her smile was radiant, and he looked quite satisfied too.

"There's nothing like a Viennese waltz to get the blood flowing!" He gave Stephen's arm a playful jab, the way guys do. "You should try it."

"I will, very soon." Stephen nodded at him, then tipped his head toward the corner where Michael Fodor stood. Christina was wedged in next to him now, but he was still talking, ignoring her. "First though, I think we may need to say 'Hello' to Christina's friend, don't you?"

Janos muttered something under his breath, which sounded like, "I'd like to say a lot more than 'Hello,'" but he had spoken so softly that I might not have heard him correctly. He was already headed across the room, while Sophie stared after him.

"I thought he was going to get me something to drink. What's he doing?"

"I'm not sure." I handed her my half empty glass. "Here, you can finish this."

Stephen had taken my hand and was pulling me across the room toward the group Janos had already joined. We had to squeeze our way through the crowd at the bar, and by the time we joined Janos and Christina, the men Michael Fodor had been conversing with had moved away, and Michael was talking to Janos about his import/export business. Christina stood next to him, but he paid no attention to her whatsoever.

"Yes, it's quite a thriving enterprise," he was saying. "My main connection is in Chicago. I have family there."

"Do you?" Janos seemed very pleased by this disclosure. "So do I. What a coincidence!"

He went on to talk about various neighborhoods and Hungarian immigrant groups in that city. Stephen stood silently, and held me close. Sophie had joined us and was watching Janos while sipping her champagne. Christina, standing stiffly erect between Michael and Janos, appeared tense and uneasy; the faraway dreamy look she'd had in her eyes earlier had been replaced by one of stark sorrow, the same look I'd seen that day when she'd talked to us about Lars. I cleared my throat, ready to steer the conversation in a different direction, but Stephen squeezed my arm and silenced me with a quick glance. Janos was asking about furniture now, and Michael was reaching into his coat pocket.

"Yes, we do buy and sell hand painted cupboards; unfortunately, we're in the process of packing our current stock into containers to ship out tomorrow afternoon. Let me give you my business card. We should be getting some more in next week. You can call and set up an appointment with one of my cousins to look at them." He handed the card to Janos, who made a great show of examining it before he put it into his own pocket. He didn't look like the type who'd go in for antique painted cupboards, but then again I don't know that much about Janos.

"Thank-you so much. I'll do that." He smiled at Michael Fodor, nodded at Stephen, and then spoke to all of us. "What do you say we go back to the grand ballroom? Stephen and Lily haven't even had a chance to waltz yet. I'd hate for his private lesson to have been wasted."

"Lesson? You had a waltz lesson?'

Stephen looked embarrassed. "Janos doesn't know when to keep his mouth shut."

The man Stephen was talking about was leading the way back to the ballroom, his arm around Sophie. Christina and Michael were ahead of them and were heading for the dance floor. Stephen's arm was around my waist; he pulled me close as we threaded our way through the crowd and found a space among the couples already gathered, waiting for the orchestra to sound the first notes of the waltz.

I turned to face Stephen and placed one hand on his shoulder, the other one in his. He spun us into the throng of whirling dancers as if he'd been doing this his entire life, but he couldn't have been. I wondered who'd given him a lesson. The Viennese waltz is far more demanding than the simple box waltz most of us have learned back home; it requires much greater speed and constant turning in circles. At least he got to move forward, while I had to spiral backward in my high heels; nevertheless, I was impressed by his skill. I would have told him so if I'd had the breath and concentration to do so. I didn't. It was exhilarating spinning around the room like this, held securely in his arms, but I began to think that I might enjoy a more sedate slow dance with him, once this one was over.

When the waltz ended, we made our way to the side of the room, out of the way of the couples who were already whirling around the room again. Talk about stamina. My head was still spinning from just one waltz. Stephen may have been practicing this demanding dance, but I had not. He must have noticed that I couldn't walk a straight line yet. He kept a firm grip on me, and whispered in my ear.

"I have to talk to Janos. Do you see him?"

I scanned the room, turned my head until I'd examined the entire circumference. Only then did I notice Janos standing directly behind Stephen.

"He's right behind you."

Stephen pivoted and took me with him. I bumped into Sophie, who was pressed up against Janos looking alarmingly preoccupied. I didn't even want to consider what she could be dreaming of doing.

The two men had their heads together. I leaned toward them, but even though I have excellent hearing it was hard to make out what they were saying. With the melodies of Strauss and the buzz of conversations surrounding us all I could hear were a few disconnected words: "midnight," Hungarian estate," "Vienna warehouse," "arrests."

What could they be talking about? I was trying to piece together a logical explanation, when Stephen turned his attention back to me and began to steer me across the crowded ballroom, toward the doorway.

"We need to take a little break, Lily."

"Take a break? We've only had one waltz."

He rubbed his hand up and down my arm, as if to soothe me. That's not precisely the effect his touch had on me, but I admit that he did alter my focus.

"We'll have another dance, Lily. Don't worry. Janos and I just have a couple of calls to make. Why don't you and Sophie freshen up and we'll meet you back here in . . ." He glanced at his watch. "About ten minutes."

With that, he and Janos hurried away, leaving Sophie and me to stare after them. At least she remembered the way to the nearest women's room. I followed her as she threaded her way through the crush of people and joined the inevitable line at our destination. By the time we'd combed our hair and applied fresh lipstick, more than ten minutes had passed.

Sophie had remained uncharacteristically quiet during all of those minutes, except to say, "I wonder what they could be doing."

I decided not to share with her the puzzling words I'd overheard. Who knew what she might make of them in her present distracted state.

Instead I said, "Oh, you never know with guys, do you?"

Actually, that was a true statement, but I went on with another one, which probably wasn't, at least as far as I knew. "They could be planning a surprise for us."

It was much later that I found out that they had indeed been planning a big surprise, just not for us. When we returned to the spot where they'd left us, Stephen and Janos were already there, standing shoulder to shoulder, arms crossed, giving no indication that they'd been doing anything other than waiting for us to return from powdering our noses.

Stephen spoke first, acted as if he'd been hanging around for quite a while, as if he hadn't been the one to send us away in the first place.

"Finally. There you are. Are you ready for another dance now?"

"Well, of course." I took his hand.

"Let's try one of the other ballrooms. I don't think I can manage another waltz yet. I'm in the mood for a different kind of dancing."

"Me too."

That was Janos speaking, and he took Sophie's arm, and the lead. We followed them, watched the way they leaned toward each other, almost touching noses as they talked, totally absorbed in one another as they worked their way through the crowded spaces. The rooms inside the Hofburg connect directly to each other, without long hallways in between them, so it's possible to walk from a chamber resonating with waltzes, through a bar or eating area, to another ballroom nearby vibrating with much more modern music. It can be a bit startling, like moving from one century to another, with very little transition time. The other ballrooms aren't as big as the one in which we'd danced the Viennese waltz, and have different, smaller bands.

If you walk through all of the interconnecting chambers, you make a circle, and eventually end up where you started, near the grand staircase. We followed Sophie and Janos as we made our way, but I scanned every room we passed through, looking for Christina. I hadn't seen her since we'd all started to waltz in the grand ballroom, and I felt strangely apprehensive about her tonight. Something didn't seem right between her and Michael Fodor.

"Have you seen Christina and Michael?" I whispered this to Stephen, who bent his head toward me. "He doesn't seem to be treating her very well tonight." Stephen didn't answer, so I had to ask him directly. "What do you think is going on?"

"Any number of things could be going on, Lily." He took my arm and guided me toward the dance floor. We had just entered one of the smaller ballrooms. "But let's not worry about it right now."

Clearly, he didn't want to talk about Christina and Michael right now, or about anything else, for that matter. I might have pursued the subject with him, but the band in this room was playing a lovely selection. The tempo was perfect for what we would have called a slow dance back in high school. Stephen pulled me close, brought both of my hands to his shoulders, placed his at my waist, and began to move to the music. My head was not quite even with his, even though I was wearing high heels, so I leaned my forehead against his cheek, inhaled the woodsy scent of his cologne, let myself relax against him. I could feel every movement he made, feel the rhythm of the dance pass from his body to mine. It was heavenly, even better than listening to Schubert in the Lichtental Kirche, and that's about as close to bliss as anything for me.

His lips were tracing a line from my temple to that sensitive place just above my ear; his hands were sliding up and down my back; our bodies were molded so closely together that when he exhaled my breath caught in my throat. It's probably a good thing that the music ended when it did, that we had a moment to collect ourselves before the next dance began. He pulled away slightly, took a deep breath, said something which sounded like, "incredible," though maybe I just thought that's what he said, because that's how I was feeling.

The band started playing another tune, and this one was a faster one, probably a good thing for us, so that we could spend a few moments with a little space between our overheated bodies. I'm not sure that it really helped, though, because we were still perfectly in rhythm with one another, our hands and eyes in constant contact. I forgot about everyone else, about Sophie and Janos, about Christina and the count who was treating her so rudely tonight. The world, for at least a little while, consisted only of Stephen and me and the music which provided the accompaniment to our courtship.

One dance blended into another; our bodies moved in such synchrony that we were barely aware of our surroundings, let alone of the passage of time. Who knows how long we might have gone on like that if Sophie hadn't appeared next to us, out of breath, her words emerging on a gasp.

"There you are. Janos was right; you never left this room." She paused to catch her breath. "You've been in here quite a while, you know."

I admit that I was having a hard time focusing on Sophie, with my body pressed as closely as it was to Stephen's, my every movement in rhythm with his. She spoke again, louder this time.

"Hello. Do you hear me? Either of you?"

I heard her. I just couldn't seem to respond to her. Stephen, though, eventually managed to clear his throat, take my hands in his, guide my body into place beside his, and say, "What's going on? Why have you been looking for us?"

He seemed to be having a little trouble talking, so I tried to help him out.

"We've been right here dancing. It's not as if we've been hiding from anyone."

Sophie nodded. "I'm sure you haven't. It's just that Stephen hasn't been answering his cell phone, and we have a bit of a crisis on our hands." Without waiting for us to ask what the crisis was, she went on. "While you've been in this one small ballroom, doing whatever you've been doing." She raised her eyebrows. "We've not only had wine and hors d'oeuvres, but also danced three waltzes in the grand ballroom. It's lucky we did, because while we were in there, we bumped into Christina. When Janos couldn't reach Stephen, he sent me to find you."

"And? You do have a point here somewhere, don't you?"

Sophie frowned at me.

"Of course I have a point. Something has happened to Christina, while you've been busy in your own small world. She's extremely upset. Janos says that we should get her away from here."

That got my attention.

"Get her away from here? Now?"

Sophie had already turned around, and she threw her next words over her shoulder.

"Yes, right now. Janos is getting our coats. Let's go."

I was thinking that I had preferred Sophie in her earlier dreamy state, distracted by whatever thoughts she'd been having about Janos. Sophie in this mood of alarm and anxiety was not a pleasant person. Nevertheless, her message had finally penetrated the bubble of bliss I'd been inhabiting with Stephen, who was pulling his cell phone from his pocket and starting to check his messages.

"I can't believe I didn't hear it."

"Of course you didn't hear it. Loud music, strong beat. You were dancing with me, remember?" I decided not to mention everything else he'd been doing while we'd been pressed so close to each other, and instead gave voice to my own rising concern for Christina.

"If Michael Fodor has done something to hurt her, I'll . . ."

"You'll do what?"

"I don't know, but it won't be nice."

"I'm sure it won't."

Stephen put his arm around me, and we followed Sophie back through the circle of rooms to the grand staircase. We descended them, and then, without uttering another word, we put on our coats, or in my case, Mitzi's mink jacket, and stepped out into the cold, dark night. Janos was waiting, holding open the door of a taxi, and we hurried to join him.

CHAPTER TWENTY

A hazy cloud cover had replaced the stars, and a few snowflakes fell on our heads as we rushed toward Janos. The taxi was not an elegant silver Mercedes like the cab we'd arrived in, but one of those large yellow vehicles which can hold several people. It reminded me of the minivans driven by car pooling parents back in Minnesota, except for its outrageously bright color.

"Couldn't you have chosen something less noticeable?" That was Stephen, grumbling to Janos as he waited for me to maneuver myself into the back seat.

"We were lucky it was here. Usually you have to order these big ones over the phone." Janos sounded a bit gruff. "We couldn't have fit into a smaller taxi."

I scooted across the seat and came to a stop next to Christina, who was sitting very erect and staring straight ahead. In front of her, in the middle seat, was Sophie, who seemed to have gotten her anxiety under control, now that we were all outside. She had turned around and was scrutinizing Christina's sumptuous white coat. It really did look as if it could be Minnesota rabbit fur, but it was probably something much more rare and expensive. Fortunately, Sophie's awareness of Christina's precarious state of mind must have triumphed over her sentiments about the wearing of fur, because she kept her mouth shut and turned around when the taxi door slammed and Janos slid in next to her.

I watched as he put his arm around her and pulled her close. She let her head drop to his shoulder, and seemed not to notice that he was using his free hand to tap out a text message on his phone. The man could multi-task as well as Stephen. I was longing to poke Sophie and ask her to read and remember whatever message he was so busy typing, but there was no way that I could do that, not while Stephen had one arm around me and was leaning across me to look at Christina, effectively imprisoning me in his solid warmth.

I looked around him as the taxi pulled away from the curb and passed the statue of Prince Eugene of Savoy on his horse. He's the guy who saved Vienna from the Turks in 1683 and built the Belvedere palace, but tonight, through the frosty windows of the taxi, he looked a bit soft around the edges, as if all the fighting had worn him down. Across from him, on the other side of the Heldenplatz, Archduke Karl sat on his own rearing horse, his head dusted with snow. Behind him, the façade of the Hofburg formed a stately silhouette against the night sky; in front of him, a steady stream of cars moved through the square. We drove through one of the arches of the Heldentor, the Hero's Gateway, and turned right onto the Ring.

Stephen had placed his hand on Christina's arm, and his voice was gentle as he spoke to her.

"What happened, Christina?"

She blinked, turned her head slowly, and looked at Stephen. Her mouth opened and closed, but no sound emerged.

"Take a deep breath, Christina." His voice was low and soothing; he was stroking her hands now.

She made a soft sniffling sound as she inhaled some of the steamy air inside the cab, and then puffed it back out with a quivery gasp.

"That's good. One more."

I was beginning to have a little trouble with my own breathing as Stephen's arm pressed against me. His face was so close that I could see the thick, dark fringe of his eyelashes, the tightening of the muscle in his jaw when Christina finally answered him.

"You were right about him. I've been a fool." Her voice trembled at first, but she seemed to gain strength as she spoke. "I overheard him talking to one of his cousins." She paused to explain. "They were behind one of the pillars in the ballroom and didn't see me. I was coming back from the ladies room." She took in another deep breath. "He was talking about me. He said . . ."

She stopped speaking for a moment. Tears were running down her cheeks. I found a tissue in my evening bag and handed it to her. She pulled her hands out from under Stephen's, wiped her eyes, and then continued.

"He said that I was becoming a nuisance, that I was always underfoot, that I was asking too many questions about his business." She stopped and blew her nose. "How could I have been so stupid? I actually thought that he cared about me."

She had begun to cry again. It was a couple of minutes before she was able to continue.

"That's not the worst of it though."

Stephen sat very still, as we waited for her next words, but I could feel his breath on my cheek, the heat from his body where it touched mine. I struggled to concentrate on Christina, tried not to think about how good it felt to have him beside me. I looked at her hair, which appeared much better controlled than her emotions at the moment. Not a strand was out of place. I pushed my own off my face where it had fallen during the dash to the taxi, as she finished her story in a burst of shocking words.

"He said that he'd have to find a way to get rid of me, that I could ruin everything!"

"Get rid of you?" That was my voice. It wasn't exactly a shriek, but I wouldn't call it my calmest voice. "Are you sure that's what he said?" Even if you gave him the benefit of the doubt, and assumed that he was talking about breaking up with Christina, rather than doing her physical harm, Michael Fodor's words were appallingly nasty.

Stephen removed his hand from Christina's, pulled me close, and whispered, "Hush. Everything will be all right," in my ear, as if he were soothing a frightened child. I clamped my mouth shut and tried to concentrate on what Christina was saying.

"Of course I'm sure." She spoke through her tears. "I can't go back to that apartment. I don't want to be anywhere near him."

"Don't worry, Christina. You're never going to have to see him again, at least if we can help it."

How could Stephen be so sure of that? Christina lives on the floor above Michael Fodor, in the elegant building on the Metternichgasse where I'd attended the *Schubertiade*. She'd certainly have to go back to her apartment at some point, even if it was just to pack her suitcases, and she might see him on the stairway, or in that antique lift. We weren't headed that way right now though. Janos must have known what was going on, known where to take her, before he gave instructions to the taxi driver.

We were on Nussdorferstrasse, heading out toward Döbling, and it was snowing harder now. Shimmering rings of light radiated from the street lamps as the flakes swirled around them. It would have felt cozy inside the taxi, even without the wintry weather just outside our windows. I was sitting so close to Christina that I could see the dampness left by the tears on her cheeks and feel each quivering breath she took, as she continued to cry softly. I wasn't sure what to do, other than to continue to hand her tissues.

"What should we do now? She can't seem to stop crying." I whispered these words into Stephen's ear, which was barely an inch from my mouth.

He turned his head just enough so that he could direct his voice toward me, rather than toward Christina.

"Of course she's still crying." His lips were so close to mine that his next words felt almost like a kiss, and I couldn't stop the tremor which rippled through me. "She's had a terrible shock. I hope that she'll feel a little better once we get her settled, once she realizes that she's safe and that Michael Fodor can't hurt her, at least not any more than he already has."

He did kiss me gently then, right before he pulled away from me. I was left to wonder how he knew so much about Michael Fodor. I would have wondered about our destination too, about his certainty that Christina would feel safe there, if I hadn't looked out the window as soon as he moved away from me. The taxi had stopped in front of a large house. It was not the Villa Christina, as I had expected, but I did recognize this place. We were parked in front of Trudi and Helmut Vogl's home.

Janos was the first person to move. He opened the door and stepped out. Stephen and I followed, and then Janos leaned back in to help Christina. Sophie remained in her seat.

"You stay here." He directed this statement to Stephen. "I'll walk her to the door."

Stephen and I slipped back into the cab and shut the door. We all watched as Janos guided Christina through the electronically controlled gate and up the walk to the Vogl's front door. It opened immediately, as if they'd been watching for her; she and Janos stepped inside quickly.

"Whose house is this anyway? Did you notice the security camera and the buzzer system at the gate?"

That was Sophie, who was squinting to see through the swirling snow.

"It belongs to Helmut and Trudi Vogl."

"Helmut Vogl, the Minister of Interior of Austria?'

"The very one."

"How do you know that?"

"I've been here."

"Well, that's interesting."

Normally, Sophie would have demanded details, but she must have been distracted by the reappearance of Janos on the front steps.

Instead it was Stephen who said, "What in the world were you doing here?"

"I'll tell you all about it later."

I did tell him, after the taxi had dropped us off at my apartment building and we'd settled ourselves at my kitchen table. I would have told him during our drive back to my apartment, but as soon as Janos had gotten back into the taxi and sat down next to Sophie, he and she had been otherwise occupied, and Stephen and I had followed their example. While I was longing to question Stephen about those words I'd overheard tonight, not to mention all the phone calls he and Janos had been making, and his newly revealed knowledge of Michael Fodor's character, I wasn't able to resist his kisses. Blame it on pheromones, or on the champagne I'd drunk, or on the universal laws of attraction; whatever the reason, the pleasures of the moment took precedence over my need for answers. While I was suspicious that both men might be using diversionary tactics to distract Sophie and me from the unusual events of this evening, what was happening between Stephen and me was a true no-brainer. I promised myself the same thing Stephen had told me a few times already, "I'll explain it all to you later." I decided I'd have to put together the pieces of tonight's intriguing puzzle some other time, but I vowed that it would be as soon as possible.

I'd heated up some goulash, and Stephen had poured beer for both of us. Janos and Sophie had refused my invitation to join us; he'd said they had other plans, and she had not objected. I know it seems as if I eat a lot of goulash, but that's because it's the perfect winter meal in Vienna. It also happens to be the traditional post ball food here. We were just having it a bit earlier than the rest of the ball goers of Vienna, who were no doubt still dancing.

Stephen had leaned back into the taxi to confer with Janos while I'd opened the door to my building, and he'd paced around my apartment speaking sotto voce into his cell phone while I'd been preparing the food. To say that I was bursting with curiosity about whatever he was up to is putting it mildly, but he was the one questioning me about the Vogls and the Schubert manuscript after I'd explained why and how I'd been to the Vogl's house before. I wouldn't say that he was skeptical exactly, but he did look a bit worried.

"Has it occurred to you to wonder why Helmut Vogl would choose you of all people to publicize this material?"

I took a swallow of my beer before I answered him. "Of course."

"And?"

"He seems to like me." I paused. "And then of course there's his wife Trudi's friendship with Christina. That could have something to do with it."

"Lily." He leaned toward me. "He's a politician. Whether or not he or his wife likes you has nothing to do with his decisions."

"That's very cynical of you."

"I'd call it realistic, not cynical."

"Well, for your information, that health scare he had at Mitzi's seems to have been a life changing event." To my own ears I sounded as if I were picking a fight with one of my brothers, but I continued. "He told me so himself."

The sound emerging from Stephen's throat sounded suspiciously like laughter, but if it was, he covered it with a quick cough, and then reached over to brush a crumb from my upper lip.

"I'm certain that he may have to change some of his behaviors, Lily, but that doesn't mean that he's had a miraculous character transformation."

I licked my lip where he'd just touched it. "Maybe not, but he seemed quite sincere to me."

"Did he really?" Stephen broke off a piece of the crusty roll he held and dipped it into the last of his goulash. "Haven't you wondered why he would choose an American professor to verify the rumors about Schubert's sexual preferences? Why wouldn't he just contact the appropriate scholars here in Austria? Do you think he might be hoping to deflect any negative publicity toward you, away from himself and his family?"

"Mmm." My mouth was full, so he just kept talking.

"The Austrians are not known for their open minded acceptance of homosexuality. They'd rather pretend it doesn't exist." He took a sip of beer. "Just look at that famous politician who died in a car wreck last year. His admirers ignored his life style, forced him to pretend he was the macho guy they wanted him to be."

"Well, no one has ever said that Schubert was a macho guy, only that he was a gifted composer. I just can't see why this would be a problem these days, especially since so many scholars already think it's true."

I pushed back my chair and picked up my plate. Stephen watched me for a moment before he stood up and joined me at the sink. He put his plate next to mine and then put his hands on my shoulders, his lips to my ear.

"I just don't want you to get hurt, Lily. At least think about sharing the authorship of the article with an Austrian, won't you? What about that guy who went to the cemetery with you?"

It was awfully hard to think about Kurt, or Schubert, or publishing academic articles, while Stephen was doing what he was doing, but I tried.

"Sure, okay." I whispered, and then I turned around and met his lips with my own.

That's how we began our next dance of the evening, not a Viennese waltz, or even another slow dance, but something else entirely, a tantalizing sequence of kisses and turns which led us from the kitchen sink to my bedroom. We left a trail behind us, my shoes in the front hall, his necktie in the living room, followed by his evening jacket and cufflinks. I was working on his shirt buttons while he was feathering kisses along my collarbone and unzipping my ball gown. The man was good with his hands, I have to say, though I'm pretty dexterous myself. It probably comes from the musical training.

We were able to do this while making up our own steps to the music floating softly through the room; he must have turned on my CD player while he was pacing around the apartment earlier. I admit that I had imagined what making love with Stephen might be like, and I have a very creative imagination. However, the reality was beyond anything even I could invent. I should have realized that would be the case when I quivered at his first gentle touch, or when my heart skipped a few beats once we'd finally shed our clothes and moved our dance to my bed.

I could describe every stroke, every kiss, but I won't, except to say that he took my breath away and then gave it back again, that I had never, until that night, understood what people meant when they talked about ecstasy so intense you thought you'd died and then come to life again. That's how good it was. I was still vibrating in the aftermath of the experience, losing myself in those blue eyes, trying to regain control of my breathing, when I heard the unmistakable sound of my favorite baritone singing a Mozart aria. It wasn't coming from my CD player, which was playing something by Puccini. No, it came from upstairs. It was Thursday, Fritz Gerling's night with Mitzi.

Stephen lifted his head. "Did you hear that?"

"Hear what? The Puccini?"

"No, it sounds like Mozart, and it sounds like it's coming from upstairs."

He turned on his side and took me with him; I nestled my head against his shoulder.

"You're right. I think it's from *The Marriage of Figaro.*"

Fritz was singing louder now, reaching a musical climax, and possibly another kind as well.

"Why would someone be singing upstairs? Isn't that where Mitzi lives?"

He had to know perfectly well that's where Mitzi lived. He'd been there himself.

"Yes. It's one of her clients. He comes every Thursday."

"I'll bet he does." And then Stephen started to laugh, a deep rumbling sound I could feel throughout my body. "Unbelievable. I'll have to tell my mother. She'll love it."

"You're planning to tell your mother about tonight?"

"Only about the singing. She loves opera." He was dropping kisses from my eyebrow to my earlobe, and I was trying hard to concentrate. "The rest of it is just between us."

And then he stopped talking and moved on to other pleasures. By the time we'd proven that we could experience that heart-stopping sensation twice in a row, I was feeling as if I'd just played a concerto. It was the kind of bone melting satisfaction which leaves me barely able to move. Fortunately I didn't need to. We were snuggled together under my down comforter, listening to the rest of the Puccini CD. His fingers were stroking that tender spot just under my ear. My head was on his chest, and his heartbeat provided a steady accompaniment to the music. It was Rodolfo and Mimi again, singing of their love.

"You do know that it ends tragically, don't you?"

His voice whispered through my thoughts.

"Yes, but at least she dies knowing that he truly loves her."

"Ah."

That's all he said, not, "Well, of course he does," or the admittedly unlikely, "Just as I've come to love you, Lily."

What did I expect? After all, we barely knew each other. What I was feeling was no doubt attributable to desire, to that sudden unexpected force which pulses through your entire being, filling you with longing and wiping out rational thought. Yes, that's what it was. Love was something else again, as my Grandpa Lindstrom used to say.

"It's a daily commitment, Lily, like practicing an instrument. The wonderful thing about it is that whether you're practicing piano, or working at loving someone even when they might not be at their most loveable, you can end up with something beautiful. It could be a well formed melody, or it could be a life well lived."

"Your Grandpa was a wise man." Stephen spoke softly. I must have been thinking out loud again. He turned toward me and kissed me once more. Actually, he did more than just kiss me. I couldn't think when he did what he was doing.

"Do you think we should practice?"

I didn't answer him. I was incapable of speech.

It was much later when the commotion started. We had been sleeping, and there had been no sound in the room except for our breathing and the occasional soft rustling of the comforter as we moved. Fritz had finished his aria long ago, and my CD player had turned itself off. I opened my eyes and squinted through the darkness at my clock; everything was blurry, because I'd left my contacts in again. It was an understandable oversight under the circumstances really.

"What's happening? What time is it?'

"I don't know. I can't see my clock." I sat up and reached for the robe I'd left on my chair that morning. "It sounds like someone is running up and down the stairs."

Stephen swore in German. I won't translate. He lunged from the bed and pulled on his pants and shirt while I was still fumbling with the sash on my robe.

"Where did I leave my phone?"

The soft chiming sound led him to the pocket of his coat. He pulled it out and put it to his ear, while I made my way to the bathroom. By the time I'd removed my contacts, brushed my hair out of my face, and found my glasses, he was putting on his shoes and unlocking my front door.

"Stay here, Lily." He turned and frowned at me. Had he ever seen me in my glasses before? "Don't even think of following me." He opened the door and stepped into the stairwell. "Lock the door behind me."

The man was a master at giving orders. I did close the door, but I didn't intend to lock it. I planned to wait a minute before sneaking out to see what was happening.

"Lily, lock it." Stephen's voice came from the hallway, and I could see his throat when I looked through my peephole. I turned the deadbolt.

"Good, now stay in there."

CHAPTER TWENTY-ONE

I stood there until he moved away from the door, and then hurried to my bedroom and pulled on a pair of slacks and a sweater. I was back in the front hallway lacing my shoes when I heard a groan, followed by a loud thump, and then the sound of footsteps on the stairs outside my apartment. I looked through the peephole, but I couldn't see a thing, so I unlocked the deadbolt and turned the doorknob as quietly as I could. Before I stepped into the stairwell I grabbed the only weapon I could find, my umbrella.

I tiptoed to the center of the stairwell, leaned over the railing next to the lift, and peered down, then up the stone enclosed space. I couldn't see anything down below, but up above I could see Stephen's legs, and someone else's feet. There was a low murmur of voices drifting downward, plus a few odd sounds which I couldn't identify, a series of muffled bumps and thuds. I held my umbrella in front of me as if it were a sword as I climbed the steps, but when I emerged on the landing in front of Mitzi's apartment, it was clear that I didn't need it after all.

The scene awaiting me could have come from a comic opera, except that the costumes needed a bit of work. Fritz Gerling, wearing one of those scoop necked, sleeveless undershirts like my Grandpa's brother Thor used to wear when he mowed his grass during the short

Minnesota summers, was sitting on top of Michael Fodor's cousin Sandor. Except for that one glimpse of Fritz I'd gotten when he was coming down the stairway last week, I'd only ever seen him from a distance, dressed up like Papageno or one of the other characters he was famous for. He looked totally different now, with coarse grey chest hairs springing out above his undershirt, and skinny white legs bent on either side of Sandor's belly.

Mitzi was kneeling on the floor next to the two of them, locking a pair of elegant silver handcuffs around Sandor's ankles. He already had a pair holding his wrists together over his head.

"Where in the world did she get those?"

"I'm sure she can tell you later, Lily."

Stephen whispered those words in my ear, right before he put his hands at my waist and moved me off to the side and a few feet away from where Frau Frassl stood with one booted foot on Andreas' chest and the other between his legs, perilously close to that part of the body most men feel quite vulnerable about. He was not moving or making a sound, except for a muted whimper emerging from his mouth, probably caused by the large revolver Frau Frassl was pointing at the same sensitive part of his body her foot was so close to.

"I thought guns were illegal in Austria."

"They are. It's probably not real."

Stephen said that while he was tying Andreas' hands together with the lasso Frau Frassl usually kept hanging on the back wall of her shop next to her Willy Nelson CD collection. He had just started securing Andreas' ankles when the gun went off. The shot reverberated in the stairwell along with Mitzi's screams and Andreas' shouts of pain. Sandor bellowed something in Hungarian, and Fritz gave voice to a piercing lyric. It sounded like something from *Aïda*. It was all so cacophonous that I covered my ears, but my eyes were wide open, so I saw the blood bubbling from Andreas' wound and watched as Stephen ripped off his own shirt to staunch the flow.

Fortunately, Frau Frassl had a poor aim, or else she had moved the gun by the time she pulled the trigger. She had not hit that part of Andreas' body she'd been pointing at, but she'd still managed to put a significant hole in his thigh.

She was hopping from one foot to another now, saying, *"Es tut mir leid! Ich weiss nicht wie es geschehen ist!"* "I'm sorry. I don't know how it happened." Then she dropped the gun; it slid over the edge of the landing and fell with an echoing crash to the ground floor.

Stephen was trying to tell me something. I knew that, because I could see his lips moving when he turned his head toward me. It was a moment before the ringing in my ears subsided enough for me to understand what he was saying though.

"Lily. Get my phone out of my pocket. Call 144." That's the number for an ambulance nationwide. I extracted his phone as carefully as I could, and made the call. Stephen was still pressing his shirt against Andreas' wound. Andreas had quit shouting and, in fact, looked as if he might have passed out.

"Good. Now, on your way downstairs to open the door for them, call Janos to tell him what's happened. His number is in my contact list under Kovacs. Whatever you do, don't touch the gun."

"Right."

I found Janos' number, placed the call, and started down the steps. Janos answered on the third ring, listened carefully, and told me he'd take care of everything. He also gave me a short message for Stephen; it was, "Mission Accomplished."

I couldn't help wondering what he meant. I hoped that it had nothing to do with Sophie, but I'd think about that later. Right now, I could hear the sound of the ambulance approaching, that perfect fourth which gets higher in pitch as it comes closer, a result of a shift in frequency of the sound waves, the Doppler Effect. Why do I think of things like that at moments of crisis?

Despite Stephen's command not to touch the gun, I used my foot to nudge it into a corner behind the mailboxes on my way to the outer door. I really didn't want anyone to take Frau Frassl to jail. She was close behind me on the steps, still saying that she was sorry and that she hadn't meant to pull the trigger, that the revolver had been a gift from a nephew who'd lived in America, the land of guns. Please don't let them take her to jail. She was only trying to help. You get the idea. She was still right behind me, still babbling, when the ambulance arrived.

I held the door open while the paramedics rushed inside.

"They're on the fourth floor landing," I told them, in German of course. "You're going to need a stretcher though."

They ignored that information; oh well, they'd figure it out soon enough. I was just about to close the door, when a VW Passat skidded to a stop behind the ambulance, and a man clothed in a dark wool suit vaulted out of it and rushed toward me. He flashed a badge as he crossed the threshold and said, "Police," before he began running up the stairs behind the medics.

I would have closed the door at that point and followed him, if Frau Frassl hadn't grabbed my arm.

"*Bitte,*" she whispered. "*Was soll ich jetz tun?*" That means, "Please, what should I do now?" It was a good question. I wish I'd had an equally good answer. While I was thinking about it, the paramedics came running back down the steps, fetched a stretcher from the ambulance and started back up again.

"Let's go to your shop. You can restock your shelves while I find out whether the policeman needs to talk to you. Lock your door, and don't open it, unless it's one of us."

I left her there, arranging magazines and chocolates, and headed back to my building. The medics were just emerging with the stretcher on which Andreas lay, pale, apparently unconscious, covered with a blanket. They slid the stretcher into the ambulance, slammed the doors and sped away. Now the perfect fourth of the siren sounded lower as it moved farther away, toward the Allgemeine Krankenhaus.

Stephen stood at the foot of the stairs, shoeless, his chest bare, talking to the man in the dark wool suit. He ran his fingers through his hair as he talked, and I watched his movements, the way his muscles flexed, the sculpted firmness of his body. I must have sighed in admiration, or made some other sound, because they both turned to look at me.

"Lily. There you are. I was just telling Inspector Krenek about Frau Frassl and the gun she mistakenly thought was a toy. Do you know where she is?" He held out one arm to me and I moved over to stand close to him. "And what happened to the gun? I thought it fell down here, but I don't see it."

Great story. I hoped I'd have a chance to fill Frau Frassl in before the Inspector questioned her. In the meantime, I busied myself looking all around the entrance, as if I didn't know perfectly well where the gun was hiding.

"Oh, there it is, under the mailboxes."

"I wonder how it got there." Stephen took a step toward it, but the Inspector stopped him, pulled some disposable gloves and a plastic bag from his coat pocket, very carefully picked up the gun and then emptied the bullets into the bag before dropping the gun into it.

"It must have been kicked to the side by the paramedics."

"Oh, maybe so." Stephen looked up the stairwell and then over to the mailboxes as if trying to follow the path of the falling gun. Then he turned to look at me again. "And where is Frau Frassl?"

"She's in her shop. She was very upset, and I thought she'd feel more at ease there."

"Good thinking. Can you show the Inspector the way, while I get my shoes and coat?"

"There's a sweater in my armoire that might fit you." I called that to him over my shoulder as I led the Inspector toward the door. "The blue one on the top shelf to the right. Oh, and I have a message for you from Janos."

He stopped on his way to the stairway. "What is it?"

"Mission Accomplished. Not very original."

He smiled. "Maybe not, but it's very good news." Then he started up the steps, two at a time.

The Inspector followed me to Frau Frassl's shop. I had to bang on the doorway to get her attention. She had her back turned and even through the closed door I could hear Willie Nelson singing. "My heroes have always been cowboys. They still are it seems." Perfect.

As soon as she opened the door I said, "Dr. Cameron was just telling the Inspector that you thought the gun was a toy." I had hoped to be able to whisper this to her, but the Inspector was close behind me and showing no sign of giving me the time or space to speak privately to Frau Frassl.

He cleared his throat as soon as I finished my sentence. "Perhaps you can leave me alone with Frau Frassl now, Dr. Lindstrom." His tone of voice left no doubt that he expected me to leave.

"Oh yes. Certainly." I wanted to give her some encouraging sign of my support before I left, but the Inspector was holding the door open for me. His eyes never left me. I had no choice except to leave her there with him, but as soon as I got back to my building, I started running up the stairway, calling for Stephen.

As it happened, he was on his way down, and I ran right into him. He grabbed me and pulled me to his chest, now covered in my Grandpa's old blue wool sweater.

"Whoa. Careful." He leaned against the wall and brought me even closer, dropped a kiss on my lips before I could say another word. "What's the matter?"

"It's Frau Frassl. I had to leave her alone with the Inspector. I'm afraid he'll arrest her."

He stroked my back while I talked, kept his eyes on me. "Don't worry, Lily. He's on our side."

"Our side?"

"Yes, he's part of the operation. I explained to him that I had brought Frau Frassl in to help."

"Operation? What operation?"

He proceeded to utter those words he'd used so many times before. "I'll explain it to you later. Right now, I have a few more things to attend to, starting with getting Sandor out of here. I left Mitzi and Fritz guarding him."

"Good grief. I hope the Inspector didn't recognize Fritz Gerling!"

"If he did, he'll keep it to himself, but really, who would recognize him looking like that?"

"Good point. I hope you're right. We'll just have to hope that he doesn't start singing again."

He didn't, at least not at that moment. Just then Inspector Krenek appeared in the doorway; he was putting a small notebook into his pocket as he spoke to Stephen.

"I think I have all the information I need right now. Do you need a ride to headquarters?"

"Yes, but we can't forget Sandor."

"Of course. They should have come for him by now. I'll call again." He pulled his phone out and placed the call, while Stephen started giving me instructions.

"I'll call you as soon as I'm finished. I think it would be best for you to lock yourself in and catch up on your sleep."

I probably would have protested this advice if he hadn't kept my mouth otherwise occupied. The man is an exceptional kisser. Only the sound of Inspector Krenek clearing his throat reminded us that we were not alone.

"I'll wait outside. They should arrive in a few minutes."

They did, and I watched as two officers escorted Sandor down the steps and out to a waiting police van. They had replaced Mitzi's fancy wrist and ankle cuffs with a sturdier pair of their own, which confined only his wrists. They'd freed his ankles so that he could walk, of course. I caught a glimpse of the medallion he wore around his neck as he shuffled past me, along with a whiff of the garlic and tobacco which infused his clothing. He didn't glance my way, but stared straight ahead as he was led away.

I rubbed the place on my forehead which had been cut by his medallion.

"It doesn't still hurt, does it?" Stephen pushed my hair away from the spot and leaned in for a closer look.

"No." I caught his hand in my own. "I was just remembering. That's all."

The Inspector called to him from the open doorway.

"I'd better go. See you later."

I watched until the taillights of Inspector Krenek's car disappeared around the corner, and then I headed straight for Frau Frassl's shop. I planned to be back in my apartment before Stephen even knew I hadn't followed his advice to the letter. I was greeted by Willie Nelson's voice, rather than Frau Frassl's. "There's nothing I can do about it now," he sang. Frau Frassl was standing on a stool behind the counter, hanging her lasso back on its hook.

I greeted her, and then closed and locked the door behind me. I could follow at least a part of Stephen's list of instructions.

She climbed down from the stool, and moved to her customary place behind the cash register, where she stood as if waiting for me to ask for my morning newspapers.

"I just came to see if you were all right, Frau Frassl."

"Es geht mir ganz gut, danke." This was exactly the same reply I'd given to Helmut Vogl not that long ago, after I'd been knocked down by Sandor and Andreas in front of my building. It means, "I'm doing just fine, thank-you," but Frau Frassl looked exhausted and her hand shook slightly as she handed me a chocolate bar. I took it from her, tore open the wrapper, and bit into it before I said anything else. I never refused chocolate, unless I was very sick.

"What did the Inspector say about the gun?"

"Oh, he said that I can't have it back, because I don't have a permit for it." Her eyes looked a bit moist. "I didn't mean to hurt anyone, but when Dr. Cameron called me tonight to tell me to watch for the Hungarians, I thought it would help me look like a real deputy."

"A real deputy?" This conversation was entirely in German, and I wanted to be sure that I was interpreting her words correctly.

I seemed to be, because she went on to say, "Oh, yes, he brought me into the operation last week. He even gave me a badge." She unbuttoned her heavy wool sweater and showed me the tarnished star pinned to the smock she wore beneath it. I leaned across the counter to examine it up close. It said, "Deputy Sheriff," and looked like the kind of prize my brothers used to find in cereal boxes, but I'd seen some just like it in one of those little costume shops you see around town during ball season. That must be where Stephen had found it. Very clever of him.

"Amazing."

"Yes," she said as she buttoned her sweater up again. "He said that I could help bring these criminals to justice."

"Well, you certainly did your job, Frau Frassl."

She beamed, and her smile was almost as bright as the frizzy red hair on her head. I was a bit astounded at Stephen's audacity, but decided to keep my thoughts to myself, at least until I saw him again.

"Yes, and the Inspector said that even though I can't have the gun back, he would make sure that his commanding officers would hear about the important part I played in tonight's arrests."

What could I say after that, except, "Congratulations, Frau Frassl." I had finished my chocolate bar, and I placed the wrapper into the hand she held out across the counter.

She nodded; we bid each other "Good Night," and I walked back to my building. It was very quiet in the stairwell; the only sound I could hear was the echo of my own footsteps. I admit that I was tempted to go up to the fourth floor, to see if there was any trace of blood or other sign of what had happened such a short time ago, but instead I entered my own apartment, locked and bolted the door behind me, and headed for my bedroom. I carried the vase of Stephen's flowers with me, inhaled their sweet fragrance as I placed them on the night stand.

My bed was still rumpled from our lovemaking, and Stephen had left behind the scent of his aftershave along with the imprint of his head on my pillow. I stripped off my clothes, crawled under the down duvet, and drifted into a sweet sleep, filled with tantalizing images of a blue eyed, dark haired double doctor from Georgia, if that's who he really was.

When I awoke, however, I did not hear the seductive whisper of Stephen's voice in my ear, but rather the reverberating sonority of Fritz Gerling's baritone in the stairwell. He wasn't singing a cheerful Mozart tune this time, or even a tender melody by Schubert. He was belting out the Toreador Song from Bizet's *Carmen*. Either he'd had a spectacular experience with Mitzi, or he was reliving last night's capture and arrest of Sandor and Andreas, with much drama and emotion.

I pulled on my robe, thrust my feet into my slippers, and hurried through the apartment. I didn't fling open the door, but instead put my eye to the peephole and waited to catch a glimpse of the singer as he passed by. I was in luck; I could see his ruddy cheeks, the strong curve of his open mouth, even the swelling of his chest as he took a breath. For some reason, he had come to a stop directly in front of my door. He paused, looked directly at the peephole, as if he knew I was behind it, smiled, and then continued on his way. I didn't realize I'd been holding my breath until I released it in a soft puff after he'd moved on.

Only after I heard the Toreador's final notes, followed by the slam of the front door down below, did I notice that my phone was ringing, well, not really ringing. It was playing the melody I'd assigned to Stephen, my favorite Puccini love song, of course. I'd begun to associate it with him.

If I'd been hoping for sweet words of love from Stephen though, I'd have to wait, who knows for how long. What he said was, "I'm on my way. I'll be there in ten minutes."

He hung up before I could reply, but that was okay. I barely had time to wash my face and throw on some clothes before he arrived.

CHAPTER TWENTY-TWO

I had just pressed the brew button on my coffee maker when the buzzer sounded at the front door. It was Stephen, but he wasn't alone.

"Janos is with me. Are you dressed?"

"Yes. Come on up."

I opened my door and listened to their footsteps as they climbed the stairs. They stopped to greet me, but then kept climbing to the fourth floor.

"Janos wants to see where it happened."

I watched their feet as they ascended to the landing outside Mitzi's apartment. They were talking, but I couldn't make out what they were saying, not until they started back down.

"At least there's no blood left to clean up."

"Too bad about my shirt though. It was new."

Janos laughed. "Surely you can add that to your expense account."

"Are you kidding? They're cutting back on everything these days. I don't think they'll pay for a dress shirt I wore to a Viennese ball, even if it was in the line of duty."

"Line of duty? Taking me to the ball was in the line of duty?" I swear I could feel that terrible squeezing in my chest that preceded a broken heart, but I didn't want to believe it. The quiver in my voice must have alerted Stephen.

He turned from Janos to me, took a step toward me, and held out one hand, palm up.

"Now, Lily. I didn't mean it that way."

"How exactly did you mean it then?"

I backed away from him. He started to follow me, but stopped and spoke to Janos, who had closed the door to my apartment and was standing very still in my foyer, holding a bag from the market down the street, watching both of us.

"Maybe you can do something useful in the kitchen for awhile, Janos."

"Right. Sure. No problem."

He left us alone, and Stephen closed the gap between the two of us, physically at least. He stood so close to me that I could feel his breath when he exhaled but he didn't touch me.

"I need to explain, Lily."

"Okay."

I continued to move away from him, until he grabbed me and pulled me down next to him on the couch in my living room. It took all of my will power not to melt into his arms, but I'd had a bit of practice in situations like this.

He loosened his grip on me, but he didn't back away, not at all. In fact, if anything, he leaned in even closer, until we were eyeball to eyeball. Our noses were touching, and I could see the reflection of my own eyes in his.

"I'm going to tell you the entire story, Lily, everything I can about my assignment here in Vienna. Janos can corroborate my explanation later and add some important details. First though, I need to clarify my remark about the ball."

"Yes, you do."

"And before I do that, I need to remind you of something very important."

Of course he kissed me. I knew he would. He was gentle, but he was insistent, and by the time he disengaged his lips from mine, I had begun to soften, but not much.

"I can't think straight when you kiss me."

"I know."

He rubbed my lips with his finger, probably to keep me from talking. It worked.

"Lily, I did have work to do at the ball. I wish that I could have spent the entire evening thinking only about you, dancing with you, holding you close, that there had been nothing else to worry about, but it was something I couldn't help."

He leaned back, ran his fingers through his hair, took a deep breath.

"If it makes you feel any better, I can't think straight when I'm with you either."

I smiled. I couldn't help it. "Yes, it does make me feel better."

"As it was, I could have ruined part of the operation taking place last night, if Mitzi and Frau Frassl hadn't taken things into their own hands."

"So Mitzi was in on your project too?"

"Yes, ever since that close call with Helmut Vogl."

He must have caught the question in my eyes, because he shook his head.

"Falling asleep with you; in fact, everything else I did with you, was not part of the plan." He started to laugh. I began to feel some of my former bad temper returning. He stopped laughing, and did something better with his mouth. I was the one who pulled away this time.

"What plan?"

"I'll tell you, but can we have some coffee first?" He stood up. "And we should probably let Janos out of your kitchen before he eats all the chocolate croissants we brought with us."

"That's blackmail."

"I know."

Even after two cups of coffee, a chocolate croissant, several orange slices, a boiled egg, and lengthy explanations from Stephen and Janos, I was still not entirely clear about what they called "Operation Hard Rocks." I snickered at the name, but they didn't even smile. They told me about the deaths in Chicago, and, it turns out, in other cities as well, about the cooperation between the CDC and the DEA, and then the involvement of Interpol and Europol once the illegal drugs were traced to Europe.

"You know that I was following Sandor and Andreas the night I met you?"

I nodded, and Stephen kept talking.

"I was tracing the deliveries here in Vienna; Janos, meanwhile, was working out the connection between Europe and the United States. It all came together with Michael Fodor, his estate in Hungary, where the aphrodisiac was manufactured, his import/export business, which provided a perfect avenue for shipping the drugs, and his many cousins, some of whom added the lucrative trade in ersatz Viagra to the business. They were shipping it in through the Balkans, and incidentally, it was in one of those shipments that the shellfish which caused your allergic reaction arrived."

"Shellfish isn't illegal, is it?"

"Not usually, and in this case, it provided the cover for the off market Viagra."

Then Stephen explained that the Viagra, manufactured in unregulated labs in northern Africa, was far more potent, and thus dangerous, than that supplied by regulated prescriptions from pharmacies.

"Even without the addition of the aphrodisiac, which includes such imaginative ingredients as dried toad secretions and mushrooms, Viagra at that strength can be dangerous, especially for middle aged and older men who have underlying heart conditions."

"The very category of men who might seek out women like Mitzi."

Stephen raised his eyebrows, but continued.

"Exactly. And in Chicago, and elsewhere, the directions included with the aphrodisiac weren't followed, probably because they were written in Hungarian."

He did smile then, and shook his head. "It would be funny, if it weren't so stupid."

"How stupid?"

"The aphrodisiac was intended to be applied externally." He paused here and looked at Janos, rather than at me. "To certain sensitive and important body parts."

I could feel the blush rising up my neck, but I didn't move or say a word. I was waiting for the punch line.

"Unfortunately, they swallowed it instead."

"And that's what killed them?"

"Yes."

"How awful."

"All because they failed to include a translation." Janos put his coffee cup down with a thump. "Unbelievable."

"It was just one of many mistakes they made, but together it all adds up to murder, even though that was not the intention."

The intention, of course, was to make money, lots of it. It had all started after the fall of communism in Eastern Europe. Michael Fodor certainly wasn't the only one who had found himself suddenly responsible for the renovation and upkeep of an old family estate, property returned by the new government of an Eastern block country. He also wasn't the only one who had found a lucrative and illegal means of funding this new responsibility. The cousins who had turned up on his doorstep needed work too, and they had no idea how to go about finding a job in this unfamiliar new system.

It was Janos who explained all of this. "The transition from communism to a free market economy hasn't exactly been smooth," he finished, "and corruption seems to be firmly imbedded in the fabric of life in some of these countries." He paused and smiled at me. "Of course, you have plenty of corruption in your country too."

I agreed. What else could I do? It was true. You could pick up a newspaper at home any day of the week and read about another official who'd accepted bribes, or worse.

"I'm still not totally clear on how you put it all together." I had decided to make another pot of coffee, and was pouring more into Stephen's cup. He nodded his thanks, before he answered me.

"Well, to be honest, Lily, it was you who provided the unexpected and, as it turned out, essential missing link, who helped us connect all of the separate threads we'd been trying to weave together."

"Me? How did I do that?"

"You inadvertently stepped into the middle of everything, and I stepped into it with you, as soon as I met you on the streetcar that fateful day. What a stroke of luck! Without you, Lily, we might not have discovered the connection between Michael Fodor and the drug smuggling operation." He looked very pleased with himself. "Now I can go home to Atlanta with at least one big case solved. What a relief!"

"You're going home to Atlanta? You're relieved?"

It was Janos who picked up on my tone of voice, or perhaps he noticed the look on my face as Stephen talked.

"He doesn't mean it that way, Lily. He's usually much smoother with his tongue. He didn't get much sleep last night."

"I know exactly how smooth he usually is with his tongue, and I also know what he was doing last night!"

"Oh."

Janos looked away, scooted his chair back from the table, and took his coffee cup to the sink.

A deep, rumbling sigh emanated from Stephen.

"He's right, Lily. I'm exhausted, and none of this is coming out the way I want it to." He turned those blue eyes on me and I looked straight into them. He did look awfully tired, but it wasn't just fatigue I saw in those eyes; there was another message there as well. It was that one which caused me to admit my own irritability today.

"I know." I reached for his hand. "I'm worn out too."

We were leaning toward each other and would have been in each other's arms in another second, if Janos hadn't spoken.

"Now that you two understand each other, maybe Stephen and I can get back to work."

"Thanks, Janos." Stephen managed a quick kiss before he stood up. Janos didn't seem a bit perturbed by Stephen's tone of voice.

"We have some statements to make, reports to file, loose ends to tie up."

"Right. I wouldn't want to keep you."

Stephen did pull me into his arms then. "Get some rest, Lily. I'll call you later."

I followed him to my foyer, watched him shrug into his jacket. "Not too much later. I'm going out for dinner." I answered the question in his eyes. "With a group from the college." I heard Janos clearing his throat behind me. "You and Janos would be welcome too, of course."

"And what about Sophie?" Stephen was looking over my head at Janos. "He seems to have become very fond of her."

Janos coughed, but he didn't say anything.

"Fond? Of Sophie?" I'd have to call her as soon as they left. "Of course she can come along. We're meeting at Mayer am Pfarrplatz, at six."

Janos, already halfway out the door, paused.

"Should we pick you up on the way?"

"Sure. That would be perfect."

Stephen gave me another sweet kiss, right before he said, "Oh, I'll bring back your sweater then too. I went off without it this morning."

And with those words, he was out the door, hurrying down the steps behind Janos.

If I hadn't been watching them leave, I wouldn't have noticed the priest from the Lichtental Kirche making his way up the steps, Mitzi's priest, Joseph Spohr. I backed up into my foyer and closed the door as quietly as I could.

CHAPTER TWENTY-THREE

When I awoke from my nap, the sky outside my window was a smoky blue grey color; *Die Blaue Stunden* had arrived. I squinted at the clock beside my bed. Four thirty. I'd better get up and take a shower.

I had just stepped out of the tub and wrapped a towel around myself when the buzzer sounded. It was Stephen, and he was awfully early, but I couldn't complain, especially not after he peeled the damp towel from my body and began to kiss a trail from my earlobe to my collarbone. One thing led to another, and we were snuggled under my duvet, limbs entwined, hearts still racing, when the buzzer sounded again. He groaned and looked at his watch.

"It's probably Janos. I'll go."

He pulled on his clothes and headed to the foyer. I heard him talking through the speaker, but no one came up the steps, and he reappeared in the bedroom a moment later.

"He and Sophie are here, but I told them I'd come down. I have to talk to Frau Frassl anyway." He leaned over to kiss me once more. "It won't take you long to get dressed, will it?"

I gave him the reply he expected, "No, I'll hurry." Then I tossed aside the duvet and stood up facing him. I wasn't wearing anything, so you can imagine how we occupied ourselves for a few minutes. The buzzer sounded again, and he pulled away.

He seemed to be having a hard time putting a sentence together, but finally he said, "Good. We'll wait down below then." He turned for one last look at me before he left. "Oh, I almost forgot. I left the sweater on the table in your foyer."

I dressed as fast as I could, brushed my hair, applied just a little make-up. My cheeks were so rosy from our lovemaking that I didn't need much. I had just pulled on my coat when the buzzer sounded once more. It was Sophie this time.

"Are you coming or not?"

"Yes, I'm on my way."

I grabbed my shoulder bag, locked my door, and started down the steps. It was dark already, so I pushed the button on my landing to turn on the lights. It couldn't have taken me more than a couple of minutes to get down, and I assumed they'd all be waiting in Janos' little grey Skoda, which was parked at the curb. It was empty though, and I looked to the left and then to the right, not sure where they'd gone. I might have guessed that they'd gathered at Frau Frassl's shop, but I could never have imagined what they were doing right now.

There on the sidewalk in front of the small store, circling slowly on the snow covered pavement, the four of them were dancing to the voice of Willie Nelson.

"Georgia, Georgia," he sang. "Just an old sweet song keeps Georgia on my mind."

Sophie and Janos swayed in time to the music, their heads close together, their faces illuminated by the soft glow of the street lamp. Stephen and Frau Frassl glided back and forth just outside her door, which was propped open to let the music drift out. Head tilted back, she gazed up at him as if he were her favorite cowboy, and he smiled down at her with what can only be described as indulgent affection. It was all very sweet, and I have to admit that I was touched.

The song came to an end. Stephen stepped back from Frau Frassl and then lifted her hand to his lips. The man had learned a thing or two from the Viennese apparently. I hoped he wouldn't click his heels together and say something ridiculous. He didn't. He just said "Thank-you," but it was enough. Frau Frassl absolutely glowed. I wondered if I did that when he turned his Southern charm on me. Probably. I decided I ought to let them know I was there.

"Here I am, everybody!"

Stephen nodded to acknowledge me, and then followed Frau Frassl back into her shop. Through the front window I could see him pull something from his pocket and hand it to her. I hoped it wasn't another toy badge. Whatever it was, it pleased Frau Frassl so much that she put her hands on his shoulders and brushed a kiss on each cheek. He said something else, which I couldn't hear, unfortunately, and then he turned and left the shop, closing the door behind him.

Sophie and Janos were still swaying under the streetlight. Did they even realize that the music had stopped? Stephen tapped Janos on the shoulder and then walked over to me, opened the car door, and slid in behind me. We watched Sophie and Janos approach the car, hand in hand, leaning into each other.

"Boy, that was fast. They only met yesterday."

Stephen laughed. "Look who's talking. How long have we known each other?"

I was saved from having to answer him by the slamming of the car door, and Sophie's immediate questions.

"Did you know about all of this, Lily? About the drug smuggling and the aphrodisiac deaths and the Hungarian connection?" She kept going without waiting for a response. "I mean, how brilliant are these guys? To plan that entire operation, to set up those raids and arrests to happen all at the same time last night, and to act as if the only thing they had on their minds was dancing with us at a Viennese ball?"

What could I say? "Yes, it was all quite amazing." I turned to look at Stephen, who was gazing out the window as if he wasn't even listening to Sophie's commentary.

"And to have it all go absolutely smoothly." Sophie paused. "Except for that one unfortunate fatality, of course."

"Unfortunate fatality?" I grabbed Stephen's hand. "Did Andreas die from the gunshot wound?"

"No, it wasn't Andreas. He's in intensive care, but he's expected to survive." That was all he said, but he did turn my hand over in his and begin to stroke it gently.

"Well, who was it then?"

"Don't you ever listen to the news, Lily?" Sophie hated it that I still only read newspapers, instead of watching cable news or listening to the radio.

"I try not to."

"Well, it was quite shocking really. The man died in the arms of a high class call girl, died after using the very same aphrodisiac which killed those people in Chicago, and started Janos and Stephen on this investigation."

"You heard all of that on the news?"

"Not all of it. Janos told me about the aphrodisiac."

"Do you know the name of the man who died?"

I was thinking of Helmut Vogl, but I was pretty sure he wouldn't have done anything so stupid after his recent close call. Nevertheless, I had to ask.

"His name was Otto Heimberger, and he was the Chief of Staff at the Department of Interior."

"I know who he was. I've met him."

I thought back to that evening at Michael Fodor's apartment, to that moment in the hallway when I'd seen Otto Heimberger talking with Sandor and Andreas.

"He was in on it, wasn't he?" I addressed this question to Stephen. "He was in on the drug smuggling."

"We think that he was, but we have to leave that part of the investigation up to Europol and the Austrians."

"He didn't swallow it, did he?" I whispered this in Stephen's ear.

"No, the aphrodisiac was used correctly, at least as far as we know. We'll have to wait for the autopsy results to be sure, but according to the woman he was with when this happened, he also took a dose of that black market Viagra. That's probably what caused his heart to stop."

Janos let out a snort of laughter. "That or the woman he was with!"

"I wonder if it was Mitzi's friend."

"It's probably better that you don't know."

I didn't agree, but I decided not to argue the point. I could just ask her later.

"So what is going to happen to Michael Fodor and his cousins?"

"They'll be tried for the drug smuggling, and now, with the death of Otto Heimberger, there could be a wrongful death charge added as well." Stephen was rubbing his thumb from my wrist to my palm now, and I relaxed against him.

While we were talking, Janos had been driving north, through Döbling, toward the vineyards and restaurants of the Vienna Woods. We were on Grinzingerstrasse now, in the village of Heiligenstadt. Janos turned off on Nestlebachgasse, proceeded up the narrow street to Pfarrplatz, and brought the Skoda to a stop in the cobblestone paved parking area of Mayer am Pfarrplatz.

It's a lovely old house, with a pale yellow façade and arched doorways. They say that it hasn't changed since Beethoven lived in it during the summer of 1817. It's one of many *Heurigen*, or wine taverns, located in the villages of the Vienna Woods, places where the Viennese gather to drink the wine produced in the vineyards surrounding the restaurants, to eat food from the well stocked buffets, and to listen to the distinctive music performed in some of them, called *Schrammelmusik*. Mayer is one of the best and most famous. In the summer its courtyard is filled with patrons enjoying their food and wine outside in the fresh air, but tonight we walked straight through this charming enclosed area and into the restaurant.

I led the way, spoke to the dirndl clad server who greeted us, followed her to a long wooden table in one of the back rooms where the group from the college was gathered. Eva sat at one end of the table, with Christina to her right. Tom sat at the other end, with Arthur on his left. The students occupied the chairs in between them along the sides of the table, but they had saved enough seats for us. Stephen helped me out of my coat before he sat down beside me, across from Kevin Carlson and Arthur. I didn't even want to think of all of the possible awkward moments ahead of me, at least not until I'd had a glass of Riesling, which I ordered as soon as a server appeared next to the table.

Christina had already greeted Stephen, and, in fact, had taken over the task of introducing him to the group. She was careful not to mention anything about our relationship, but I was fairly certain that the students had noticed the way he draped his arm around my shoulders, the way his lips brushed my earlobe when he leaned in to speak to me. Kevin was glaring at him from across the table, and Arthur barely acknowledged him when Christina performed the introductions, but at least they hadn't said anything to embarrass me, not yet.

Fortunately, Sophie and Janos stood up as soon as they'd ordered their wine.

"We need to go straight to the buffet. We've hardly eaten all day."

That was Janos speaking, but I was only too grateful to follow his lead. The distinctive wines, cultivated in their own vineyards, aren't the only temptations of the *Heurigen*. They also have hot and cold buffets, packed with everything from cucumber salads to grilled chicken, sliced ham, and roast pork. Then, of course, there are countless varieties of cheeses, sausages, crusty rolls and hearty breads. My plate was completely filled by the time I made my way back to our table, and I hadn't even looked at the dessert counter yet. I'd have to pace myself.

While I ate, I listened to the conversation at the table. Christina, who looked pale and tired, was telling Eva about her travel plans.

"Yes, I've decided to leave Vienna sooner than I'd planned. The weather, you know, is so dismal here this time of year."

Eva nodded, but her mouth was full, so she didn't reply. It didn't matter, because Christina continued talking.

"I'm going to sublet my apartment here, pack everything up, and fly to my home in Florida on Sunday. It's near Naples." She paused and took a sip of her wine. "Have you ever been there?"

"No, but I've heard that it's lovely."

"It is, and even though I'll miss Lars, I have friends there." She smiled at Eva but her eyes held a tinge of sadness. "I'd love to have you come visit sometime though."

Eva thanked her, and said that she'd love to do that someday. "This year, of course, we've promised to stay in Vienna through the spring semester."

"Of course. What would the students do without you?" Christina looked down the table at me then. "I do think that Lily could handle things, though, if you ever needed to get away."

I had to swallow a mouthful of chicken before I could say anything, but really, what choice did I have, except to agree. "Always glad to help out."

I would have said more, but the warmth of Stephen's thigh pressing against mine under the table was distracting me, that and the conversation coming from the other end of the table. Arthur was telling Tom about his idea for an article for a music history journal.

"I think I'll call it 'Unrequited Love: The Significance of Loss in *Lieder*, from Blondel to Schubert.' I may even turn it into a book."

"Well, that's sure to be a bestseller." Fortunately, Janos spoke softly enough that Arthur didn't seem to hear him. Kevin, however, became animated at the mention of Blondel, and practically shouted his response to Arthur's idea.

"*Blondel!* I loved that show! I had no idea you were into rock opera, Professor Larson."

Arthur blinked and turned his puzzled gaze toward Kevin. "*Blondel* is the name of a rock opera?"

The man had missed a lot while he was in the library studying copies of medieval manuscripts and articles about them. I decided not to emphasize that point though, because I didn't want to aggravate Arthur tonight. Besides, it really wasn't a well-known show. It had been performed in London, but not on Broadway. Nevertheless, it was a favorite of college theater groups back home; maybe I could get Arthur to suggest it to our drama department. While I was thinking about this, Janos brought up an even less famous reference to Arthur's favorite minstrel.

"Not just a rock opera, but an acoustic band. You know, Amazing Blondel, an early seventies group." Janos looked around the table, as if waiting for someone else to share this memory. These kids hadn't even been born then; come to think of it, Janos didn't look all that old either. "My dad loved it," he explained.

"Of course he did." Sophie acted as if everyone back then had loved this group, but then she changed the subject.

"But why end your research with Schubert, Arthur? Why doesn't anyone ever mention Alma Mahler's love songs?"

"It's not as if she ever suffered from unrequited love, Sophie, at least as far as we know." Even though I didn't want to antagonize Arthur, I rarely worried about annoying Sophie, so I added one more sentence. "That and the fact that no one can keep track of all her names."

I'm sure that Sophie would have come up with a persuasive response. She's always ready to defend Alma, along with Gustav, but Arthur re-entered the conversation at that point. His pale blue eyes were fixed on me, even though I hadn't pointed out how self indulgent I thought his proposed title was. I didn't like the look in those eyes.

"I was hoping that Lily might want to work with me on this."

There was a sudden silence around the table, and all eyes were on me. Did everyone except Janos and Stephen know what had happened between Arthur and me? Had I even remembered to fill Sophie in on the latest episode?

I swallowed my wine, set my glass down carefully, and cleared my throat.

"Actually, Arthur, I have a project of my own to work on right now, but of course I'd be glad to contribute to the section about Schubert, once I've finished."

"Your own project? Lily! Does this mean that you've finally discovered a lost love song?" Arthur had put down his wine glass and was leaning as far as he could across the table toward me.

"It has yet to be authenticated, Arthur, but if it turns out be genuine, then the answer is yes. That's all I can say about it right now."

"All you can say?"

He looked as if he wanted to leap across the table, but as he stretched out his arm toward me, he grimaced, and then grunted with pain, before he subsided into his chair again. I whispered an explanation to Stephen.

"Arthur suffered an unfortunate injury a few days ago, Stephen. Fractured his tailbone. I'll tell you how it happened later." It occurred to me that there were quite a few other things I needed to tell Stephen as well. It had been an eventful week. We just seemed to find other things to do whenever we were together.

His grin cheered me significantly. "I'll look forward to it." He said that right into my ear, and the warmth of his breath skidded along my jawbone, distracting me from Arthur's next words.

"Can you tell me, at least, if you've found any hint of who he loved?" Arthur was listing to his right now, and his head was close to Kevin's shoulder. "Any letters? Any secret paramour?"

Sophie saved me, at least for the moment. "Why does everyone think that all composers had some mysterious 'Immortal Beloved'? Just because of Beethoven? Really, there's nothing that hidden about the love lives of most composers."

"Certainly not about Alma's anyway."

"At least she was a woman who followed her own heart." As Sophie said this, she moved even closer to Janos, who already held her hand in his.

The fortunate thing about Sophie's mention of Beethoven is that it turned the conversation at the table away from Schubert, and toward the man who had lived in this house, and, in fact, had worked on his Ninth Symphony here. He'd written his Sixth symphony, "The Pastoral" during an earlier stay in Heiligenstadt. While I was telling the students about this, Kevin was pushing at Arthur, trying to return him to an upright position. He groaned, and swayed toward Tom, who put a steadying hand on his shoulder and helped him sit up straight. His eyes were strangely unfocused though, and I began to worry about what the potent *Heuriger* wine might be doing to his emotional equilibrium, or lack thereof, how it might be mixing with whatever painkillers he had taken earlier.

I found out a moment later when the musicians started playing. Viennese *Schrammelmusik* is named after the brothers who made it famous during the nineteenth century. Johann and Josef Schrammel were classically trained violinists who were born in Vienna and grew up hearing traditional Viennese folk music. They were joined in their performances by a clarinet and a bass guitar, a thirteen-stringed instrument with two necks. Their playing was so beautiful that they developed a first class reputation and gave the music its name.

Tonight an accordionist and a violinist took the place of the original quartet of instruments. As soon as the musicians launched into their first polka, Arthur began to tap his fingers on the table and to nod his head in time to the music. I breathed a sigh of relief. Tom caught my eye and smiled. I watched as he replaced Arthur's wine glass with one full of mineral water.

"Now we just need to get some chocolate into him."

That was Stephen whispering in my ear again. "Let's go get some dessert."

We did, and by the time we returned to the table, Arthur wasn't the only one in the room enjoying the music. Toes were tapping and a few people were humming along. One robust customer at the table next to ours was actually singing.

"Probably had too much wine."

"Maybe so, but at least he has a good voice."

Stephen had placed a piece of chocolate cake in front of Arthur, who managed to get a forkful to his mouth while he kept the beat. Even Kevin looked happier now.

"This reminds me of my cousin's wedding reception in St. Cloud last summer," he said. "They had a great polka band."

"Polka?" Stephen sounded shocked. "Is that what people do at wedding receptions in Minnesota?"

I tried not to read too much into Stephen's interest in Minnesota weddings, and instead responded to the polka part of his question.

"Not always, but it's pretty common." I caught his hand under the table. "What do you do in Georgia?"

"Ah, Lily." He was stroking the inside of my wrist now, and I was struggling to focus on his words. "Have you ever heard of beach music, of moves so smooth it's as if you're dancing in the sand?"

Smooth moves I could certainly believe, but I'd never seen a Georgia beach. My only frame of reference was the shore of my favorite fishing lake back home. I couldn't imagine dancing on it, even during the short Minnesota summer, and I said so.

"No, we don't do that back home."

"When you come to Georgia, I'll show you what I mean." His lips were so close to my ear that I shivered in response.

"I'll look forward to it." That was an understatement. I wondered when he thought I'd visit him, but Christina interrupted my thoughts.

"If you really want a beautiful beach, you'll have to come see me, Lily. There's nothing in Georgia that can compare to Sanibel."

Stephen moved his lips far enough from my ear that he could discuss beautiful beaches of the south with Christina. There's no telling how long they might have gone on discussing seashells and white sand, if Janos hadn't intervened.

"It all sounds warm and wonderful, especially on such a cold winter night. Unfortunately, I need to head back out into that wintry world."

He turned to Stephen and me then. "Do you want to come now, or would you rather stay and take a taxi home later?"

Stephen didn't even ask my opinion.

"Now, of course."

So we said our good-byes to everyone, hugged Christina, put on our coats, and made our way back through the restaurant, through the stucco and wood paneled rooms, past multiple sets of antlers hanging high on the walls, out the arched entrance and under the fresh pine bough hanging over it which was the trademark of the *Heurigen*.

"So Lily," Janos grinned at me. "Do you have something you'd like to tell us? Something about Arthur, and that angry looking young man sitting next to him?"

What could I do? I really had no choice, with all of them looking at me as if I'd been keeping a stupendous secret. So on the way back to my apartment I told them everything, starting with Kevin and the opera and not stopping until I'd finished the account of the disastrous trip to Dürnstein. Janos and Sophie loved the downhill slide part of the story best, but Stephen seemed to be stuck on the ending, the kiss in the car.

"Arthur kissed you?"

CHAPTER TWENTY-FOUR

"Yes. I didn't expect it, though I probably should have, after that awful proposal last year. He did it before I could stop him. Did you miss the part where I smacked him on the head to get him to let me go?"

We were back in my apartment now, hanging our coats on hooks in the foyer, pulling off our boots.

"Proposal?" Stephen was helping me with my boots, and his hand had stopped on my ankle. Ordinarily I loved the feel of his hands on my body, but his grip on my ankle was disconcertingly tight.

"Yes, a year ago. I turned him down, of course, but unfortunately he hasn't been able to let go of his fantasy that I'll fall in love with him. Maybe this article he's writing will help him work through his feelings."

Stephen had loosened his grip on my ankle, and now he was massaging my foot. I had to lean against the wall in my foyer to keep my balance, but if his hands didn't quit creeping upward, I had a feeling I wouldn't be standing much longer. He kept talking, even while he pulled himself up from his knees to his feet, moved those expert hands from my calves to my shoulders. His voice was dangerously soft.

"Are there any others I should know about, Lily? Anyone you've forgotten to mention who might be in love with you?"

I was beginning to have a bit of trouble organizing my thoughts, but I managed to say, "Not that I know of," before his lips closed over mine.

It was a few minutes later when he stopped kissing me long enough to say, "I think there may be one more." He smiled, and his eyes told me who it was.

"Oh, oh." I had to search for the right words. "That's very good news."

When we woke up the next morning, it was to that gentle stillness which accompanies a snowfall. Stephen rose from the bed, walked to my bedroom window, rubbed a circle on the frosty glass, and looked out. I was admiring another view, the way his well formed back tapered to his waist, the way the muscles of his thighs flexed when he moved from one foot to another.

"If this keeps up, I may not be able to fly out tomorrow."

"You're leaving tomorrow?"

He turned to face me, and what I was looking at now almost diverted me from his announcement, but not quite. "Can't you stay, just for a few more days?"

"Lily, there's nothing I'd like better, but my assignment in Vienna is over." He had returned to bed and was leaning over me now, smoothing my hair. "I have work waiting for me at home in Atlanta. I have to go."

I pulled him close, wrapped myself around him, let him know how I felt with my body and my words. "I'll miss you." And then, even though I tried not to, I started to cry.

I would like to be able to say that he reassured me so well that I felt just fine about the fact that I'd finally fallen in love with a man who seemed to love me too, that I believed him when he said that we'd figure out how to see each other again, but I definitely had my doubts.

"Lily, you're going to have to trust me when I tell you that this is not the end for us. We're just beginning, you and I."

I held those words close to my heart as I watched him walk away the next day. They sounded like the first line of a song, but I'm not sure if it would have been a song by Schubert, or one by Willie Nelson. I was as dazed by the swiftness of his departure as I had been by the suddenness of his arrival.

I coped that winter by going to as many concerts as I could afford, by teaching my students as much as I knew about Viennese composers, and by showing them around the city I loved. I worked on the article about the newly discovered Schubert song, once it had been authenticated. Kurt worked with me; he would share the authorship and the credit.

Frau Frassl still listened to Willie Nelson every day; I went with her to his concert when he performed in Vienna a few weeks after Stephen left. He had been handing her the tickets while I had watched them through the shop window after their dance in the snow. She didn't have her gun anymore, but she still wore the badge under her sweater, and glowed with pride whenever I mentioned her part in the arrests that night. She'd even talked me into buying an autographed CD at the concert, and I was becoming almost as fond of some of Willie's songs as I was of Schubert's.

Mitzi had gone to live with her aunt in Villach while she awaited the birth of her baby. There was a cellist living in her apartment now, so instead of hearing arias sung by Fritz Gerling, I awoke to Bach's Solo Sonatas. They were very soothing and reminded me of my mother's playing, but I missed Mitzi. She'd given me a full bottle of slivovitz before she left, along with another gift, those fancy handcuffs she'd used on Sandor the night of the arrests. She said she thought my doctor friend might enjoy them, but Stephen just laughed when I told him, and said we didn't need them. I ended up giving them to Frau Frassl, who hung them up next to her lasso. I had seen Joseph Spohr, Mitzi's priest, from a distance, but I had never spoken to him again, or asked for another sermon.

Sophie still saw Janos whenever his work brought him to Vienna, which was almost every week. I had never seen her so enthralled with anyone. *"Er hebt mich aus den Schuhen!"* she exclaimed one night over a glass of wine. In English, that's "He lifts me out of my shoes," though back in Minnesota, we'd say, "He knocks my socks off," if we still talked like that. My Great Aunt Hulda used to say that about her husband Thor, but my generation tends to use different phrases. Sophie didn't stop with that revealing statement though; she followed up with, "I just wish he weren't so mysterious about his work, wish he'd stay put in Vienna, instead of coming and going constantly the way he does." He stopped by to see me now and then too, when he had time. He reassured me that Christina had indeed been able to pack her suitcases, with Trudi Vogl's help, and to leave town without having to see Michael Fodor again. That's because he was in jail, of course.

I socialized with Tom and Eva, and even went out a few times with men they introduced me to, but it didn't stop me from missing Stephen. We talked almost every day via the Internet, except during those weeks when he was out of town on assignments and unable to communicate with me. He never told me where he went or what he did, and I still wondered if it was really the CDC he worked for, or someone else. When we did connect, his face was right in front of me on my computer screen, and his voice reached out to me, but it wasn't the same as touching him, having him hold me.

To comfort myself, I wore my Grandpa's old sweater, the one I'd loaned to Stephen the night he'd ruined his shirt soaking up Andreas' blood. Now it not only reminded me of my Grandpa, it also enfolded me in the memory of Stephen, wrapped me in his scent and his warmth.

Those who were closest to me tried to console me with well-worn clichés and small pieces of advice. I like to think that they meant well.

"Absence makes the heart grow fonder," said my mom. "Of course, I've never met anyone from Georgia, so I'm not sure whether it's true for him, but he does sound like a very nice young man."

"Out of sight, out of mind," my dad told me. I hoped that he was teasing me, but a part of me feared that he was telling the truth, from the male standpoint, that he was trying to prepare me for the worst. He'd always done that for me.

I won't even mention what my overprotective brothers said about how guys come and go, and how women are expecting too much if they think they'll somehow love them forever.

Sophie, of course, had her own distinctive viewpoint, which pretty much reflected Alma's life choices. "It's wonderful that you enjoyed your time with him so much," she said. "Now, move on and find someone else. He's certainly not coming back to Vienna anytime soon."

I knew that they were trying to help me, and I listened politely to all of them. Well, usually I listened politely. I didn't tell any of them, though, what it was that actually comforted me the most during that long cold winter. It wasn't their words. It was Schubert, of course, as channeled through Stephen.

He'd tucked the envelope inside Grandpa's sweater, so I didn't find it until after he'd left on that snowy Sunday. Inside was a hand-written message for me, and attached to that message was a list of some of Schubert's songs, a list which cited specific stanzas and lines, the way Lutherans print the Bible verses to be studied during the week in Sunday's bulletin.

The first one was *"Ihr Bild,"* with a text by Heinrich Heine, one of Schubert's favorite poets. It means "Her Portrait," and he included all three verses of this one. It was about a man staring at the portrait of his beloved, looking at the teardrops in her eyes and missing her. I guess it had not been surprising to him that I cried when he left.

I won't enumerate the rest of them, except to say that there were enough to keep me going for quite a long time. Schubert did write more than six hundred songs, after all, though of course Stephen didn't include nearly that many in his list. I will say that my favorite among the ones he chose was the famous "Serenade," partly because I could hum it easily, but mostly because of its words. *"Liebchen, komm zu mir,"* I sang every day, in my subdued alto. "Beloved, come to me."

For weeks I was so touched by the poignancy of my memories of Stephen as evoked by Schubert's songs, that I thought only vaguely of how and where we'd actually manage to get together again. I suppose that, despite Sophie's warning, I somehow thought he'd magically reappear on my doorstep someday. By the time I realized that he wasn't coming back to Vienna any time soon, the lilacs had bloomed, the May Music Festival had come and gone, and I was packing to return to Minnesota.

I had dried the rose petals from the bouquet he'd brought me the night of the ball, and I tucked those into my suitcase along with the note he'd written, the one he'd folded inside Grandpa's sweater. It was Grandpa's voice I heard in my head during the long flight home, that voice which had always offered me comfort and wisdom while he was alive, and continued to do so, even though he'd been gone for more than a year now.

He was saying, "Never give up, Lily. Never give up."

I held that thought as closely as I held my dreams of Stephen, all the way home.